CAPTAIN
DUTCH

Also by Robert J. Conley
in Large Print:

The Gunfighter
Outside the Law
Strange Company
To Make a Killing
Wilder & Wilder
A Cold Hard Trail
Fugitive's Trail

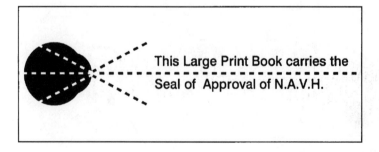

This Large Print Book carries the
Seal of Approval of N.A.V.H.

CAPTAIN DUTCH

ROBERT J. CONLEY

WHEELER
PUBLISHING

Published in 2005 by arrangement with
Cherry Weiner Literary Agency.

Wheeler Large Print Western.

The text of this Large Print edition is unabridged.
Other aspects of the book may vary from the original edition.

Set in 16 pt. Plantin.

Printed in the United States on permanent paper.

Library of Congress Cataloging-in-Publication Data

Conley, Robert J.
    Captain Dutch / by Robert J. Conley.
       p. cm. — (Wheeler Publishing large print western)
    ISBN 1-58724-959-6 (lg. print : sc : alk. paper)
    1. Cherokee Indians — Fiction. 2. Osage Indians —
Fiction. 3. Texas — Fiction. 4. Large type books.
I. Title. II. Wheeler large print western series.
PS3553.O494C37 2005
  813'.54—dc22   2005001333

CAPTAIN
DUTCH

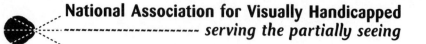
National Association for Visually Handicapped
---------------------- *serving the partially seeing*

As the Founder/CEO of NAVH, the only national health agency solely devoted to those who, although not totally blind, have an eye disease which could lead to serious visual impairment, I am pleased to recognize Thorndike Press* as one of the leading publishers in the large print field.

Founded in 1954 in San Francisco to prepare large print textbooks for partially seeing children, NAVH became the pioneer and standard setting agency in the preparation of large type.

Today, those publishers who meet our standards carry the prestigious "Seal of Approval" indicating high quality large print. We are delighted that Thorndike Press is one of the publishers whose titles meet these standards. We are also pleased to recognize the significant contribution Thorndike Press is making in this important and growing field.

Lorraine H. Marchi, L.H.D.
Founder/CEO
NAVH

* Thorndike Press encompasses the following imprints: Thorndike, Wheeler, Walker and Large Print Press.

AUTHOR'S NOTE

I first thought of writing a novel about Captain Dutch because he was a fascinating, though nearly forgotten, character from history who deserved more attention than he has received. The more I got into the story, the more I realized that I was dealing with not only a neglected individual but also with a whole period of nearly forgotten history, all the more amazing in that it was packed full of adventure and peopled by a whole cast of very prominent historical figures, including Sequoyah, Sam Houston, Washington Irving, George Catlin, and Jefferson Davis.

This is the early history of the Cherokees in the West, a story of Cherokees who moved west on their own for a variety of reasons before the infamous Trail of Tears forced the rest to follow. Beginning in 1794 and continuing until 1848, *Captain Dutch* is a story involving conflict between those Cherokee Early Settlers and the Osages who had preceded them to the part of the U.S. that is now western Arkansas and eastern Oklahoma. It is a story of

7

conflict between the Cherokees and the United States and it is ultimately a story of inner conflict — Cherokees against Cherokees. And that's just part of the rich fabric of these fifty or so years of history.

In putting together this novel, I depended heavily and necessarily on the work of others who have gone before me. I owe a particular debt of gratitude to the work of Grant Foreman, who dug deep into primary source material such as old newspapers and government files, particularly those of the War Department and the Office of Indian Affairs, to rescue the details of those years from obscurity. Foreman's books dealing particularly with this period are *Indians and Pioneers*, *Advancing the Frontier*, and *The Five Civilized Tribes*.

I should say here, however, that I note throughout Foreman's work a decidedly anti–Western-Cherokee bias, first in favor of the Osages, and later in favor of the Cherokee government of John Ross. Descriptions of the battles between Cherokees and Osages in which the Cherokees came out victorious are labeled massacres by Foreman. His descriptions of these "massacres," to be sure, came from the records of the War Department. But it is instructive to know how they got there.

The battles thus described were first reported by Osages to either one of the Chouteaus or to Pryor, traders and friends to the Osages. The Osage-friendly traders then reported to the U.S. Army, and the Osage point of view became the official record. I have taken these battle descriptions with a grain of salt and make no apologies for my Cherokee point of view.

Readers interested in the other perspective who have not already done so are encouraged to read Foreman and the Osage writer Mathews (see below).

Foreman's wife, Carolyn Thomas Foreman, wrote perhaps the only biography of Dutch for a 1949 issue of *The Chronicles of Oklahoma*. But George Catlin, who met Dutch, painted his portrait, and probably got to know him fairly well, was fascinated with him and included remarks on his bearing, character, and exploits in *Letters and Notes on the Manners, Customs, and Conditions of the North American Indians*. Extremely valuable for some firsthand observations of some of the events and people of the time is *Reminiscences of the Indians* by the Rev. Cephas Washburn. He was there and he knew the people he wrote about.

Some other published sources for this

compelling historical period and the people involved that helped me with this work and that I recommend for any readers interested in further pursuit of the topics dealt with here are the following: *Jesse Chisholm: Ambassador of the Plains* by Stan Hoig, *Sam Houston with the Cherokees: 1829–1833*, by Jack Gregory and Rennard Strickland, *Chief Bowles and the Texas Cherokees*, by Mary Whatley Clarke, and the *Osages: Children of the Middle Waters*, by John Joseph Mathews.

I am fortunate to have a good many friends who are both rich sources of information on Cherokee history and generous with their time and knowledge. In the course of writing *Captain Dutch* I had valuable conversations with W. Lee O'Daniel Robbins, John Strange, Mary O'Brien, Leon Gilmore, Chad Smith, and Murv Jacob. My thanks to them all.

Special thanks are due to Bruce Ross, then of the Fort Gibson Military Park, to Robert Finch of the Tahleqwah Public Library, and to members of the library staff at Northeastern State University, especially Dolores Sumner of the Special Collections Room, for their valuable and unselfish assistance to me during my research into the life and times of Captain Dutch.

And, as always, to my first editor, most severe critic, and best advisor, Guwist' Elaqui, my wife, Evelyn Snell. *Wado, Wado, Wado.*

"I promise you that the life of this man furnishes the best materials for a popular tale, that are now to be procured on the Western frontier."

— George Catlin (on Captain Dutch)

PROLOGUE

Muscle Shoals, Alabama
1794

His name was Diwali, but he was known in English as Bowl, the Bowl, Chief Bowls, Captain Bowles, and sometimes even Colonel John Bowles. He was war chief of Running Water, one of the Five Lower Towns of the Cherokees known as Chickamaugas.

Only about thirty-four years old, Bowles, raised Cherokee, was half white, with auburn hair and blue eyes. Stout and of medium height, Bowles, like the other Cherokee men with him, wore traditional moccasins and leggings with breechcloth. But he also wore a white linen shirt and a colorful cloth hunting jacket with a woven sash tied around his waist. His head was wrapped in a bright-colored cloth turban.

At the conclusion of the American Revolution, the Chickamaugas, who had sided with the British, continued to fight against the new United States until 1794, when they finally signed a treaty of peace at a place called Tellico Blockhouse.

At the treaty signing, gifts, including guns, ammunition, and cash, were made to the Indians. Diwali and other residents of Running Water were on the way home from this meeting, and they stopped to camp at a place called Muscle Shoals on the Tennessee River. The river was low at the shoals, and the beach was wide and sandy, but behind the camp the woods were thick and green. Just as they were settling down for the night, the Chickamaugas saw a string of flatboats coming down the river. As they watched, the boats tied up at the bank at the head of the shoals.

Bowles could see the white men on the first boat looking in the direction of the Cherokee camp. While it was true that Bowles and his followers had spent their last several years at war with the colonies and then with the United States, they had been allies of the British and had among them several mixed-bloods and even a few white men, Tories who had cast their lot with the Chickamaugas at the end of the war.

The boatmen were a rugged-looking lot, barefoot, with trousers rolled up to their knees, but they had along with them some women and children and some black slaves. Bowles was not afraid of them, but he was a bit suspicious. As he watched, one of the boatmen waved and shouted, a broad grin on his hairy face. He was wearing a white shirt, ripped open at one shoulder, and a red rag was tied around his head.

"Ahoy, you on the shore," he called. "Any of you talk English?"

Bowles looked behind him toward a man named Hicks, whose appearance was more white than Indian, and Hicks stepped forward.

"Sure, I talk English," he yelled back at the boatman. "What do you want of us?"

"Just being friendly," called the boatman. "That's all. I'm William Scott, a trader bound for New Orleans with my goods. Would you be coming from the treaty talks at Tellico?"

"We are," said Hicks.

"Then you must have some cash about you," said Scott. "Would you care to look over our goods? You're welcome to come aboard. You'll have the first choice. The stuff ain't been picked over yet."

Hicks turned toward his traveling companions and repeated in Cherokee the gist of what Scott had said.

"Let's see what they have," said one man. Others added their voices to his. They had money and were anxious to spend it. They were also interested in any diversion on their long trip. Bowles studied the boats for a moment. Besides Scott, there were five other white men, three white women, four white children, and about twenty slaves. He shrugged, and the party of curious Chickamaugas headed anxiously for the flatboats, ready and eager to spend their money.

The Indians boarded the boats, smiling and shaking hands with the white man and looking at the piles of trade goods there in boxes and barrels and bundles. Scott immediately cracked open a keg of whiskey and offered free drinks all around. Bowles, Hicks, and the others readily accepted. They drank the whiskey. They joked with one another and with the white men as the *wisgi* burned its way down their throats. They laughed. And they spent their money. They bought bolts of cloth and strings of glass beads. And they drank more whiskey. They had a wonderful time.

The next morning, the Chickamaugas woke up with heavy heads and empty pockets. They looked at the cheap, almost worthless goods they had spent their money on.

"What did I buy this for?" said one called Water Dog.

"Did I buy this?" said Hicks.

"The white men cheated us."

"I spent all my money."

"So did I."

"That man gave us *wisgi* to get us drunk so he could get all of our money."

"It was a trick."

"Come on," said Bowles. "Bring all of the things you bought. We'll ask them to give us back our money."

Their heads throbbing, they followed Bowles back to the boats, carrying with them all the trinkets they had bought the night before. When Scott saw them coming, he did not look as friendly as he had before, when he had been so free with his whiskey.

"What do you want?" he said. "You spent all your money last night."

Hicks spoke for the Cherokees. "That's what we want to talk to you about," he said. "We don't want these things you sold us. We only bought them because we were drunk on your whiskey. We want you to take them back and return our money."

"All sales are final on this boat," said

Scott. "If you didn't want the stuff, you shouldn't have bought it. Besides, you drank up a whole barrel of my whiskey."

Hicks conferred briefly with Bowles in Cherokee, then turned back toward Scott. "Take back these things," he said, "and give us our money back, and we'll pay you for all the whiskey we drank."

"I've already told you no," said Scott. "Now get the hell off my boat."

The Indians went back to their campsite. For a while they fidgeted around. They mumbled. Then one said, "We ought to kill the white men."

"Wait," said Bowles. "I'll talk to them one more time."

He took Hicks and Water Dog with him back to the boat where Scott and the other white men were, and they boarded it once more.

"What now?" said Scott. "I already told you I ain't giving back no money."

"We came to prevent a fight," said Hicks. "The others want to kill you if you don't give back the money. We don't want that to happen. That's what we came to tell you."

"You mean to rob me," said Scott. "Is that it?"

"No," said Hicks. "We want to give back

the goods. We don't want to fight, but the others want to."

"If it's a fight you want," shouted Scott, grabbing a long boat pole, "we'll give you a fight."

Another boatman also grabbed a pole. He swung it hard, cracking Water Dog's skull and knocking him off the boat and into the shallow river. Scott rammed the metal-tipped end of his long pole into the chest of Hicks, tearing through muscle and bone and sinew, spewing blood. Bowles dived into the water and splashed to shore, running back toward his camp.

"Kill them all!" someone shouted.

"No," said Bowles. But the Cherokees, armed with long rifles, were already running toward the boats. "Only the white men!" he shouted after them.

The five white men on the boat scrambled for weapons, but the Cherokees, with their long rifles, shot them down easily. Women and children screamed and slaves ducked for cover, but as soon as the white men were all dead, the shooting stopped.

Bowles had the women and children, along with four slaves, put onto one boat, with all of the belongings they said were theirs and with ample supplies. He sent them on their way unharmed. Then he and his followers took for themselves the rest of the boats, the rest of the goods, and the rest of the slaves.

"We won't go back to Running Water," he said. "Not only will the white men claim that we broke the treaty we just signed, but our own people will be mad at us for killing these white men."

"Where will we go then?" asked one.

"We'll go west," said Bowles, "where there aren't so many white people."

They settled along the St. Francis River in Missouri near the northwest part of the territory of Arkansas and built a new town of rude log cabins, much like those of frontier whites. The hunting was good. The land was much like what they were used to, hilly and covered with lush forests. They were not too much bothered by white people there. The climate was good, and they were out of the jurisdiction of the United States. The French claimed this Missouri country as their own. Bowles thought that he and his people could get along with the French, and the French might even protect them from the Americans. There were occasional clashes with other Indians, but that did not bother Bowles and his followers. Life had always been like that, and the Chickamaugas were fierce fighters. They especially fought with the Osages. Cherokees had wandered this far west before on hunting trips, and always they had fought the Osages.

They wondered from time to time if they would vanish, like the Lost Cherokees and Dangerous Man, who had led his followers west after the Cherokees first signed a treaty with Carolina back in 1721. They had sent messages back from time to time, but eventually the messages ceased. No one had ever heard from them again.

Bowles and his followers had not been in Missouri more than a year when they were joined by other Chickamaugas from the old country. One of Bowles's people had gone back home for a visit, and these new arrivals had been attracted by his tales of the abundance of game in the west and the absence of whites. They had come from Turkey Town on the Coosa River, and among them was a man of mixed blood named Thomas Taylor. He had brought with him his widowed sister, Lisi, and her son, five years old, called Tahchee.

True to their Cherokee traditions, Taylor, the boy's maternal uncle, took on the responsibility of raising the lad to be a man. He took him into the woods and told him the names of the different plants they found there, and he showed the boy how to make use of them.

He told him the names of the birds and taught him to recognize them by sight or by the sound of their songs. He taught the boy about the animals and their habits. Taylor made a little bow and some arrows for the boy, and he made him a blow gun and darts. Tahchee wanted to shoot his uncle's long rifle, but Taylor said that he was not yet big enough for that.

Taylor taught him to speak English as well as Cherokee, for he said, "The whites will be around again. Sooner or later they'll follow us out here. You need to be able to talk to them and to understand what they say." And when he was talking English to the lad, he called him Dutch, because it sounded something like his real name.

Everything went well for the Cherokees in Missouri until the day in 1811 when the ground began to shake. Log cabins were torn apart and sometimes splintered. Trees were uprooted. Large boulders rolled down the hillsides. Great slabs of the earth sank. Everywhere the ground lurched and trembled beneath the people's feet, sometimes knocking them to the ground, sometimes dropping out from under them.

There was no place to run. There was no place to hide. When the trembling stopped at last, they looked around at the devastation, at their ruined homes, at the broken ground, at the misplaced boulders and fallen trees, and then they looked at one another.

"This is not a good place to live," said Bowles.

PART 1

Cherokees West

1

The Mouth of the Verdigris River
June 1, 1816

It was a strange-looking camp with a hodge-podge of temporary dwellings — a few U.S. army tents were pitched along the bank of the river, not far away were several Osage tipis, their temporary dwellings while away from home, and, on the other side of the tents, were some lean-tos and brush arbors constructed by the Cherokees, a few tipis in their midst. The Cherokees had picked up some Plains Indian habits in their years out West. Both the Washashe, called Wasasi, or Ani-Wasasi in the plural form, by Cherokees and called Osages by whites, and the Cherokees had arrived early. They'd camped a good way apart and stared hard across the space at each other, waiting for the arrival of Lovely.

The U.S. soldiers, in the space between the two groups of longtime enemies, were uneasy. Their presence probably helped to ward off any sudden outbreaks of violence, but they were keenly aware that if such an outbreak should occur, they were vastly outnumbered.

On the one side the Osage paced, the men nearly naked, some wearing breechcloths and leggings, some only breechcloths, the scalp locks on their otherwise shaven heads adorned with feathers. The Osage weapons were all primitive, bows and arrows, lances, war clubs.

On the other side the Cherokees waited, dressed in buckskins much like those of frontier whites, but on their heads they wore colorful cloth turbans, some of them decorated with loose-hanging waterfowl feathers. Almost all of them were armed with long rifles, steel knives, and steel trade tomahawks of European manufacture. Some had pistols.

The Osages were headed by their great chief Clermont, a red deer-tail roach on his shaved head. He wore leggings fringed with scalps and a breechcloth, but was naked from the waist up. Several strings of beads and one round medal on a piece of rawhide hung around his neck. He had a wide brass band on his upper right arm and bracelets on both wrists. His ears were adorned with rings of beads, and his face was painted with vermilion. He carried a large red blanket, sometimes wrapped around his waist, sometimes slung loosely over one shoulder, and a wooden war club as long as his leg, with a metal blade fastened to one side. In spite of his medium stature, he cut a formidable figure indeed.

Tahlonteskee, half white, newly elected chief, represented the Western Cherokees. No taller than Clermont, he was dressed like a white man, except for his hunting jacket and turban. And Dutch, twenty-one years old, was present, watching everything with keen and fascinated eyes. He especially watched a young Osage woman across the way, and he wanted desperately to get closer to her, to get a better look.

Even from his distance, though, he knew that she was beautiful. He could tell by her step that she was young and strong. And he liked her step and the way her hips swayed when she walked. She wore a white fringed-buckskin dress and moccasins. Nothing more. Her hair was long and straight and shining black.

While he watched her, the young men on both sides began to get restless. Any small thing could have started a fight. William L. Lovely, agent to the Cherokees in Arkansas for three short years, arrived just in time, for both the Osages and Cherokees were getting impatient, and they were starting to give each other harder and harder looks across the way.

Lovely had served earlier as assistant to the Cherokee agent in Tennessee, and when the government had decided that it needed a Cherokee agent in the West, Lovely had seemed the likeliest candidate in spite of his advanced years and failing health. Indians, after all, were great respecters of age.

More and more Cherokees were arriving in the West all the time, getting tired of the pressures for removal back home. Both the state and federal governments were trying to talk all the Indians in the east into moving to new locations west of the Mississippi River. Sam Houston, who in his youth had been adopted by Tahlonteskee's brother John Jolly, had helped persuade Tahlonteskee and his followers, three hundred or so, to make the move in 1809, only six years after the Louisiana Purchase had been concluded.

Still, the vast majority of the Cherokees were standing firm behind Chief John Ross, insisting that they would never leave their homelands, now claimed by the states of Alabama, Georgia, Tennessee, Kentucky, Virginia, West Virginia, North Carolina, and South Carolina. It was becoming more crucial all the time to settle the troubles between the Osages and the Western Cherokees. It was difficult enough trying to get the rest of the Cherokees to move west, without the added problem of a major war being fought right where they were being asked to go. William Lovely had a plan.

"It was the French," he said, "who instigated these problems between you. I know that both the Cherokees and the Osages want peace. As things are now, no Cherokee or Osage woman or child is safe. You want to raise your families in peace."

Clermont, the Osage chief, rose up to speak. "The last time we came to talk to you of peace," he said, "on our way home we were attacked by our enemies." He only glanced toward the Cherokees present, but everyone knew that it was they he meant. "Ten Washashe warriors were killed," he continued. "Who is to say that such a thing won't happen to us again when we go home from this place?"

Then Tahlonteskee took his turn. "Under the faith of the president of the United States," he said, "I and my people came out here to this land, and we have been industrious. All I want is my house and my field, and to be friendly with my neighbors, but I am overwhelmed on all sides by strangers. Clermont and the other Ani-Wasasi say that we're hunting on their land. Where is my land that the president promised me? Our young men can't go out hunting without fearing for their lives."

"It's not the young men of my village who attack the That Thing on Their Heads People," Clermont responded, using the Osage designation for Cherokees, a reference to the turbans that they wore. "It's White Hair and some of the other chiefs. I only want peace."

Dutch looked at the scalps dangling from Clermont's leggings and wondered, in spite of the chief's protestations, how many of them were from Cherokee heads.

"My friends," said William Lovely, "the United States acquired this land from France only a few short years ago, and I was sent out here to work with you on these matters only three years back. These things take time, but I am here to make things right for everyone concerned.

"The Cherokees and the white people in these parts," he continued slowly, turning toward Clermont, "have claims against your people. The claims amount to a great deal of money, and I know that you have no money. But if you accept my offer, the United States will pay your claims for you, and we will have peace."

Lovely then outlined a piece of Osage land, between the Verdigris River and the place where the Cherokees were living in Arkansas. It was a vast territory. Though no one lived there, the Osage frequently hunted this land. The Osage towns were mostly to its northwest, and the Western Cherokee settlements of Spadra Bluff, Webbers, Point Remove, and Dardanelle were east, along the Arkansas River.

"Give that to the United States for the use of the Cherokees," said Agent Lovely, "and your claims will be paid."

To the amazement of Dutch and the other Cherokees, Clermont agreed, and Tahlonteskee, with the consent of all the Cherokees present, agreed to a peace. The war with the Osages had come to an end, and the Cherokees' land area was at last accurately defined. At the same time, it had been greatly increased.

Dutch did notice, with some amusement, that while the Indian agent was talking so hard to convince both sides to follow his plan, a young Osage man slipped behind the army tents, mounted the horse that Lovely had arrived on, and rode away on its back.

Then with the formal conclusion of the peace, a festive mood swept over the entire camp. A few Osages walked toward the Cherokee camp and a few Cherokees walked over toward the Osages. They shook hands and invited each other to share their food.

Dutch took advantage of the situation to search out the young woman in the Osage camp he had been admiring from afar. He came upon her just as she was coming out of a tipi with a pot of stew in her hand.

"Hello," he said to her, speaking in her own language. "I'm glad we've made this peace. Are you?"

She ducked her head modestly and answered him in a low, timid voice.

"Yes," she said. "I'm glad."

She wondered about this strange young man who spoke her language so naturally. Like most of the rest of his people, he wore moccasins and leggings, but he wore a white man's shirt under his buckskin jacket, and he had his head wrapped in cloth.

"I'm glad," said Dutch, "because it gives me a chance to talk to you. I've been watching you from over there."

She blushed a bit, keeping her head down. "You speak my language," she said.

"I've lived near your people since I was a child," said Dutch.

She gave a nod as if to say that his explanation was satisfactory, but she said nothing, and she did not look up.

"You know," he said, "I think the way to make this peace between your people and mine really last would be to have some marriages between Washashe and That Thing on Their Heads People. Don't you think that would be good?"

"I don't know," she said.

"If I had Washashe brothers-in-law," he said, "I wouldn't want to fight them. Do you have brothers?"

"Yes."

"You don't talk much, do you?" Dutch paused, waiting for a reply. "Where's your father?"

The girl pointed with her lips and eyes toward a tall, bare-chested Osage man with a painted face who was approaching, striding directly toward Dutch. He carried a short bow in his left hand and wore a quiver of arrows on his back.

Dutch turned to face the man. "I'm Tahchee," he said, "and I want to marry your daughter. How many horses would you want?"

"How many Washashes have you killed?"

the old man asked, frowning.

"How many That Thing on Their Heads People have you killed?" countered Dutch. "It doesn't matter any more. We have peace now. All that is behind us. How many horses?"

"Seven and seven," said the Osage, with a smirk. "Do you have so many horses?"

"I have one horse," said Dutch, "but I'll bring you twice that many. I'll be back. What's your name?"

"I'm Spotted Horse," said the Osage. "I don't need your name. I don't expect to see you again."

"I've already told you my name. It's Tahchee. Sometimes they call me Dutch. And you will see me again." He turned to the girl then. "And what are you called?" he asked.

"She's Wind in the Meadow," said Spotted Horse. "Now we have to pack our things. We're going to hunt the buffalo."

"Are there some near?"

"Of course," said Spotted Horse. "We saw them on the way over here. Clermont said we'd get some on the way home."

"Let me ride with you," said Dutch. "What I kill, you can have."

Dutch raced alongside the frightened

herd, neck and neck with the beast he had chosen to kill. He had not hunted buffalo in this manner before. Even though the Western Cherokees had been in the West for over thirty years, for more than his own lifetime, their manner of hunting had not changed that much, for they still lived in wooded hills, venturing out onto the plains only occasionally to hunt.

Cherokees had hunted the eastern buffalo for hundreds of years, either by sneaking up on them on hands and knees to get a close shot, or by driving small herds over the edge of a cliff. This plains style of running the buffalo and shooting from horseback was new to Dutch. It was exciting and exhilarating.

The frightened, great, shaggy beasts snorted and blew as they raced madly and blindly for their lives, churning up great chunks of earth with their sharp hooves and creating a cloud of dust that choked both beast and man. Like the Osages with their short bows, Dutch rode in close to the pounding herd.

He took careful aim with his Model 1803 Harper's Ferry long rifle and dropped a fine bull with one shot. Dutch managed to reload the rifle while staying in the saddle, the horse still running. It took all of his concentration, but he did it. Then, rifle once more ready, he looked over the beasts on his side of the herd and picked out another one.

In front of him and behind him and on the other side of the thundering herd, Osage hunters were dropping the animals with well placed arrows. A great cloud of dust hovered over everything. Dutch moved in again, catching up exactly with the animal he had chosen. He rode in close, rode along beside it. He aimed his rifle and killed it, again with one shot.

When the day was done, they counted their kill, and he had not gotten the most, but neither had he got the least. Even so, he noticed the Osage hunters scoffing at him. He approached his chosen father-in-law.

"I give you all these buffalo," he said.

Spotted Horse snorted.

"I know that your hunters are disparaging me," said Dutch, "but I got more than some. And you should know that this was the first time I have hunted buffalo according to your style. I think I did not do so badly."

"You killed these buffalo with a white man's gun," said Spotted Horse. "That's no way to hunt the buffalo. These others all used bows. These are good hunters."

Dutch's face burned red with humiliation and rage. Why hadn't the old man told him that before? Still, it wasn't too late. The herd was still in sight, although the sun was getting low in the sky.

"Let me use your bow and some arrows," he said.

"The hunt is over," said Spotted Horse.

"No it isn't," said Dutch. "I haven't quit yet."

"You can't catch the buffalo now. Your horse is tired."

"Are you afraid to let me try? Are you afraid that I can do better than your Washashe hunters?"

Dutch wondered if he was being too bold with these Osage people. He alone, of the Cherokees, had come away with them. They could kill him easily; the peace was not yet old enough for anyone to be used to it. They hated him still, he could tell. Perhaps, he thought, he shouldn't push too hard or fast. But something drove him on. He couldn't help himself.

"Let me have a bow and some arrows," he said. "I'll show you what a That Thing on Their Heads person can do."

He was racing after the herd, bow in hand, quiver of arrows on his back. The horse was tired, and he knew that he was asking much of it, but he had to show Spotted Horse and the other Osage hunters that he could do as well as they. He had to show Wind in the Meadow. He couldn't stand having been humiliated in front of her. He would run the horse to death if he had to.

His lungs felt as if they would burst as they sucked in dust with the air. His muscles ached, and he knew that the horse beneath him felt the same way. They would both rest later, and he would reward the horse, if it lived.

He caught up with the herd at last, and he rode up beside a cow. Something told him he ought to give it up, but he couldn't. He nocked an arrow, drew back the bow, and aimed. He drove the arrow deep, just behind the shoulder, and she fell. He spotted a bull, and he rode hard up beside it. He let fly another arrow, and he had another kill. And another. And another.

At last he dismounted and led his panting horse around to let it snort and blow. He too was panting. His chest was heaving up and down. But he had killed eight buffalo more, and all of these with Osage arrows. The leading Osage hunter had killed sixteen that day. Dutch had killed seven with his rifle, and now eight more. He wondered if it would be enough. Probably not. The seven killed with rifle balls didn't seem to count. Had he continued any longer, though, his horse would have dropped over for sure, and he himself might not have gotten up again after the fall.

He looked back over his shoulder, and he saw Spotted Horse and a few more men coming in his direction. They did not seem to be in a hurry. He continued walking his tired horse and waited for them to arrive. He noticed that Spotted Horse, each time he and the others passed by a dead animal, would stop and point to it with his staff. Finally he came close.

"I'm claiming all my buffalo," he said.

"I didn't get so many after all," said Dutch.

"You didn't do so bad," said Spotted Horse.

Dutch pulled off the quiver and held it and the bow out toward Spotted Horse.

"Thank you for the use of the bow," he said.

"It's yours," said Spotted Horse. "You used it well. Stay with us tonight and eat."

2

Dutch rode west. He had stayed with the Osages for one night in Clermont's Town, a town of one hundred fifty rectangular, curved roof, mat and skin covered dwellings of ten to fifteen people each. He had eaten with them and had been treated well enough, although many of the people had remained distant. He hadn't let that bother him. It was to be expected. After all, his people and theirs had, until recently, been killing one another.

He had slept that night in the home of Spotted Horse, the man who had invited him to stay. Wind in the Meadow slept the whole night in the same house, across from him beside the opposite wall. He had lain awake much of the night thinking about her, frustrated by her nearness, imagining her charms. In the morning he had thanked Spotted Horse for his hospitality, mounted up, and ridden out of Clermont's Town. He had not wanted to waste more time.

He rode west. There were things to be

done before he could get his wife. He had horses to acquire, and he had no money. Besides, he knew enough about these plains people to know how they acquired horses, and if they could do it, he told himself, he could, too. He had been on the edge of the prairie already with the Osages, but as he rode west, the land became noticeably flatter, and there were fewer and fewer trees. He felt vulnerable out in the open, for he was used to the tree-covered hills of the Arkansas country. He knew that he was as good a man as any, and if it came to a fight, in the forest or in the open, he would take it on.

After six days of cautious riding, he came across a village of conical, skin-covered lodges. He wasn't sure, but he thought that it must be Comanche. The village was beside a river, and a large herd of horses grazed contentedly just beside some trees that grew along the bank. Dutch hid himself and his horse in among a clump of trees in a place where the ground rose slightly. From there he could watch the village.

There were sixty or more lodges, and plumes of smoke rose from the holes of them all. A few boys and young men rode around the village on horseback, while dogs chased and barked. Small children seemed to be everywhere, running naked, laughing and playing. Women worked on hides, either staked out on the ground or stretched upright on frameworks of poles, and strips of meat hung drying on racks. A group of men sat cross-legged in a circle on the ground, apparently engaged in some sort of gambling game.

Dutch thought about the beautiful Wind in the Meadow. He recalled her voice, how it was like her name, and he tried to picture the details of her face and of her body under the buckskin dress. He watched again in his mind the movements of her body as she walked. She was the reason for this quest. He realized that, for him, she had become everything. And then he thought of the horses and he watched the herd and the village once more.

The horses were beautiful and strong and healthy. They all looked good, and he was glad of that, for he would probably not have time to pick and choose from among them. He estimated that the village could have as many as one hundred warriors, and, of course, as soon as they detected him, they would all be after him. He didn't want to fight. He wanted to get the horses and run away.

He tried to formulate a plan. If he could

find a way to get himself down to the herd undetected and drive off all the herd at once, he would have a chance, for any pursuit would have to be on foot. But then he noticed for the first time that there were some horses tied up close to lodges within the village.

They must be, he thought, favorite horses that certain of the warriors keep close by. They might even be kept close just because of a plan such as his. So even if he somehow should manage to drive off the herd, there would be a few warriors still able to follow him on horseback. He could see four, no six, such horses. Six warriors then. That, he decided, would not be so bad. He could deal with six.

He knew that he could ride hard and still reload his long rifle. He had learned that during the Osage buffalo run. But aiming and firing at a run was a different matter. With the buffalo, he had ridden close alongside his target. He would not be able to do that with six pursuing Comanche warriors who would also be shooting at him.

He watched the village overnight, all throughout the next day, and overnight again. The next morning, he was surprised to see close to sixty warriors mount up and ride away. The odds were suddenly much better, much more in his favor, and the horse herd still numbered, he estimated, over one hundred.

He waited until the mounted warriors were well out of sight and beyond knowing what was going on at the village. There would be no better time. He mounted his horse and rode hard for the herd, whooping and yelling. Women, children, and a few young men of fighting age ran out of their lodges to see what was going on.

Dutch was close to the herd, and two young men were running toward him from the village. He aimed his long rifle and fired above their heads. They dropped to the ground on their bellies. Dutch was now among the excited horses, still yelling. He jerked loose the tethers of the few that were thus secured and started them running east. Then he reloaded his rifle as quickly as he could, glancing back toward the village. The two young men were up and running toward him again. All the horses were running now.

Dutch aimed his rifle, and the two young men dropped to the ground again. He did not fire. Instead he turned to ride with the herd. He looked back over his shoulder

46

and saw two horsemen riding after him. This time, he knew, he would have to make a shot count. He reined in his mount and jumped to the ground. Taking careful aim, he fired, and the nearest rider toppled backward off his horse.

Dutch reloaded quickly, watching the second rider all the while. When his companion fell, the other had slowed. He looked down at his companion, then looked ahead at Dutch. He could see that Dutch was reloading. He screamed a war cry and rode hard toward Dutch, waving a war club over his head. Dutch rammed home the lead ball, pulled the rod out, and looked up just as the rider was close enough to ready his club for a downward swing. Dutch raised his rifle and fired. There wasn't time to aim. The ball tore into the rider's bare chest, leaving an ugly black hole. The man screamed out in pain and fell at Dutch's feet as his horse raced on by.

Dutch reloaded and climbed onto his horse's back. There were at least four more possible pursuers in the village. He raced after his newly acquired herd of horses.

Tom Taylor was amazed at the size of the herd of horses that came running into his yard. He squinted through the dust to see who it was driving this herd, and then he saw his nephew.

"Dutch," he called.

"Uncle Tom," said Dutch, "help me gather them and settle them down. Where do you want them?"

"In the corral," Taylor shouted.

Taylor's corral was overcrowded with the herd. The two men leaned on the top rail and looked the animals over.

"We'll have to build a larger corral," said Taylor.

"I'm going to take out twenty-eight of them," said Dutch.

"Twenty-eight?" said Taylor. "We'll still need a bigger corral. These are good looking horses, Dutch."

Taylor was curious. He wondered where his nephew had gotten such a herd of horses, but he didn't want to ask him directly.

Dutch knew that Taylor was angling for an explanation. He smiled. "They're western horses," he said. "Comanche, I think."

Taylor nodded knowingly. "And you're taking twenty-eight of them out?" he said.

"I'm giving them to Spotted Horse over in Clermont's Town," said Dutch. "I've asked him for his daughter."

"You want a Wasasi wife?" his uncle asked.

"I want Wind in the Meadow," Dutch said. "She's the most beautiful woman I've ever seen. I don't care what she is, Uncle Tom. I've got to have her. Besides, we're at peace with the Ani-Wasasi now. We're supposed to be friends."

"Being at peace is one thing," said Taylor. "Being friends is another. I'm afraid this will lead to trouble."

"If Cherokees and Ani-Wasasi marry each other," said Dutch, "then pretty soon we'll all have relatives on both sides. No one wants to fight his relatives."

Taylor wrinkled his brow in deep thought and stared out into the crowded corral where horses stamped and snorted, bumping into one another, tossing their heads, nickering and occasionally whinnying loudly as if proclaiming something to the world at large.

"I don't know," he said. "It worries me, but you might be right, Dutch. Anyhow, you're always welcome here, and if you get that girl for your wife, she'll be welcome here, too."

"*Wado*, Uncle," said Dutch.

Spotted Horse was stunned into total

silence when he saw twenty-eight horses headed for his lodge. The whole village came out to watch, and soon they all knew that the horses had been driven in by the Cherokee known as Dutch. In the midst of the swirl of activity, Dutch rode up close to the lodge of Spotted Horse and jumped off his mount to stand in front of the amazed old man.

"Twice two sevens," he said. "I've come to ask you for your daughter."

Spotted Horse had no love for Cherokees, but this young man was interesting: bold, impulsive, determined, and skillful. And the war with the Cherokees was supposed to have ended. Grudgingly, he told himself that perhaps it would all be for the best.

"My daughter is not for sale," he said. "She's not a slave. She alone will decide who she will marry. All I can do is consent to your asking her. Wait here."

Wind in the Meadow was hiding inside the lodge. She, like everyone else in Clermont's Town, knew why Dutch had driven in the twenty-eight horses. She glanced up briefly as her father came inside.

"That Thing on Their Heads person they call Dutch is here," he said. "He brought the horses he promised me. I didn't think that he would. Do you want to talk to him?"

She glanced up again at her father, then looked back down.

"Yes," she said.

They walked beside the river and talked. Dutch felt as if he were soaring in the clouds. He wanted to take her in his arms and hold her. He wanted, at the very least, to hold her hand in his. He did not. Eyes were on them from the village. It was not yet time.

"I want you to be my wife," he said.

"You don't know me."

"I know enough to know that I want you, and I want to know you better. I rode all the way to the Comanche country in the West to get those horses for your father. I risked my life for love of you."

"Maybe it was for love of excitement," she said. "All of our young men steal horses. It's what they do for fun."

"I love you, Wind in the Meadow," he said, "and I want you for my wife. There is no other woman I want. There is no other woman I will ever want. I'll build you a house and I'll get for you everything you want. I'll take care of you, and I'll never mistreat you."

"Would you take me to live with the That Thing on Their Heads People and build me a house like a white man's house?"

Dutch hesitated a moment. He realized that she might have laid a trap for him with that question. "My uncle said that we would be welcome at his settlement," he said.

"I'd be afraid," she said. "It would all be too different for me. This is the only life I know."

"Then I'll live here with you," he said. "I'll learn to live the way you do."

"If you'll do that," she said, "I'll marry you."

3

1817

They had been the happiest of people for a time, and Dutch had been more than content living there in Clermont's Town with Wind in the Meadow, the most beautiful woman he had ever known, the love of his life, living with her as an Osage. He would have gone around the world to live with her. But now their happiness had been shattered by the news of the violent death of her father. And he had not been alone.

He had gone out with a party of forty-eight Osage warriors into the western plains, and there they had encountered a small group of Pawnees. The Pawnees, though badly outnumbered, had boldly made a fight, then turned to run. The angry Osages had raced after them, shooting arrows as they rode, and the fleeing Pawnees had turned on their running horses' backs and sent their arrows flying back toward their Osage pursuers. Not many arrows found their marks in this running fight.

But the Pawnees had not been retreating, as it had appeared. Instead, they had been leading the unsuspecting Osages into a carefully laid trap. Four hundred Pawnees waited ahead in ambush, and the Osages had not even suspected it until they found themselves suddenly overwhelmed. The rest of the battle had been brief, decisive, and deadly. Forty-seven Osages had been killed, among them Spotted Horse. One had escaped to return home and tell the tale. No doubt the Pawnees had let him escape for exactly that purpose.

Dutch eagerly joined in the Osage war dance, painted himself for battle, and rode out with one hundred Osage men seeking revenge for the deaths. He did so for his wife and for her lost father. He took with him his long rifle as well as a bow and arrows, and he carried a steel knife and a steel war ax. The trip north into Pawnee country in the plains of Kansas took several days, but the fervor for revenge did not abate. The Osage weapons were thirsty for Pawnee blood.

It was midmorning when the Osage scout came riding back to the main group to report a Pawnee village not far ahead. It was down along the river, and they could see it from up above, he said. They followed the scout to the top of a rise overlooking the river valley and the unsuspecting town. It was just as he had said. No one among them knew if the Pawnees who had killed Spotted Horse and the others were in this village or even from it. No one cared. It was the first Pawnee village they had discovered, and they had waited long enough. It would do for their revenge as well as any other.

The leader of the anxious Osage war party studied the town for a brief moment, then raising his war club high above his head, let out a loud and fearsome shriek and began racing his horse down the slope. The others, Dutch foremost among them, followed.

Below, the Pawnees heard the frightening noise. Men ran for their weapons. Women grabbed up small children and raced for the river. Dogs barked and snarled and ran in circles, trying to decide whether to fight or flee. And the Osages, in a frenzy of vengeance, shot or struck at anything that moved.

They raced through the town, shooting arrows, swinging war clubs, killing any Pawnee they could reach, man or woman, young or old. It didn't seem to matter.

Dutch was appalled at the killing of women and children, but there was, of course, nothing he could do other than refrain from joining in. Besides, things were happening too fast, and some Pawnees were managing to shoot back.

Dutch searched for warrior targets for his arrows. He had fired his long rifle once, early in the attack, and had not bothered to reload it. His one spent rifle ball had dropped a Pawnee man just as he had come out of his house with a bow and arrows in his hand. Dutch had then quickly sheathed the rifle, and another Pawnee man had run toward him, brandishing a war club. Dutch had whipped out his steel war ax and split open the man's skull with one swipe. Then he had readied his bow.

The bloody fight was quickly done. Soon all the living Pawnees were in the river, trying desperately to reach at least the imagined safety of the other side. Some Osages rode into the water after them, swinging war clubs. Others shot arrows from the bank. Many Pawnees died in the water. Dutch sat in his saddle and watched. He liked a good fight as well as any man, but this kind of killing was distasteful to him. He soon turned away from it. He had seen enough.

Some of the Pawnees managed to escape across the river, and some small children were taken by the Osage men as captives. The rest were dead, and the Osages looted the town for anything of use to them, then set the rest on fire. They rode away in triumph, driving all the horses from the Pawnee village before them. Spotted Horse and the others had been avenged.

And Dutch's new life had taken yet another new turn, for the Osages had many enemies on the southern and western plains. He had gone out with them once, and after that, they expected him to go again. There were raids against the Wichita, the Comanche, the Kansa, the Caddo, and the Quapaw, and Dutch joined his adopted people on many of these raids. Sometimes they were raids for revenge, sometimes for stealing horses. Often they were just for the sake of adventure.

And then another and a newer threat to the Osage domain made itself known. More and more, white hunters were encroaching into the hunting territory claimed by the Osages, lands they had often fought and died for, defending them against various neighboring tribes. Clermont and other Osages saw this as a major problem, and one to be dealt with soon, before it got worse.

"Let's chase the Heavy Eyebrows out," he said, but he did not want to provoke the wrath of the United States by killing white men. So small bands of Osages, Dutch sometimes among them, sought out the camps of these intruders, and, sweeping down among them and taking them by surprise, they would steal all their traps and all their blankets and lead, even their horses, leaving them helpless far out on the inhospitable plains.

"That should discourage them," Clermont said.

Between the raids and the hunting trips, Dutch spent quiet, happy hours with Wind in the Meadow. He was now speaking the Osage language as if he had been born to it, and he had joined fully in the Osage cycle of life. He learned the songs and the dances, and he took part in all the ceremonies of his wife's people. It had always been the Cherokee way for a man to live with his wife's people, and Dutch had made the move wholeheartedly and without hesitation.

And because he had fought with them against their enemies, most of the Osages seemed at last to have accepted him as one of their own. Only a few remained distant. None insulted him or challenged him openly in any way, and he might have lived the rest of his life among them, there in Clermont's Town, with Wind in the Meadow, the woman he loved.

No one ever knew exactly what happened, or just who it was who actually broke the fragile peace. The Osages, already tense and edgy because of constant warfare with so many neighboring tribes and the more recent trouble with the white intruders, said that Cherokees, not satisfied with Lovely's Purchase, had been hunting on their lands again. The Cherokees, in turn, claimed that Osages had murdered some Cherokee hunters. Whatever the case, the peace between the two people, always uneasy at best, was broken after one short year.

Dutch was away from home when the Osage men went to his house there in Clermont's Town. Wind in the Meadow was just outside the house busy with domestic chores. Things seemed normal in the town. She did not suspect that she was in any danger there among her own people, in her own home. She smiled at the men as they approached her and gave them a friendly greeting. She had known all of them her entire life.

One man walked around behind her. She

thought nothing of it until she noticed the grim expressions on the other three faces.

"Is something wrong?" she asked.

"We've come to kill you," one said.

"But why? What have I done?"

"You took a That Thing on Their Heads person for a husband, a killer of Washashes."

She started to protest that her husband had lived among them as one of them for a year now, that he had come to live with them during a time of peace between their two peoples and had been with them ever since, even riding out to fight with them against their enemies. She started to say these things, but she never got the chance. The thoughts only flashed through her mind an instant before the man behind her crushed her skull with his war club. They left her lying there.

It was late evening, and Dutch was about to ride into Clermont's Town, but something made him pause. He had an uneasy feeling that something was not right in the Osage town. He told himself that he was being foolish, that his uncle Tom Taylor had simply made him nervous during Dutch's visit back at the Cherokee settlement that day. Taylor had told him that he

had better be careful, that he should probably bring his wife back to the Cherokee
settlements, because the trouble between
the Cherokees and Osages was heating up
again.

"They'll kill you just because you're
Cherokee," Taylor had said.

"I'm almost like one of them," Dutch
had protested. "I've fought with them
against Comanches, Pawnees. I've hunted
with them. I've lived with them for a year
now."

"What will you do when they ask you to
ride with them against some Cherokees?"
Taylor had asked. Dutch had no answer,
and Taylor had added, "That question will
be on their minds now, too."

Dutch sat on his horse, looking toward
the town, thinking about the things his
uncle had said. Perhaps Uncle Tom was
right, he thought. He decided that early
the next morning, he would take Wind in
the Meadow away from Clermont's Town
and move back to the Cherokee settlement. They would be safe there, living
near his uncle. Wind in the Meadow might
protest, but for once he would be firm. He
made up his mind. They would move.

He was about to ride on in, when four
mounted Osage men rode toward him,

whooping and brandishing war clubs. He took his long rifle by the barrel, and as the first rider came up beside him, he swung the rifle, knocking the man off his horse. The man wasn't dead, but he was out of commission. He was on his knees holding his head in his hands.

The other three riders weren't far behind, and Dutch raised the rifle to his shoulder and fired. The heavy lead ball tore a gaping hole in the chest of one of the riders, sending him rolling backwards off his horse. The remaining two kept coming. Dutch swung his rifle again, unhorsing a third Osage. Then, dropping the rifle and pulling out his war ax, he turned his horse toward the fourth rider and kicked it into a run.

War club and ax came together and locked, and both men toppled from their mounts, landing hard in the dirt. Dutch hit the ground, rolled, and came to his feet. The other rider was just a little slower, and as he was coming to his feet, Dutch split his head with the ax. He looked around. The man he had last unhorsed was up on unsteady feet, still holding his war club in his hand.

"Why have you attacked me?" Dutch asked him. "What's this all about?"

Just then six more riders came toward him, riding fast from the town and whooping as they rode.

"We'll kill you," said the man. "You might kill me, but those will get you."

Dutch picked up his rifle, jumped onto his horse's back and fled. The six riders kept after him. It was getting darker, and Dutch was riding hard, but he thought that he saw even more coming up behind the six. He loaded his rifle on the run, then pulled up beside a large boulder and dismounted. He took careful aim at the nearest rider and dropped him. Then he remounted and rode again.

As darkness fell, Dutch easily eluded his Osage pursuers, but then he worried about his wife. He could not simply ride away and leave her. He decided that he would wait a few hours to make the Osages think that he had gotten well away. Then he would slip back into Clermont's Town and get her. The two of them would steal away under the cover of darkness.

He left his horse well out of town, hidden in a cluster of trees, and he crawled the distance to his house, his belly pressed against the ground. He found her there as they had left her. Dutch took her in his arms and wept. He wanted to cry out, but if he had, they would have heard him and killed him, and he did not want to die, not until he had killed at least a hundred for what they had done.

Then he wanted to wrap her up and carry her gently back to his horse and take her away for a proper burial, but he knew that he could not even do that. They would see him or hear him. What he finally decided to do was risky enough. Slowly, carefully, as quietly as he could, he dragged her into the house and placed her on their bed. Tears were streaming down his cheeks.

He didn't want to leave her, even then, but he knew that he must. He left the house and returned to his horse the same way he had gone into the town, crawling on his belly. When he reached the grove of trees, he stood up and looked back at the sleeping town.

Several small fires still burned in front of homes. He would make use of them. He mounted his horse and rode out from under the trees, his rifle ready in his right hand. He surveyed the situation for a moment, then kicked his horse into a run and headed straight for the town.

As he rode into the town, he let out the shrill war whoop of the Cherokees, the piercing sound of the wild turkey's gobble, and he rode directly for the nearest of the small fires. Not slowing down, he leaned far to his left and swooped up a burning log from the fire. In one smooth movement, he slung the brand through the open door of the house that had been his home.

Continuing to the next fire, he grabbed up another brand and tossed it onto a nearby roof, and he managed the same trick at a third fire. By that time he was almost through the town, and he could hear people yelling behind him. He turned his horse sharply and saw an Osage man come out of a house. He lifted his rifle and fired, and the man fell back inside.

"It's Dutch!" someone shouted.

Dutch started riding back through the town. The three houses he had tossed firebrands at were all burning, and people ran screaming out of the two that had been occupied by the living. A big man holding a war club stepped out into the road, braced for attack, and Dutch rode him down. Another man waited ahead, and Dutch struck that one down with his rifle butt. He raced on through the town, and this time, he continued on.

A few men sent angry arrows after him, but they were shooting into the dark. They couldn't see their target, so their arrows were as useless as the names they shouted after him. A short way out, Dutch reined in his mount and turned around to look at the damage he had done. Clermont's Town was in chaos. Everyone was shouting, and people were running in different directions. He knew they wouldn't chase him, not in the dark.

He calmly reloaded the long rifle and took another look. A man was standing in the middle of the town, waving his arms as if shouting orders. He was illuminated by the firelight. It was a long shot, but it was worth a try. Dutch thumbed back the hammer, raised the rifle to his shoulder, and took careful aim. He squeezed the trigger and the man's arms waved one last time before he fell over on his back. The chaos intensified as a result of that final shot. Dutch watched for another moment.

"That was only the beginning," he vowed, and he turned his horse and rode east toward the Cherokee settlements along the Arkansas River.

4

Dutch saw the fire in the clearing in the woods ahead. Given the area he was traveling in, it could have belonged to almost anyone: Cherokee or Osage hunters, even white men traveling through. He decided to investigate cautiously. If he found that it was a friendly camp, he would announce himself and wait to be invited in. There was a slight chill in the night air, and they might have hot coffee over their fire. If not, well . . .

He left his horse well back in the woods and made his quiet approach to the camp. He carried his new 1814 .54 caliber Derringer rifle, and in the sash around his waist were tucked a brace of 1805 model .54 caliber Harper's Ferry flintlock pistols. All three weapons were loaded, primed, and ready to fire. He moved through the woods so slowly he seemed not to be moving at all.

Standing half behind a wide tree trunk, he looked into the small camp. Four Osage hunters sat around a fire. The smoldering hatred in his heart flared up. He thought about Wind in the Meadow, and he held his rifle ready in his hands.

"Hello, you in the camp," he called out, speaking in the Osage language.

The startled hunters all moved to one side of the fire to face the voice they had heard. Each man picked up a war club and readied himself for defense.

"Who is there?" one asked.

"It's late," said Dutch. "May I come into the camp?"

"Who are you?"

"You know me," said Dutch, and he stepped not quite out of the woods, raising his rifle to his shoulder.

"Dutch!" shouted one of the four, and Dutch squeezed the trigger, sending the .54 caliber lead ball into the man's bare chest. As their companion fell back dead, the other three vaulted across their small campfire to race toward Dutch, their war clubs high overhead.

Dutch smoothly and quickly leaned his empty rifle against the tree trunk and drew the pistols out of his sash. He let the men get close and then he fired first one and then the other. Two men dropped almost at his feet. He flipped the pistol over in his right hand, catching it by the barrel. He was ready to use it as a club to fight the last Osage, but when the warrior suddenly found himself facing Dutch alone, the man turned and bolted into the woods.

It's just as well, Dutch thought. Let him go home and tell the tale. He tucked the pistols back into his sash and withdrew his long steel knife from its sheath. He knelt beside the nearest body and grasped the scalp lock firmly in his left hand. He made a quick cut across the skin just in front of the hair, then jerked hard with his left hand, tearing loose the scalp. Then he stood up and moved over to the next body.

Tahlonteskee had called an emergency meeting of the national council of the Western Cherokee Nation to discuss the problem with the Osages. Two more parties of Cherokees had been attacked and killed by Osages while hunting in the area known as Lovely's Purchase. He also wanted to present to everyone who attended the meeting the venerable Degadoga, recently arrived from the old country.

"We have done everything we can to live in peace with our neighbors," Tahlonteskee said, addressing the assemblage there. "All we want is to live in peace, to raise our crops and our livestock. We want to raise our families in peace. We moved out here when this land was French, and then the United States government bought it from the French. They said they wanted us to live in peace, and so they bought Lovely's Purchase for our use, and they said that we were free to hunt over it as we please. We even signed a treaty with the Ani-Wasasi for Agent Lovely.

"But every day we hear another sad story. The Ani-Wasasi have killed another woman's husband, another mother's son. I say that it's time for us to declare war on the whole nation of Ani-Wasasi, and I urge you all to vote with me on this matter."

Old Degadoga rose to speak following the chief's address, and everyone present was respectfully silent and attentive. He was an impressive figure, tall and straight, even in his advanced years. His wrinkled skin was dark and his eyes were piercing and almost black. Long white hair fell over his shoulders. Standing about five feet and nine inches tall, he was at least sixty years old. He was wrapped in a blanket and wore a turban on his head. His right hand clutched a long staff, but he did not seem to lean on it.

"Listen to the words of your elected chief," he said. "The Ani-Wasasi have proved themselves to be a nation of liars.

What good does it do to talk with liars? None, of course. What good to treat with them? Even less. The only thing to do is fight them. Fight them to the death. Fight them and kill them until there is not one Wasasi left alive on this earth.

"And you will not be alone in this fight. I've been talking to the Quapaw, the Delaware, the Choctaw, and the Chickasaw. All of them hate the Ani-Wasasi and will join with you in this war to wipe them out.

"And your brothers in the old country have not forgotten you. They pity you in your time of trouble. If you give me leave, I can send word back east and boatloads of Cherokee warriors will come out here to join you in this fight. I say, let there be perpetual war against the Osages."

The vote was taken, and it was overwhelmingly for war. Because the Cherokees knew that the United States was opposed to war between them and the Osages, and that government had been a party to the previous treaty between the two, Tahlonteskee decided that it would be wise to inform the government, through Agent Lovely, of the Cherokees' formal declaration of war, of their intentions, and their justification. He sent a letter to accomplish that end. At the same time, Degadoga sent word back east.

71

★ ★ ★

The United States government, following urgent pleas from Agent Lovely, sent Major William Bradford, in command of a detachment of eighty-two riflemen, to establish a military presence in the Western Cherokee country, with the express purpose of enforcing the peace between the Osages and the Cherokees. While Bradford and his troops were en route from St. Louis, an army of six hundred rode out of the Cherokee settlements headed for the Osage country.

In addition to Tahlonteskee, Bowles, Dutch, old Degadoga and the other Western Cherokees, along with eleven white men who lived among them, there was a company of recently arrived Eastern Cherokees led by Captain John McLemore, a veteran of the Creek War, who had fought under the command of General Andrew Jackson. With them also were Delaware, Choctaw, Chickasaw, Koasati, Tonkawa, and Comanche warriors. Degadoga had been true to his word. Dutch took the point and led the way to Clermont's Town.

Dutch had not been back to Clermont's Town since that awful night almost one year earlier when he had discovered the body of his murdered wife and had made a desperate, lone swipe through the town. He had killed other Osages since that night, but he had not been back to Clermont's Town.

Riding back there at the head of an army, Dutch burned inside for revenge. He would kill an Osage any place and any time, but Clermont's Town held a special place of hatred in his heart. He longed to wipe it from the face of the earth. Perhaps that would erase the constant pain he felt for those lost days with his lost love.

Clermont, with more than two hundred men from Clermont's Town, was several days' ride away from home, having gone north and west in search of Pawnee or Comanche horses. They were not thinking of the Cherokees, and even if they had been, it would not have occurred to them that the Cherokees would ever be able to muster such a large force for a direct attack on the largest of their towns, in the heart of the Osage country.

It was business as usual in Clermont's Town. Children ran and played. Dogs barked or slept in the shade. Men, old and young, lounged about here and there. A group of young boys at the edge of town were busy with a game of hoops and sticks.

Women worked at various jobs, cooking, cleaning hides, chasing and scolding mischievous children. The young men who lounged about the town had recently returned from a long and tiring excursion. Now they rested while another group was on the trail.

Suddenly their peace was shattered by shrill war whoops and clattering hooves. They looked up from whatever they were doing to see the unthinkable sight of six hundred mounted men rushing toward their town. The massive daytime attack, unlike anything they had ever seen, was unbelievably frightening.

Children ran screaming for their mothers, and mothers searched frantically for their children. Men ran desperately for weapons. Many people of all ages and both sexes ran for the river, thinking that it might afford an avenue of escape. Some ran into houses, others came running out.

Some others ran for horses and mounted up to run away. The Cherokee-led army raced through the town, shooting and hacking unmercifully. Anyone who wielded any excuse for a weapon, even a piece of firewood, was cut down on the spot. The air was filled with hideous shrieks, war cries on the one side, screams of fear on the other, and howls of pain and moans of the dying from both sides.

Horses snorted and stamped, whinnied out their own animal fears and confusion, and screamed their screams of pain when hurt. Dogs barked and snarled and yelped, running here and there in the chaotic swirl of dust and blood, avoiding running human feet and stamping horses' hooves as best they could. Some of the bolder ones nipped at the legs of the invading horses.

Some of the attackers, perhaps a hundred or more, raced after those Osages who had gotten themselves horsed and were trying to escape. They shot at the backs of the fleeing people with guns and arrows, successfully knocking some of them from the backs of their horses.

Others lined up along the bank of the river, shooting at the ones who were trying to escape. Most still rode through the town, seeking out targets there.

At last the killing was done.

Several Cherokees had been wounded, not too severely, but none had been killed. One Delaware was dead. Fourteen retreating Osages had been shot from their horses' backs, and in the town and in the river, another sixty-nine were dead. Some of them were women and children, some old men. Over one hundred captives were taken. The rest of the population of Clermont's Town had managed to escape.

The victors then went through the town, checking in every house for anything of value. During their search, they discovered a number of scalps of Indians and twenty-five scalps of white men that Osage warriors had taken. Dutch was not among those searching the houses for loot. He was busy collecting his own scalps from the dead. He did not know how many Osages he had killed that day.

Captives and plunder secured, they set fire to all of the houses and trampled the crops in the field. What they did not intend to carry away, they destroyed. As they turned to ride back east, Dutch moved out of the line. Sitting on his horse's back he watched as the town that had once been his home was completely reduced to ashes.

He had thought that this day's business would bring him a feeling of elation, but it did not. He recalled the pleasant days when he had lived in Clermont's Town, when he had run the buffalo in the company of Osage hunters; when he had raided Pawnees, Comanches, and others with Osage companions; when he had shared a warm buffalo robe with Wind in the Meadow.

He looked at the ruins of Clermont's Town, watching it smolder, and a tear rolled down his cheek, and he knew that he was not yet done with this bloody business.

They were sitting around the yard in front of Tahlonteskee's house, Bowles, Dutch, the Egg, old Degadoga, a young man named John Smith, and some others, including the white man John Chisholm. McLemore and his company had already gone back to the old Cherokee country in the east, and they had taken with them most of the Osage captives from the recent battle. Chisholm had just returned from a visit to Fort Smith, newly established in Arkansas Territory.

"Major Bradford, the commander there," Chisholm said, speaking in Cherokee, "is very angry with us."

"We sent a letter to the government declaring our intentions and detailing our grievances against the Osage," said Tahlonteskee. "Why should this Bradford be angry with us?"

"He thinks that we behaved like the worst kind of savages," said Chisholm. "He says that we sent a friendly letter into Clermont's Town inviting them to come out and make a treaty with us. Then, he

77

says, one lone old Wasasi chief came out to meet with us and Bowles here crushed his skull. Then we attacked the town."

"No such thing happened over there," said Tahlonteskee, incredulous. "How could we send a letter to them anyway? None of us had paper or pen and ink."

"Then he says that there were no warriors in the town. He says the young men were all away on a buffalo hunt, and we killed only defenseless old men, women, and children."

"How can he say these things?" asked Bowles. "He wasn't there to see what happened."

"Major Bradford got his story from that Frenchman, Chouteau, and Chouteau got it straight from his friend Clermont."

"Clermont wasn't even there," said the Egg. "If he had been we'd have killed him."

"I wish he had been there," said Bowles.

"This Bradford must be a fool," said Tahlonteskee. "Does he really think that six hundred of us would bother to call out one old chief to kill before we attacked the town? What purpose would that serve? And does he believe that Clermont would take all of his fighting men away at once and leave his town completely unprotected, and go hunt buffalo without the women along to take the hides and cut up the meat?"

"I think that Major Bradford was really so upset," said Chisholm, "because his government sent him out here to stop the war and he didn't get here in time to stop us. He failed. Anyhow, he heard the tale first from Clermont."

"The Ani-Wasasi are all liars," said Degadoga, "and the man is indeed a fool to believe anything they say."

5

1818

Back in the ancestral lands of the Cherokees in the east, in the states of North Carolina, South Carolina, Georgia, Tennessee, and Alabama, the pressures on the Cherokees were growing. The United States had promised to exchange land in the West for any land given up by Cherokees in the east. A new treaty in 1817 had promised guns, powder, lead, traps, kettles, and blankets to anyone who would voluntarily move.

Tahlonteskee's brother, Ooloodega, also known as John Jolly, accepted the terms. He had good reason. Not only was his brother chief of the Western Cherokee Nation, his adopted son, Sam Houston, had been appointed sub-agent to the Cherokees in the east, and as a government employee, part of Houston's job was to help convince the Cherokees to move.

John Jolly led three hundred thirty-one Cherokees west. Just over a hundred of them were warriors, and each of them, according to the terms of the treaty, had a new 1814 model .54 caliber Henry Deringer rifle. The contingent traveled on thirteen flatboats and four keel boats, and it took them about seventy days to make the trip. Before leaving the old country, Jolly had written a letter to the U.S. secretary of war, John C. Calhoun.

He promised the secretary that he and his people would not revert to the "savage" life out west, and he asked that "missionary schools or some other teachers" be sent to teach the Western Cherokee children. He expressed the opinion that, by intermarriage, the Cherokees and the whites were "gradually becoming one people." And, he said, "We shall live in peace and friendship with all the Indian tribes west of the Mississippi River if in our power, and it is our wish that our difference with the Osage Nation may be amicably adjusted."

At the time he wrote the letter, Jolly was but a private Cherokee citizen. However, he and his followers were not long in the West before his brother, Tahlonteskee, old and tired, died.

They had a meeting then to elect a new chief, and two men got up to speak. One of them nominated John Jolly to be their new chief, and the other nominated someone else. Speeches were made in favor of each man, and then the two nominees were led away to a place where they could not see or hear what was going on.

Back at the meeting the two nominators stood far apart, and the people began to move to one side or the other to stand with the man with whom they agreed. When everyone had taken a position, the two groups of people were counted, and John Jolly was elected chief.

They met at St. Louis: an Osage delegation headed by Mad Buffalo, son of Clermont; Major Bradford; William Clark, brother of George Rogers Clark and famous on his own for his part in the Lewis and Clark expedition, and the recently appointed governor of the Territory of Missouri, which included Arkansas Territory; John Jolly and other leaders of the Western Cherokee Nation; and, since old Lovely had at last succumbed to the ravages of age, the new agent for the Western Cherokees, the much younger Reuben Lewis.

Because the meeting was ostensibly to come to some sort of agreement with the Osage, Degadoga refused to attend. Dutch also stayed home. When Jolly and the

Western Cherokees arrived, the Osage representatives had been waiting there with Governor Clark and Major Bradford for a week. Mad Buffalo's patience was at an end.

"We have not killed any That Thing on Their Heads People," he said, when the meeting at last commenced, "except those we found hunting on our land."

The land in question, further discussion revealed, was that known as Lovely's Purchase.

"Two years ago, the government gave us that land to hunt on," protested Jolly.

"It was not the government's land to give," Mad Buffalo said.

"Excuse me," said Governor Clark, "but I believe that an agreement was reached between the Osage and the late Agent Lovely for the purchase of that land, with the understanding that the government could give the Cherokees permission to hunt there."

"Maybe the Arkansas Washashes agreed to that," said Mad Buffalo, "but we did not."

After much discussion, a new treaty was drawn up whereby the Osages present finally agreed to give up any interest in Lovely's Purchase to the United States, and the

United States, in turn, agreed once more to allow the Western Cherokees freedom to hunt there. A further payment was made to the Osages by the United States. Also by this treaty, the Osages and the Cherokees, with their Delaware and Shawnee allies, agreed to a permanent peace.

"I thought all this had been done before," said Jolly. He shrugged off the thought and told himself, maybe this time it will work.

Degadoga, Bowles, the Egg, and a few others showed up at the home of Dutch. Sequoyah, only recently arrived from the east with Jolly's group, was among them. He was quiet and contemplative, with a faraway look in his eye. Tall and slender, he was dressed, like many of the others, in leggings and breechcloth, with a linen shirt and colorful jacket. His head was wrapped in a turban. Earlier, Dutch had noticed that Sequoyah walked with a limp. They all sat around in front of the house drinking cups of strong, boiled coffee.

"I didn't know if you'd be home or not," said Degadoga, looking at Dutch slyly. "I thought that you might have gone to St. Louis with those others."

"I'm not interested in making peace with the Ani-Wasasi," said Dutch. He sipped hot coffee, trying not to think about Wind in the Meadow. He found himself growing angry with Degadoga for bringing up the subject of the Osages and the peace conference. He didn't want to talk about it. He really didn't even want to think about it.

"I think John Jolly will make a peace with them over there," said Degadoga.

"Who knows?" said Dutch with a shrug. "John Jolly's a good man."

"Yes," said Bowles, "of course, but he's only been out here for a short time. He doesn't know the Ani-Wasasi the way we do."

"They're a nation of liars," said Degadoga, a hard edge to his voice. "Perhaps, when they have made their peace with the governor back in St. Louis . . ." He paused, seemingly in deep thought. The others watched and waited for him to continue. "It would be interesting," he said, "if someone were to meet the Ani-Wasasi peacemakers on their way home from this meeting. It would be interesting if they were to be killed on their way home."

Dutch's mood suddenly changed, and he smiled just a little. "No," he said. "Not killed. Not this time. But it would be interesting if . . ."

Dutch, Bowles, the Egg, and eleven others looked down on the Osage camp. Sequoyah had not come along because of his crippled leg. A good number, Dutch thought. Twice seven. It had not been difficult to locate the returning Osage delegates. The road to St. Louis was fairly well traveled. Dutch estimated that he and his followers had intercepted them about halfway home.

It was late evening, and the Osages had made camp for the night. They were just off the road. A small stream ran almost parallel to the road on the north side. South of the road at just this point was a high and long hill, covered with trees and dense undergrowth. From this thickness up above, Dutch studied the Osage camp.

He counted forty-six men around four small fires. They seemed relaxed. They were cooking, eating, and visiting. Now and then the sound of laughter reached up into the thicket on the hillside through the cool night air.

Not far from the camp, to the east, horses browsed along the stream bank. A long rope, or a series of ropes, had been strung from tree to tree to form a temporary corral to contain the herd for the night.

Because of the number of trees that lined the stream, Dutch couldn't be sure how many horses were there, but he knew that there were more than forty-six. Forty-six for the men. Maybe ten or a dozen extra.

He turned his head to look at Bowles on his left, and he nodded.

"I think it's dark enough now," he whispered.

"Yes," Bowles agreed.

"Let's go then," said Dutch.

Bowles grinned and started moving to his left. Six men followed him. Dutch led the remaining six to the right. When he had reached a point beyond the grazing herd below, he started down the hill. Bowles and his bunch would probably be doing the same, he thought. If Dutch's plan worked, he and his group would wind up close to the stream, east of the horses. On the far side of the herd was the Osage camp. Bowles and his six men would be west of the camp.

They moved slowly and quietly to avoid detection, and when they were at last in place, not far from the herd, they waited. Dutch and two other men drew out their steel knives. The heavy sounds of the grazing horses carried through the night, and now and then voices from the camp could be heard. Somewhere in the distance a whippoorwill called. Then suddenly the serenity of the Osage camp was shattered by the booming voice of Bowles.

"Dutch is here."

The Osage men quickly grabbed their weapons and got to their feet. They looked into the darkness of the west for the source of the voice, but they saw no one out there. They spoke to one another in hurried whispers. Hoots and calls from the unseen enemy lurking in the dark taunted them.

Dutch and the two other men with knives rushed to the makeshift corral and cut the ropes. Then all six men jumped onto horses' backs. They drove the herd out of the trees onto the road and headed them east. The startled Osages ran shouting toward the road as they saw their horses passing them by. Up ahead, Bowles and his six waited until the herd came by, and they raced to leap onto the backs of running horses.

The desperate Osages ran down the road in pursuit for a distance, but soon the only evidence of the stolen animals ahead of them was the thick dust from their pounding hooves still hovering in the night air. Laughing and riding hard, Dutch and the others ran the horses until they knew that they were well beyond any possible pursuit.

Much later, with the first morning light, they counted their newly acquired herd. There were forty horses. They had lost a few. Ten or twelve, Dutch thought, no more than that. Maybe the Osages would be able to round up the strays. Even so, they would have a long, slow trip home from the peace talks.

"What the That Thing on Their Heads People did to us was cowardly and wrong," said Clermont, who, of course, had not been there when the deed was done. "We traveled to St. Louis to make a peace with them. The peace was made, and they agreed to it. Governor Clark was there and saw it done."

Major Bradford looked across his desk at Clermont. At forty-eight, Bradford was an old veteran who walked with the aid of a cane because of a five-year-old gunshot wound to his thigh received at Fort Meigs in Michigan fighting Tecumseh's Shawnees.

"Yes, I know," he said. "I too was there, and even though you were not, your information is correct. Both sides agreed to a permanent peace."

"The That Thing on Their Heads

People are just no good," said Mad Buffalo, the son of the Osage chief. "The peace is broken. We're going back to war with them."

"Now wait a minute," said the major. "I can't let you do that. You know that my government sent me out here to establish Fort Smith in order to keep your people and the Cherokees from fighting with each other. We finally achieved a peace, and it was no easy task. We have to keep it."

"We cannot," said Clermont. "The That Thing on Their Heads People broke it before the ink was dry on the paper."

"They stole our horses," Mad Buffalo protested.

"But no one was killed," said Major Bradford, his voice betraying his exasperation. After a year at Fort Smith, he was just about fed up with this nonsense between the Cherokees and Osages. It seemed so simple to reach an agreement and then live up to it. Why couldn't they? He almost longed for the days when he had been fighting with the army against Tecumseh and the Shawnees. The fighting was easier than all this bickering, he thought.

"We had a long walk home," said Mad Buffalo. "They insulted us by what they did."

"We'll get the horses back," said Bradford. "All right? How will that be? We'll get them all back for you."

"You can make the That Thing on Their Heads People give us back the horses?" Clermont asked skeptically.

"Yes," said Bradford. "I'll make them return your horses."

"All forty horses?" asked Mad Buffalo.

"I'll get all forty horses back to you."

"Well," said Clermont, "but they still have one hundred Washashe captives. We want our people returned to us as well."

The major heaved a sigh. He stood up from his chair, and, taking his cane in his right hand, limped over to look out the window.

"The Cherokees claim that all the captives are women," he said. "They claim that the women have all married Cherokee men and don't want to be returned."

"Unless our horses and our people are returned to us," said Clermont, folding his arms across his massive chest, "there can be no peace with the That Thing on Their Heads People."

91

6

1819

Tom Graves could speak Cherokee as well as any, having lived among the Cherokees for years. He was a sandy haired, blue eyed white man who had married a Cherokee woman and fathered two children. And he had been made a Cherokee by adoption. A generation or two earlier, in a different town or with a different band, Graves might have found life among the Cherokees difficult, for he was headstrong and individualistic.

But life with the Western Cherokees was loose. Their towns were not clustered together. Rather, they were made up of a number of families scattered along a riverbank, living the lives of individual small farmers. If any of them felt like getting up to greet the day by going into the water, the way Cherokees had done for countless generations, they were free to do so, but there was no one going around calling all of the people out in the mornings for that purpose. There was no compulsion.

If Graves felt more like lying late in his bed because he had drunk too much whiskey the night before, which was often the case, he was free to indulge himself. If someone held a green corn dance or some other ceremony believed to be for the benefit of all, he was free to attend or to stay away. He liked it that way.

He had not been awake long, and he was still a bit groggy. He had sat up long into the night with friends drinking whiskey. They had not stopped until the jug was empty. Graves groaned and stretched his long, thick body as he went outside to relieve himself of the uncomfortable pressure on his bladder.

Sighing over the pleasant sensation of relief, he lifted his head and saw four riders coming his way. He squinted his eyes at them, and in another moment, as they drew closer, he recognized Bowles, the Egg, and two other Cherokees. He stepped over to his water barrel, leaned over it, and splashed water on his face. When he looked up again, the riders were in his yard.

"*'Siyo,*" he said. "Coffee's boiling inside. Come in."

Inside the house, the children had just

finished their breakfast, and Graves ran them outside to play. The five men sat around the table, while Mrs. Graves poured coffee all around. She also dished out food to everyone.

About halfway through his meal, Graves spoke through a mouthful of food. "What brings you by here this morning?" he asked.

"White men are here with those things they use to measure land," said Bowles. "We want you to go talk to them and find out what they're up to."

Graves rode with the others to the surveyors' camp. For a few moments, they watched the men at work. Then Graves rode up to the tent and found the man in charge. He talked to the man for some time, then rejoined his companions. Later they met at the home of their chief, John Jolly. A large crowd had gathered there.

"He told me that they're working for the United States government," Graves told the crowd. "He said this land all belongs to the government, and they're just now getting around to measuring it off. He said that right now they're measuring the land that the government gave us to live on, and our houses are on the wrong side of the line. He said we'll have to move our homes."

"We have our fields cleared here," said Egg. "We've built our homes."

"What else can we do?" said John Jolly. "If we don't move, they'll send their soldiers out here to make us move. Do we want to fight the United States? I don't think so. Besides, when I came out here, I promised to live in peace. How soon do we have to move, and where do we have to go?"

Graves shrugged. "He didn't know those things," he said. "He told me to talk to our agent. He's only measuring the land."

"We came out here to get out of the United States," Bowles said angrily, "and now the United States has followed us to this place. Right now they're trying to talk all of our relatives in the east into moving out here with us so they can have all of our ancestral lands in the east. Are they telling them that once they get out here they'll make them move again?

"The United States is nothing but trouble. They're worse than Ani-Wasasi. They can't be trusted. Well, they can't tell me where to live. You don't want to fight them? All right. I'll move. But I'm moving clear out of the reach of the United States. I'm going to the Spanish territory."

"I'll go with you," said the Egg. "I'm tired of this United States, too."

So Bowles, the original leader of the Western Cherokees, his family, and sixty other men and their families packed up their things and left. They moved south and west into the Spanish territory, outside the jurisdiction of the United States, and soon they were known as the Texas Cherokees.

It was early 1820, in the coldest part of the winter, when young John Smith, Crane Eater, and four other Cherokee hunters were breaking camp just north of the conflux of the Canadian and Poteau Rivers in the southern tip of Lovely's Purchase. Their furs were bundled, and they were ready to head for home with the morning light.

"Ani-Wasasi," said Smith, looking up toward the river. All six dropped what they were doing and grabbed up weapons as a dozen mounted Osages, Mad Buffalo in the lead, splashed into the frigid water from the opposite shore. The Cherokees waited, long rifles held ready, as the Osages came out of the water on the near side and rode slowly but deliberately toward the small camp.

"What are you doing here?" Mad Buffalo demanded, speaking in his own language, but none of the Cherokees in the camp understood what he had said.

"'Siyo," said Smith. He indicated the bundles of furs stacked off to one side of the camp. "We've been hunting here. We're just getting ready to go home."

No one in Mad Buffalo's party could understand the Cherokee words.

"You shouldn't be here," said Mad Buffalo. "We're taking the furs."

The Cherokees did not understand the words, but they understood clearly the intentions when four of the Osages dismounted, walked boldly into the camp right past the Cherokees, and started to take the bundles.

"Hlesdi," said a Cherokee, lifting his rifle to his shoulder as he turned to aim at the fur takers. Mad Buffalo flung his war ax. Its blade buried itself between the Cherokee rifleman's shoulder blades. The man cried out, dropped his rifle, and fell forward.

The other Cherokees raised their rifles to defend themselves, but the mounted Osage warriors rushed toward them, swinging war clubs. Smith's rifle and one other went off, but the balls went amiss. Crane Eater's rifle misfired. He and the other two owners of the now useless rifles turned and ran into the woods behind them. An Osage war club struck down another rifle barrel just as its owner pulled the trigger. The rifle discharged harmlessly into the dirt, and yet another Osage smashed his war club into the man's head. The last remaining Cherokee hunter fired a rifle ball that tore an Osage ear. Then he too was beaten down by war clubs.

Some of the horsemen started to pursue the three who had run into the woods, but Mad Buffalo stopped them.

"Let them go," he said. "Let's take their furs and horses and rifles and go home. Then we'll sell the furs."

Forty men rode with Dutch. Crane Eater and John Smith, two of the three hunters who had escaped from Mad Buffalo and the other Osages on the Poteau River, were along. So was the white man Tom Graves. The rage with which Dutch had set out had turned to grim determination. The business of Lovely's Purchase had been twice settled now. There should no longer be any problem in that area, he thought. He recalled Degadoga's explanation as he rode: "The Ani-Wasasi are a nation of liars."

They were getting close to Clermont's Town, now rebuilt, on the Verdigris River. Dutch was almost certain that he would find the guilty parties there. His intention, however, was not to attack Clermont's

Town, as he had done before. His hastily raised band was more like a posse than an army. He thought to demand from Clermont the surrender of the killers and payment for the stolen goods.

He decided that, rather than riding directly to Clermont's Town, he would stop at the trading post of Nathaniel Pryor a few miles downriver. Pryor did his business almost exclusively with the Osages and had become their friend. He could easily get word into Clermont's Town, conveying Dutch's demands.

Inside Pryor's post, a long, low log structure, Mad Buffalo and the trader Pryor, a short, stocky man in his early thirties, had just concluded a mutually satisfactory trade. The furs stolen from the Cherokee hunters were stacked on the counter. A young Osage man came running in.

"Dutch is coming," he said.

"How many men are with him?" Mad Buffalo asked.

"Forty men on horses."

"Shall we fight them?" asked an Osage.

"No," said Mad Buffalo. "Forty is too many, and the That Thing on Their Heads People all have guns. Let's get away before he arrives."

"They'll be coming up over the hill very soon now," said the young man who had reported the approach of the Cherokees.

"Wait then," said Pryor. "If you ride off now, they'll see you from the hill and give pursuit. I know what to do. There are only twelve of you. You can hide, with your horses, in the trees along the river bank back behind the post. When the That Thing on Their Heads People get here, I'll try to distract them and get them off their horses. Then you can ride away fast. You'll have a better chance that way."

Mad Buffalo and the others took Pryor's suggestion and hid themselves not far behind the post. Not long after they got themselves and their mounts well into the trees, Dutch and the Cherokees came over the hill. They rode directly down to Pryor's post. Pryor stepped out the front door to greet them with a smile spread across his face.

"Hello, my friends," he said. "Welcome. Get down off your horses and rest."

The Cherokees had made a long ride, so Dutch readily accepted the white man's invitation.

"Turn your horses in the corral," said Pryor. "There's water and grain. Then come on inside to warm yourselves. There's plenty of hot coffee."

There were not enough chairs inside for the forty Cherokees, so most of them sat on the floor, but Pryor had a big fire blazing, and it was warm. He also managed to get each man a cup of steaming coffee. Pryor watched nervously as Tom Graves and a couple of others took their cups and went back outside.

"Have you had any fur business with Osages lately?" Dutch asked Pryor, speaking in English.

"No," said Pryor. "Not for a month or so."

Dutch eyed the bundles on the counter, but he said nothing about them.

Even so, Pryor noticed the glance. "Some Delawares came by this morning though," he said. "They swapped that batch there with me."

Dutch read the statement for a lie, but still he kept his opinion to himself. "A dozen Osages attacked a Cherokee hunting party down on the Poteau a few days ago," he said. "They killed three men and they stole their furs. Horses, too. Guns, traps. Some other stuff."

"And you're looking for them, are you?" asked Pryor. Dutch nodded. "Well, I don't think you'll find them up this way. I don't think that it could have been anyone from Clermont's Town."

"I'm not surprised to hear you say that," said Dutch. "They're your friends. They're your trading partners. But I'm not as sure about it as you are. I think they might be from Clermont's Town."

"Are you going to ride in there looking for them?" Pryor asked.

Dutch sipped from the tin cup in his hand. Then he shook his head. "No," he said, "I'd rather not do that. I thought maybe you could get a message in there to Clermont."

"Why, yes, I think I could do that."

"We want to be paid for the furs," said Dutch, "and we want three Osage men delivered to us for the three of ours they killed. You tell them that."

"I, uh — I'll tell them," said Pryor. "I'll send the message in right now by one of my assistants." Pryor turned and left the room.

Crane Eater walked over to Dutch. "The furs on the counter are ours," he whispered.

Dutch glanced at the furs again. "I thought so," he said.

Just then the front door burst open, and Tom Graves came running through. "Ani-Wasasi," he said. "They're down at the river. They were hid down there, and they're leaving fast!"

7

Dutch tossed aside the tin cup he held in his hand and raced for the door.

"Let's get to our horses," he shouted. The others inside the building followed him. They ran to the corral out behind the post. Their horses were either eating grain or drinking water. The ones that had been wearing saddles had been unsaddled. They were penned inside the corral, a long pole laid in place across the gateway.

Tom Graves pointed toward the river. "There!" he shouted. "There they go!"

"Let's get after them!" yelled Crane Eater.

"Catch the Ani-Wasasi!" called Smith.

Dutch looked and saw the twelve mounted Osage warriors. They had already crossed the river and were racing away, not toward Clermont's Town, but west. Some of the Cherokees, including Smith and Crane Eater, were already on the backs of their horses, riding without the benefit of saddles and crowding each other to get out of the corral. On one side of the opening, the fence collapsed, and the riders broke loose and headed for the river.

Dutch let them go. He knew that there would be no stopping them anyway, and it would only make him look foolish to shout out commands that no one would obey. The Osages were too far ahead, but those young hotheads chasing them would have to find that out for themselves.

Dutch and the rest caught up their own mounts and followed them, but Dutch was in no hurry. He had no intention of wearing out his horse for nothing. He and his level-headed group loped along at an easy pace, knowing that the hotheads would soon give up the fruitless chase. He was right.

He soon caught up with them. They were walking their horses back toward Pryor's post, grumbling to themselves and making threats about what they would do to the next Osage they encountered. Mad Buffalo and his party were no longer even in sight.

Dutch turned his mount and headed back toward the river. "Come on," he said.

The disgruntled Cherokees followed him to a spot along the river bank upstream from where the Osages had been hiding, a spot where they could not be seen from

Pryor's post. There they dismounted.

"We'll rest our horses here for a while," said Dutch. "Soon it will be dark. Then we'll pay another visit to Pryor's post. We'll teach him that a white man should not take sides in this war."

He kept to himself while the others talked in small groups around several small fires. He was calm but angry. Dutch could understand business, and he had no quarrel with Pryor for having established his post near the Osage town and for dealing with the Osage people. But the white man, he thought, had no right to be meddling in the quarrel between the Osages and the Cherokees. And it was obvious to Dutch that Pryor had meddled.

Pryor had known that the Osages were hidden down by the river. He had possibly even known that the Cherokees were coming and had told the Osages to hide. Then he had invited the Cherokees into the post, offering the use of his corral, thus allowing the Osage warriors time to escape. He had clearly taken sides, and Dutch had resolved that he would suffer the consequences of that decision.

It was shortly after dark when Dutch and the other Cherokees rode again up to

Pryor's post. No light showed through cracks in the door or windows. The post appeared to be abandoned. They halted their mounts just outside. Dutch dropped to the ground and walked up to the door. He tried to open it but found it secured by an iron padlock. By that time, Tom Graves had stepped up beside him.

"Tom," said Dutch, "can you get us in?"

Several more Cherokees had dismounted and were standing around on the porch. The night air was cold and damp, and their breath came out of their mouths in little puffs that looked like wisps of fog.

"I never seen the house that I can't get into," said Graves, sucking in a deep breath and heaving his chest. He swept his arms out to his sides as if asking for space, and Dutch and the others stepped back out of the way, giving him plenty of room.

Graves pushed on the door with his palms a couple of times, tentatively, testing its strength. The staple and hasp were both fastened tightly into the wood. He pushed at the other side of the door, where it was hinged on the inside. It too was snug. He took another deep breath, then grasped the padlock in his big right hand. He put his left palm against the wall and pulled and pushed, but to no avail. He bumped the door with his shoulder. It didn't budge. He backed off a little and bumped it harder. It was firm.

Stepping back again, he looked hard at the door, and a kind of low growl came out of his throat. He was angry, as if at an enemy.

"You son of a bitch," he said, speaking in English.

He spit on both his palms, took another deep breath, then got hold of the lock with both hands. He raised his left leg, placing the sole of his foot against the door as high up as he could get it. Then he roared out like an angry lion, pulling and twisting on the lock and pushing with his foot.

There was a loud ripping, splintering sound, and suddenly Graves flew back, falling over onto the porch, his momentum causing him to perform a complete backward roll off the edge. He landed with a belly flop hard in the dirt, sending up a cloud of dust. He lifted his head to look. The door was standing open. The lock still fastened the hasp to the staple, but the staple had been pulled loose from the door frame.

Some of the men crowded anxiously onto the porch and through the doorway into the dark interior of the post, some of them almost stepping on Graves to get there. With the unruly mob at last out of the way, Dutch, smiling, stepped over to Graves and offered him a hand up. Then the two men went inside.

It was almost too dark to see what was going on, but Dutch could tell what was happening by the sounds. They were knocking things over, running into each other and groping around to see what they could get their hands on. Dutch found an oil lamp on the counter and carried it with him to the fireplace where there were still glowing embers. He pulled a splinter off of some kindling, and soon he had a match with which he lit the lamp. He held it up and looked around the room.

"Get the furs," he said, and he had to shout to make himself heard over the din. "Get all the furs."

Some of the men began to gather the bundles of furs and take them outside to load onto the backs of their horses. Then they loaded powder and lead. Some stole cloth and some tools. They took coffee and flour and whiskey. When they had all they wanted or could manage to carry, they threw the rest on the floor, smashing and breaking what they could. They turned over counters and shelves. At last they left.

Dutch's uncle, Tom Taylor, found his nephew inside his house cleaning his pistols. He stepped over to the table, pulled out a chair across from Dutch, and sat down. Dutch glanced up.

"*'Siyo*," he said. "Help yourself to the coffee or whatever else you like. I have gun oil on my hands."

"Major Bradford is here with me," said Taylor, "with that new agent, Agent Lewis. They've come from Fort Smith to talk to you about that business at Pryor's post."

Dutch raised an eyebrow. "Well," he said, "I don't believe that I have anything to talk about with those men."

"They've had a long ride," said Taylor. "They're waiting just outside. May I bring them in? It's cold out there."

"Bring them in," said Dutch with a shrug. "I won't leave any man standing out in the cold."

He kept cleaning his pistols, even when the white men came into his house and stepped over close to the fire, even when they spoke to him. He only glanced up and nodded. It was rude, and he could tell that his uncle was embarrassed by his behavior, but these men were trying to lord it over the Cherokees, and Dutch thought that they needed to know what he thought about that. They needed to know that they could not intimidate him.

"I recently had a visit from Nathaniel Pryor," said Major Bradford. "Do you know Nathaniel Pryor?"

Dutch made no response. It was an insulting question, the kind of question one might ask a naughty child. Of course Dutch knew Pryor, and the major knew that Dutch knew him. He laid aside one pistol and picked up the other one.

Bradford cleared his throat. "Pryor's post was robbed," he said. "All of his furs were taken, as well as some other things." He paused, and still Dutch said nothing. "He — that is, Pryor," Bradford continued, "he accused you of having done the deed. You and your followers."

Dutch raised his head and looked the major in the face. The officer began to fidget under Dutch's cold stare before Dutch decided to break the silence.

"Did he see me do this deed?" asked Dutch.

"Well, no, but —"

"Did someone else see me and tell him?"

"No."

"Yet you believe him."

"No," said Major Bradford. "I —"

"When we have a complaint," said Lewis, "we have to investigate. We've only come to tell you that you were accused and to find out what you have to say."

"If Pryor didn't see me," said Dutch, "and no one else saw me and told him about it, then I think he's accusing me falsely. Don't you? He's a liar. He's been around the Osages too long."

"Pryor said that —"

"My horse was stolen while I was away from home," said Dutch, interrupting Agent Lewis. "I think that it was you who stole it, Mr. Lewis."

"Now, see here," said Bradford, blustering, and raising his walking stick as if to punctuate his speech.

"That is the way that Pryor has accused me of robbing his store," said Dutch.

"Uh, yes," said Lewis. "I can see your point. But Pryor said that you were in pursuit of some Osages and you stopped in at his post earlier that day."

Dutch put down the pistol he was working on, wiped his hands on a rag, and leaned back in his chair, his arms folded across his chest. He looked up at the U.S. government's agent for the Western Cherokees, and he thought that he had liked Agent Lovely better than he liked this man.

It was too bad that Lovely had died. But then, he had been an old man.

"You came to ask me what I know about the robbing of Pryor's post?" said Dutch.

"Yes," said Lewis. "That is correct."

"Well," said Dutch, "I did it."

"You did it?" asked Major Bradford.

"I broke into Pryor's post and took the furs."

"You admit it?" said Lewis, astonished.

Major Bradford and Lewis looked at each other and stammered. At last the agent got control of his tongue.

"But we can't have that," he said. "You can't go around stealing from white men and expect the United States government to look the other way. Pryor has a license from the government. The government has an obligation to protect its citizens."

"We have a war," said Dutch.

"The United States government is very well aware of your war with the Osage Nation," said Bradford. "I was sent out here to put a stop to it. That is the whole reason for the existence of Fort Smith."

"But you haven't stopped it," said Dutch. "Have you?"

"It is painfully obvious that I have not."

"Then, as I said, we have a war. If Nathaniel Pryor wants to be left out of this war because he is a white man with a license, then he should not take sides. That's all I have to say about it, except that any man, Indian or white, who takes sides with my enemies against me and my people may consider me his enemy from that day on."

He leaned forward over the table again and started to load his pistols, and there was a long moment of tense silence.

"Are you taking sides in this fight?" Dutch asked.

"No," said Agent Lewis.

"We're only investigating," said the major.

"Is your investigation over with?"

The officer and the agent looked questioningly at one another and shrugged simultaneously.

"Why, uh, yes," said Bradford. "I believe so."

"What will you do now?" Dutch asked.

"We'll forward a report to the war department," said Lewis. "That's the standard procedure."

"Good," said Dutch. "We'll see what your war department has to say."

Tom Taylor had sat silent throughout the discussion. Here he stood up. "Gentlemen," he said, "can you tell us what will be in your report?"

"Well," said Lewis, "it will say that Pryor

made his complaint and his accusation, and it will further say that Dutch has admitted to being the perpetrator but has also said that Nathaniel Pryor had improperly interfered in the troubles between the Cherokee and the Osage. That's all we can say."

"Good," said Dutch.

He continued working on his pistols, and Tom Taylor ushered the two officials out of the house. The interview was clearly at an end.

8

1820

Pryor simmered inside with quiet rage and righteous indignation. He had been wronged mightily, he believed, and just as firmly, he believed that his government should set things right. Dutch and his outlaw Cherokees had robbed him and broken up his store, and he had made the long and difficult trek to Fort Smith to lodge a complaint and file a claim. Then he had gone home and waited.

He knew that these things took time. He knew that neither the military Bradford nor the civilian Lewis could satisfy his claim. He knew that they would have to write to Washington and wait for a response. But he decided that he had waited long enough, and he made the trip again to Fort Smith. He found Agent Lewis in his office.

"Why, Mr. Pryor," said Lewis, standing up behind his desk. "What brings you all this way from home again so soon?"

"I don't believe that it's so soon," said Pryor. "I believe that I've waited long enough, and since neither you nor Major Bradford has seen fit to send me any kind of word, I've come back at my own expense to find out what's happened."

"You're, uh, referring to your claim against the government, I suppose," said Agent Lewis.

"Of course, I'm referring to my claim," said Pryor, just managing to control his temper. "Have you received any response from Washington?"

"Well, the report, along with your complaint and your claim, was filed with the war department," said Lewis. "The war department won't respond directly back to me on the matter. They'll go through military channels, I believe, on any claims involving Indian depredations."

"Bradford?" snapped Pryor.

"Yes," said Lewis. "I believe so."

"Have they answered him then?"

"Uh, yes. I believe they have. No. I'm sure they have."

"Well then?"

Lewis shrugged. "Well what?" he said.

"Well, what the hell did they say?"

"I'm afraid that I can't tell you," said Lewis. "The correspondence was received by Major Bradford. You'll have to ask him."

Pryor turned and headed for the door. "Well, by God, I will then," he said.

"Wait," said Lewis. "I'll go with you." But Pryor did not wait, and Lewis had to run along, trying to catch up. It was warm outside, and Lewis slapped at gnats as he ran along in the trader's footsteps. He tried to reach the door to the major's office before Pryor, but he was unsuccessful. Pryor jerked it open and stormed inside. An orderly jumped up to attention behind a small desk just as Lewis came puffing in behind.

"Can I help you, sir?"

Pryor struggled with himself for a moment, trying to decide whether to answer the orderly or to burst on into the major's office. At last he took a deep breath and, standing in the middle of the room, looked at the young soldier.

"I need to see the major," he said.

"The major's busy just now," said the orderly. He gestured toward a couple of straight-backed chairs against the far wall. "If you want to sit down and wait, I'll tell him you're here just as soon as he's free."

Pryor made a movement as if he would burst into the office anyway, then hesitated as Lewis stepped up and put a hand on his shoulder.

"Corporal, do you think the major will be long?" Lewis asked.

"Well, sir, it's hard to say. They've been in there for near an hour."

"Come on," said Lewis to Pryor. "Let's sit down and wait a little."

"Aw, hell," said Pryor, and he allowed Lewis to usher him to the chairs. Both men sat down. The orderly moved back around behind his desk and sat. Pryor was red in the face with anger, and he drummed his fingers on his thighs in his impatience.

Then the door to the inner office opened, and Dutch stepped out, followed closely by Bradford, leaning on his cane. Pryor came at once to his feet. Lewis stood up quickly and nervously. Dutch recognized Pryor immediately and smiled.

"Hello, Mr. Pryor," he said. "I haven't seen you for a while. How's business?"

Lewis could hear a rumbling come from Pryor's throat, and he put a hand on the trader's back and pushed him toward the major's office door.

"Let's go in," he said. "Come on."

Pryor scowled at the smiling Dutch as he passed by him, moving on into the office followed by Lewis, and in another moment, Major Bradford came back into the room and shut the door.

"What was that son of a bitch doing here?" Pryor demanded.

"Mr. Pryor," said Bradford, "I am not required to explain to you the business of this office, and I would appreciate it if you would keep a civil tongue in your head." He sat down behind his desk. "Please state your business," he said.

"Major," said Pryor, "I've come all the way from the Verdigris, and I would think that you would know my goddamned reasons for being here."

"I will not tolerate that kind of language here," said Bradford. "If you persist in it, I'll have you forcibly ejected from this post."

"Mr. Pryor came to ask about Washington's response to his claim," said Lewis. "I thought that you should be the one to tell him, since the correspondence came to you."

"Quite right," said Bradford. "Mr. Pryor, the war department has denied your claim."

"What?" roared Pryor. "How can they?"

"They agree entirely with the Cherokee position as expressed by Dutch," Bradford continued. He picked up a letter off the top of his desk and read from it. " 'A license to trade by no means bestows upon the licensee the right to involve himself in disputes between different tribes of Indians, and although we do not condone his actions, we agree with the Cherokee Dutch in that Mr. N. Pryor should not have taken sides in the matter. The United States government cannot be held responsible for Mr. Pryor's losses in this instance.' "

"What kind of a judgment is that?" roared Pryor. "I'll write to the president!"

"You can write to whomever you wish," said Bradford. "The matter is out of my hands."

Pryor stomped to the door and jerked it open.

"Mr. Pryor," said Bradford. Pryor stopped and looked back over his shoulder at the major. "I have only one thing more to say to you."

"Yeah?" said Pryor. "What's that?"

"Under the circumstances, I would say that you're extremely fortunate not to have been at the post when Dutch and his men returned. You might easily have been killed. Instead of complaining, you should count yourself lucky. Oh, yes, and, uh, I'd watch myself from here on out if I were you."

Pryor grumbled and stormed out of the building.

Lewis sat down and heaved a sigh of relief. "I'm glad that's over with," he said.

"Oh," said Bradford, "we haven't heard the last of Mr. Nathaniel Pryor. He probably will write to the president and to the secretary of war and anyone else he can think of. Would you like a cup of coffee, Mr. Lewis?"

"Yes. Thank you."

Major Bradford called out to the orderly to bring two cups of coffee into the office. Then he leaned back in his chair. "Relax, Mr. Lewis," he said. "As I told Mr. Pryor, it's out of our hands now. He can send letters all over the country as far as I care."

"Yes," said Lewis. "All right. He certainly was angry, though."

"In a way," said Bradford, "I suppose I can't blame him for that. He suffered some heavy losses, but he should never have gotten himself involved in a dispute between the tribes. He brought it all on himself."

"Yes," said Lewis. "He certainly did that."

The orderly brought in the coffee, placed a cup on the major's desk, and handed another to Lewis.

"That's all, Corporal," said Bradford. "Thank you."

"Thank you," said Lewis.

"Yes sir," said the orderly, and he left the

room, closing the door behind him.

Lewis took a tentative sip of coffee. It burned his tongue. "Major Bradford?" he said.

"Yes?"

"May I ask, what was Dutch doing here?"

Bradford chuckled. "The sly devil knew that Pryor was on his way here," he said. "He pretended to be interested in the war department's response to Pryor's complaint, but I suspect very strongly that his real purpose was nothing more than to further aggravate Pryor."

"If that was his intent," said Lewis, "it certainly worked."

"Yes." Bradford put his cup down on his desk and picked up a piece of paper. "I'm glad you came over," the major said. "I have another piece of correspondence here that you'll be interested in."

"Oh?"

"We have been officially organized into Arkansas Territory, and we have a new governor on his way out here to join us. A Mr. James Miller of New Hampshire."

"Is the extent of the territory what we were expecting?"

"Yes, pretty much," said Bradford. "East to the Mississippi River, west to the one-hundredth meridian."

"And Governor Miller?"

"As I said, he's on his way," said Bradford. "I also have a letter from him. He's requested us to arrange a meeting for him at Clermont's Town with the Cherokee chiefs. We're to try again to make a peace between the two tribes."

"I see," said Lewis. "I wonder if Dutch has left the post yet."

"I don't think so," said Bradford. "I asked him to wait awhile for us so we could talk about this meeting. He said he would."

"Oh, good."

"Shall we go find him?"

Major Bradford and Agent Lewis located Dutch lounging in front of the sutler's store. They pulled up chairs and joined him there in the shade.

"Dutch," said Bradford, "the United States has made us into a new territory here. It's called Arkansas Territory. And we have a new governor on the way."

"Governor Miller wants to meet with your chiefs and the Osage chiefs at Clermont's Town when he arrives," said Lewis. "He wants to talk of peace between your two tribes."

"Another peace talk?" said Dutch.

"Governor Miller wants to try to settle

this business once and for all," said Lewis. "Would you mention this to Chief Jolly?"

"I'll tell him," said Dutch.

"Good," said Bradford.

"Some Cherokees would like to live in Lovely's Purchase," said Dutch. "Not just hunt there. Maybe we could talk about that."

"Perhaps we could," said Lewis. "We'll mention that to the new governor."

"And you will ask Chief Jolly to attend the meeting?" said Bradford.

Dutch nodded. "John Jolly'll probably agree to go there," he said. "He wants peace."

"And Degadoga," said Bradford. "Will he come along?"

"I don't think so," said Dutch. "He doesn't want peace. Not with the Osages. He says they're a nation of liars, and you can't make treaties with liars."

"But he's your war chief, isn't he?" asked Bradford. "How can a treaty be made at all without his involvement?"

"We probably can't make a treaty without him," said Dutch, "but we'll go there and talk if you want us to."

"I wish you would try to convince Degadoga to join us there," said Bradford.

"If he comes back before the time for the

meeting, I'll tell him that you want him to be there."

"If he comes back?" asked Lewis.

"Where has he gone?" asked Bradford.

Dutch shrugged. "I don't know where he is," he said. "He's gone to see the Caddos and the Quapaws, I think. Maybe some other people. He's gone to ask them to help us wipe out the Osages."

"Good God," said the major. "We can't have that. Especially not now with the new governor coming and expecting us to hold a peace conference. Dutch, you've got to help us. Please. Try to stop Degadoga and the others from any further attacks on the Osage, at least until we have the meeting."

"Only a few months ago," said Lewis, "you had more families come out here from the east, did you not?"

"Yes," said Dutch. He thought of Tobacco Plant, Nofire, Traveling Wolf, Frost, Pumpkin Boy, Gunrod, Gunstocker, Ajila, Whirlwind, Broom, Angry Worm, and all the others, nearly four hundred families in all. And then he thought of Wind in the Meadow.

"The continuation of this war endangers all their lives," said Lewis. "For God's sake, Dutch, let's put a stop to it."

"When will this meeting be?" asked Dutch.

"The twentieth of April," said Bradford. "At Clermont's Town. John Jolly, Degadoga, you, perhaps one more chief."

"I'm not a chief," said Dutch.

"Nevertheless," said Bradford, "we'd like to include you. Come here first and ride along with us if you like."

"We're not afraid to ride into Clermont's Town," said Dutch.

"Then you'll be there?"

"I don't know. I'll tell the others what you said."

9

Chief John Jolly was not fit for travel. He was getting old and he was not feeling well. He needed a little rest. And Dutch, of course, had been right about Degadoga. The stubborn war chief did not want to even consider the possibility of making peace with the Osage and absolutely refused to meet with them, especially in their town.

But John Jolly was still interested in pursuing the peace. He had meant the words he had sent to Mr. Calhoun. So even though he could not make the trip to Clermont's Town himself, he sent Dutch and three others in his place with instructions to listen to the talk, make no promises, and bring back word of what had been discussed.

Dutch and the others rode toward the big Osage town on the Verdigris River. They kept a careful watch all along the way, for even though they were going to the talks, they did not trust the Osages. Some might attack them as they traveled, even with the U.S. agents in their town.

They were only a few miles from their

destination when they spotted a canvas tent beside the river. Horses were picketed there and some men were sitting out in front of the tent. A fire blazed, and a pot was on the fire. Riding closer, Dutch recognized first Agent Lewis then Major Bradford. There were other soldiers there, and he saw another civilian. The four Cherokees rode on up to the camp.

"Hello, Dutch," said Lewis. "Welcome. All of you, welcome. We're glad that you're here. Please get down and join us."

The Cherokees dismounted and a private took their horses. Dutch counted six more privates and a sergeant. He looked at the civilian stranger, tall and straight, with a military bearing even in his dark civilian suit. Dutch guessed the man to be younger than he looked. The whiteness of the short-cropped hair, he thought, was most likely premature.

"Governor Miller," said Lewis, "may I present Dutch, a very prominent member of the Western Cherokee Nation?"

"How do you do?" said Miller, and he offered his hand. Dutch took it.

"Governor Miller," he said. "Allow me to introduce the rest of my company. Crane Eater, Pumpkin Boy, and John Smith."

"I'm glad to meet all of you," said the new governor. "Please be seated. We have some fresh coffee. Would you care for some?"

"Thank you," said Dutch.

They all sat down on folding camp stools with canvas seats, and a private poured coffee all around.

"I trust you had a pleasant journey," said Lewis.

"Yes," said Dutch. "Thank you. We had no trouble. I guess the Osages are all in town for the meeting."

The other three Cherokees chuckled, but the white men pretended not to hear or not to understand the joke.

"We've been waiting here —"

Bradford started to speak, but Governor Miller cut him off by clearing his throat loudly and giving him a stern look. The major ducked his head under the hard look of the governor and then started over.

"We've been camped here now four days," the major said. "We've had a chance to talk with the Osage leaders. They say that you're still holding some of their people captive, and they want them returned. They say that there can be no peace as long as Cherokees hold Osage captives."

"We still have four of them, I think," said

Dutch. "When we told one little Osage girl that we'd be bringing her back home if we made peace, she cried and ran away to hide. She doesn't want to come back here."

"They're all children," said Pumpkin Boy. "They're all back in the eastern country and going to school. They're better off there. What would they do back here? Run barefoot and grow up ignorant? They know something better now, a better life."

"Well," said Miller, "I think the Osages will talk of peace if we can get the captives back. They are insistent on that point."

"We can be insistent, too," said Dutch. "Osages killed those three Cherokee trappers south of here in Lovely's Purchase. They gave that land to you, and you told us we could hunt there. Before we talk of peace, we want the Osage murderers. Tell them to give those men to us. Then maybe we can talk of peace."

Miller cleared his throat again. "We'll ask them about that," he said, "when we meet again in the morning. I, uh, I think it would be best if you four waited here at our camp tomorrow while we go into Clermont's Town to talk."

Dutch shrugged. "It makes no difference

to us," he said. "We've heard them talk before."

The soldiers, on orders from Major Bradford, all turned in early that night, all except one private who stood guard over the camp. The major himself and the two civilians sat up for a little while longer, but soon they too crawled into their bedrolls. Dutch and the other Cherokees had made their small fire away from the white men's camp, and they sat up late into the night, talking, laughing, and smoking. Early the following morning, when the governor and his entourage headed for Clermont's Town, leaving one private to guard the camp, most of the Cherokees were still asleep.

It was late afternoon when the delegation returned to their camp. Two of the privates prepared a large meal, and everyone ate. Then Governor Miller decided that it was time to fill the Cherokees in on the day's events.

"I mentioned what you said about the murderers of the Cherokee hunters," the governor said, "and they freely admitted that those men are among them, even now." He paused, waiting for some kind of reaction from Dutch and the other Cherokees, but he received none. "They continued to insist, however," he said, "that there can be no further progress toward peace without the return of the captives. They also said that you have some of their horses. They want those back."

"They've stolen Cherokee horses, too," said Dutch. "If we give them back their horses and the captives, will they then give us the murderers and our horses?"

"Yes," said Miller. "That was my understanding from them today, and I will insist upon it."

"The captives are in Tennessee," said Dutch.

"Let's all meet again on, say, the first of October," said Miller. "Will that give you time to bring back the captives?"

"Yes," said Dutch. "If we decide to do it."

"All right," said the governor. "We're agreed that far. We'll meet again, all of us here and representatives from the Osage Nation. We'll meet October first in Fort Smith."

"Perhaps," said Lewis, "since the journey won't be so far, you can bring Chiefs Jolly and Degadoga to join us at the next council."

Dutch drained the coffee from his cup

and dropped the cup to the ground. "Maybe so," he said. "We'll see."

"We need them to conclude this business," said Bradford.

"All I can do is ask them," said Dutch. "I can't promise you any more than that."

Dutch rode into the yard of Degadoga. Upon returning to the settlement from the meeting with the new governor, he had heard an amusing story, and he could hardly wait to confront the old chief with it and tease him a little. He was smiling as he jumped off the back of his horse. Degadoga poked his head out the door to see who was there.

"Dutch," he said. " 'Siyo. Come on inside."

Working to keep a straight face, Dutch went into the house and sat down at the table. Sequoyah was there with a cup of coffee on the table in front of him. Quiet as usual, he nodded a greeting. He and Dutch shook hands. The old man put a bowl in front of Dutch. It was *kanohena,* the traditional hominy drink offered to guests. Dutch drank from the bowl and smacked his lips.

"Say, Uncle," he said, using the word as a polite form of address to an elder, "what is this I've heard about you now? You did something while I was away."

"What?" said Degadoga. "What are you talking about?"

"Did a white man stop by your house a few nights ago?"

"A white man?" said the chief, giving Dutch a sideways look. "Yes."

"And did he ask you for directions to the home of Mrs. Lovely, the widow of our old agent?"

Degadoga chuckled. "Yes," he said. "He did."

"And what did you tell him then?"

Dutch glanced at Sequoyah, and Sequoyah smiled. The old war chief chuckled some more and sat down at the table across from Dutch. He put a coffee cup on the table in front of himself.

"You want some?" Degadoga asked.

"Not yet," said Dutch, lifting the bowl of *kanohena*. "*Wado*. I still have this. What did you do to the *yoneg*?"

"I did nothing to him," said Degadoga. "He wanted to know how to get to the widow's house, and I gave him a guide. That's all. I didn't see him after that."

"Yes," said Dutch. "Hog Stones, I think it was. That's what I heard."

Sequoyah, still smiling, nodded in agreement, as if he had heard the story, too.

"If you know this whole story already," said Degadoga, "then why are you asking me to tell it to you again?"

"So Hog Stones left with the *yoneg*," said Dutch, ignoring Degadoga's last statement, "but you spoke to Hog Stones before they left, in Cherokee, didn't you, so that the white man wouldn't understand you, and what did you tell Hog Stones to do? Did you tell him to take the white man to Mrs. Lovely's house? Did you, Uncle?"

Sequoyah chuckled a bit, barely audibly, and Degadoga smiled. It seemed as if a laugh was building up inside him, but if so, he managed to suppress it. Then, in spite of himself, Dutch grinned, but then he forced the grin away. He took a breath and tried to set a stern expression on his face again.

"You told Hog Stones," he said, "you said to him — is this right? This is what I heard. You told him to lead the white man to the trail right down the road here. The one that leads up the side of the mountain."

Degadoga laughed out loud and shook his head. "Yes," he said. "I did that to the *yoneg*."

"The trail that leads nowhere?" Dutch continued. "That one? You sent him there. And you told Hog Stones to slip into the woods and leave the white man there alone."

Degadoga stood and pompously crossed his arms over his chest. He nodded his head. "Yes," he said. "I did."

"Uncle," Dutch said, "do you know what happened to the poor *yoneg?*"

Degadoga shook his head. "I don't know," he said. "How could I? I never saw him again."

"He was lost up there for two days and nights," said Dutch. "Alone."

The old man chuckled at the thought. So did Sequoyah, and Dutch had to work even harder at keeping a straight face.

"Two days and nights," he said. "He had no food. No water. And he was already sick when he first stopped by your house to seek your help. He had a fever. You might have killed him, Uncle. Why did you do that?"

Degadoga resumed his seat. He sat up straight and put a serious expression on his face. His arms were still crossed over his chest.

"He came from that Miller," he said. "He's a government agent sent to spy on us or talk us into making peace with those Ani-Wasasi liars. Or something. I don't know. Anyhow, it's too bad I didn't kill him."

"Well, you didn't," said Dutch. "He made it somehow at last to the home of Mrs. Lovely, and he's there now sick in her bed. She's nursing him. But his skin is yellow, and he has blisters all over."

That, too, struck Degadoga as amusing, and he chuckled out loud again. Dutch pretended to ignore that.

"His name is Cephas Washburn," he said. "It seems he met our former chief two years ago back in the east, and Tahlonteskee invited him to come out here."

There followed a moment of silence, during which Degadoga looked very serious, even a little worried. Sequoyah stared at the tabletop, the expression on his face revealing nothing.

"Our chief invited him out here?" said Degadoga. "Why did he do that?"

"Mr. Washburn is not a government agent," said Dutch. "You made a mistake because he told you that he'd stopped at Fort Smith to see the governor on his way here. Lots of white men stop to see the governor when they come into a new territory. It's a courtesy. Nothing more."

"Well, what is he then?" asked the old man, a suspicious look now on his face.

"He's a missionary," said Dutch. "He's

come out here to establish a school for our children. He's come to teach our children."

For a moment, Degadoga looked stunned. He sat and stared at Dutch almost to the point of rudeness. Then he looked away again.

"A preacher?" he said. "A missionary. A teacher. *Didayohuhsgi*."

"That's right," said Dutch, "a teacher for our children."

"Ha. I thought he was working for that governor."

"And you almost killed him," said Dutch, "sending him up that blind trail."

"Hmm," Degadoga muttered. "I did almost kill him, didn't I?"

"You sure did."

"How long did you say he was lost?"

"Two days and two nights."

"A lost preacher," said Degadoga. "Wandering in the wilderness. That's even better, I think, than if he had been a government agent." And he laughed out loud. "He'll try to put breeches on all of us," he said, and he laughed some more.

"If he lives," said Sequoyah, and he laughed along with Degadoga.

10

Governor Miller had fully expected to negotiate some kind of peace agreement between the Cherokees and the Osages at the meeting scheduled for October first at Fort Smith. Instead, he received his first hard lesson in just how stubborn both sides were and how persistent the hostilities would be.

No captives were released, no murderers given up, no stolen horses returned to their owners. In fact, no Cherokees and no Osages even bothered to show up for the scheduled meeting. Instead, Miller received reports that a large party of Osages had attacked a camp of Cherokee hunters on the Poteau River. They had killed two Cherokees there, wounded another, and stolen all the horses, furs, and property of the Cherokees. Even worse was a report that Mad Buffalo and other Osage warriors had killed a party of five white hunters near the Red River.

There was plenty of bad news. Miller could see that the job ahead of him would not be an easy one. However, there was good news also. Reverend Washburn, recovering from his illness, had been joined by others from the American Board of Commissioners for Foreign Missions, and work on the buildings for the new mission to the Western Cherokees, according to reports Miller had received, was progressing nicely. It would be called Dwight Mission.

At almost the same time, Dr. Palmer and others from the United Foreign Missionary Society of New York were establishing Union Mission in the Osage country. Both groups of missionaries had stopped at Little Rock to present their credentials to Miller before moving on to their work sites, and Miller had been overjoyed to see them.

"We need all the help we can get," the governor had said, "to bring a speedy end to this bloody and senseless war."

Miller knew that the progress of the missionaries would be slow, but he hoped that it would also be sure. Perhaps they, after all, were the ones with the right approach. Perhaps only deep-rooted changes in basic beliefs could alter the age-old habits of these savage people.

There could be no one more dedicated, Miller thought, than these brave missionaries. He knew of the difficulties they had encountered on their respective trips from Boston and from New York. He knew the hardships and dangers of travel in the western wilderness, and he knew of the sickness that had overtaken both groups of missionaries. Several of their number, in both parties, had died along the way.

He admired their boldness, their faith, their selfless devotion to duty, and their obstinate enthusiasm. He was not a praying man, or he would have prayed for their success, but he did earnestly wish for it, for the success of the missionaries, he sincerely believed, would mean his own success. But, of course, he couldn't just sit back and wait for that time to come.

With a small military escort, Governor Miller traveled to the Cherokee settlements. Along the way, he stopped to visit with the missionaries at Dwight to check on their progress, wish them success, and encourage them. Then he went on to visit Chief John Jolly at his home. Jolly was glad to see the governor. He invited him in, introduced him to his family, and fed him. Then Governor Miller told Jolly why he had come. He wanted to talk about a peace between the Cherokee and Osage tribes. Jolly was sympathetic and expressed his own desire for peace.

"When first I came out here," he said, "I wrote to Mr. Calhoun, your secretary of war. I promised him that I would do all I could to remain at peace with other tribes of Indians."

He paused, and Miller could read in the tired, weak old chief's face both worry and sorrow.

"But there's nothing I can do," Jolly continued. "Degadoga is war chief, and we're at war. The matter is completely out of my hands."

Armed with a little better understanding of the roles of the Cherokee war chief and peace chief, Miller went from Jolly's house to visit with Degadoga himself. The old man did not smile when he let him in. He did offer him a chair at the table, and fed him *kanohena* and coffee, but when Miller tried to talk of peace with the Osage, Degadoga was firm.

"There is no reason for us or anyone else to even talk with them," he said. "They're all liars. They're a whole nation of liars. The only thing for us to do is kill them all. I now have many allies: Delawares and Shawnees are coming to join us in this war. Maybe even Oneida, all the way from New York. Don't you see? Everyone hates the

Ani-Wasasi. Already I have Quapaw, Choctaw, Creek, Kansa, Fox, Caddo, Comanche. Nothing can stop it now until the Ani-Wasasi have been rubbed out."

"Degadoga," said Miller, "I beg you not to attack the Osage with this force of yours. Try to understand the position I'm in. My government wants to see an end to this war. I was sent here to accomplish that end. When I talk to you, you tell me that the Osage are all liars. You tell me that they have killed your hunters.

"When I talk to the Osage, they say the hunters they killed were all on Osage land where they had no right to be. They say that you hold Osage captives and stolen horses. Who am I to believe? What am I to do?"

Degadoga filled a pipe bowl and lit it. He took several puffs, almost filling the small room with rich, thick, gray clouds of smoke. Then he turned the pipe and handed it to Miller. "When we smoke this pipe together," he said, "nothing but the truth will pass from our lips."

Miller took the pipe and puffed, and Degadoga grinned.

"I don't like your job," Degadoga said. "I don't like your government trying to tell me what to do about my enemies. I alone know my enemies. I am the only one who knows what they've done to me. Only I know what they've told me in the past, and therefore only I can know what they've done later to prove to me that they're a nation of liars.

"When my enemy lies to me, steals from me, and kills me, I don't like it for someone else, someone like you, to come along and say to me, 'I think you should make friends now with your enemy. I think you should forgive this man who stole your horse, this man who killed your brother.' "

"But if you persist in this war," said Miller, "more Cherokees will die."

"Yes," said Degadoga, "and more Ani-Wasasi, too."

"John Jolly tells me that he would like to see an end to this war," said Miller, handing the pipe back to Degadoga.

"John Jolly is a peace chief," said the old man. "Like you, that's his job. Besides, he doesn't know the Ani-Wasasi as well as I do, and I am war chief. We are at war. That puts me in charge of this business."

He puffed on the pipe while Miller sat in frustrated silence. He couldn't help but like this tough old man, but trying to talk sense with him was certainly frustrating. Then the war chief broke the silence.

"I too would like to see an end to this war," he said. "Does that surprise you? I would like to see an end to this war, because that would mean that all the Ani-Wasasi would be dead."

The sound of an approaching horse outside prevented Miller from responding to this last statement, and it was a good thing, too, he thought, because it had angered him. He clenched his teeth, tightening his jaws. Reverend Washburn and his associates certainly will have their hands full with this old savage reprobate, he thought. Degadoga had walked to the door and was looking out.

" *'Siyo,* Tahchee," he said. *"Ehiyuh ha."*

He stepped aside and Dutch walked into the house. Governor Miller stood up and held out his right hand. Dutch took it in his.

"Hello, Governor," said Dutch.

"Hello. It's good to see you again."

"Ah," said Degadoga, "you already know my captain?"

"Yes," said Miller. "Captain Dutch and I have met."

"We met near Clermont's Town," said Dutch.

"Oh," said Degadoga, grumbling. "I remember. It was a foolish trip you made."

145

"We did some hunting on the way back home," said Dutch.

"We've been trying to find some common ground for talks about a peace," said Miller to Dutch, "Degadoga and I, but I'm afraid we haven't gotten very far. He's . . . stubborn."

Degadoga smiled as he put a bowl down on the table for Dutch, and Dutch sat down. He looked up at Miller, who was still standing there.

"Governor," Dutch said, "I wonder if you know just what it is you're asking of us. We've lost friends and brothers, fathers and sons, mothers and daughters, husbands and . . . wives. You're asking us to forget all of those people that we loved."

"I do understand all of that," said Miller, picking up his hat, "and I'm not asking you to forget. One can never forget lost loved ones. War is a terrible thing. Innocent people are killed on both sides. The Osage people have also suffered the kinds of loss you mention. Somehow it has to stop."

"We've agreed on peace terms with them before," said Dutch, "more than once, and then they've killed our hunters again. It would be foolish of us to trust them again."

Miller heaved a heavy sigh. He turned to

Degadoga and held out his hand. "Thank you for your hospitality," he said. "I must be on my way. I'm going to visit your enemy now. I'm going to talk with the Osage chiefs."

"They'll only tell you lies," said Degadoga.

"You won't listen to me," said Miller. "I have to try to talk to someone."

"I've heard that the Osages have missionaries now, too," said Dutch. "Is that right?"

"Yes, it is," said Miller.

"Then talk to those white men," said Degadoga. "Tell them to get out of that country. If they stay, they might get in the way during the fight, and some of them might get killed."

Governor Miller said a brusque good-bye and went out the door. Dutch stood up, and he and the old war chief watched as the governor rejoined the military escort outside and rode away. Then they went back to the table and sat down across from one another.

"When did you make me a captain?" asked Dutch.

"Just now," said the old man. "Do you like it, Captain Dutch?"

Dutch shrugged. "It has a good sound," he said.

"Where have you been all this time?" said Degadoga. "I could have used my captain to help me argue with that governor."

"I expect you did all right without me," said Dutch. "I've just been visiting with the missionaries."

"Do they have any Indians in breeches over there yet?" asked Degadoga.

"I didn't see any," said Dutch. "The missionaries are too busy being carpenters just now to worry about that."

"Did they preach to you?"

"They asked me to bring children to school," said Dutch. "That's all."

"Of course," said Degadoga, "so they can put them in breeches."

11

1821

Governor Miller was out on his mission of peace for three long months. When he returned to Fort Smith, weary, dirty, and sore, he told Major Bradford and Agent Lewis that he had failed utterly with the Cherokees, but that he had met with some small success with the Osages at Clermont's Town. They feared another Cherokee attack, remembering the ferocity of the one they had suffered four years earlier, and they had heard about the large numbers of Indians from other tribes who were joining with Degadoga for the attack.

"I don't believe the Osage will attack the Cherokee," Miller told Bradford. "If they should, they will have lied to me, and if that should happen, then it is my intention to give my full blessing to Cherokee revenge. In the meantime, do everything you can to keep the Cherokees at home. If you can do that, and if I'm right about the

Osages, the war will be at an end."

With that, Miller had begun a trip back to New Hampshire, leaving the volatile situation in the hands of Bradford and Lewis. Bradford organized a squad of soldiers, and in their company he and Lewis headed for the Cherokee settlements. They were astonished to find large numbers of Delaware, Shawnee, and other Indians camped along the river not far from Degadoga's home.

"Look, Major," said Lewis. "Degadoga's prepared for an all-out war with the Osage Nation."

"That's what he's always wanted," said Bradford, "but that's just what we've got to try to prevent."

When Bradford and Lewis reached Degadoga's house, the old chief stepped out into the yard to greet them. He knew why they had come, and he faced them with the demeanor of a man of stone who would not be moved.

"We've come with orders from the governor," said Bradford.

"Where is my friend the governor?" asked Degadoga. "Why did he not come here to talk to me himself? He's been in my house before. He knows the way here."

"Governor Miller is away on a trip," said

Major Bradford, "but he left me with these orders."

Degadoga shrugged. "What are the orders then?" he said.

"We've come to order you not to take to the field with your warriors," said Bradford. "Keep them all here. Do not ride against the Osage. There are too many whites in the way of your attack, and if any of them are harmed in any way, it could arouse the wrath of the United States against you."

"What about *my* men that have been killed?" said Degadoga. "Am I to forget about them? Their wives and their babies are still crying."

"They should not have been hunting on Osage ground," said Bradford.

"They were hunting in Lovely's Purchase," said Degadoga. "A land you told us we could hunt on."

"We have only your word for that," said Bradford. "The Osage say that the men were on Osage hunting grounds."

"And my horses the Ani-Wasasi have stolen?"

"You have stolen Osage horses," said Major Bradford. "You also have Osage captives."

"The Ani-Wasasi we took are no longer captives," said Degadoga. "They're free to go if they please, but they do not want to go back to that nation of liars. They have learned to tell the truth. They found a better life among the Cherokees, and they love their new lives. You see, we are not savages. We treat our captives well."

"Then consider that you are even with the Osage," said Bradford, "and leave it at that. If you feel that you have any just grievances against the Osage or anyone else, go to Washington and present them to the president. Do not go to war. If the president agrees with you, then you'll be compensated for the wrongs that have been done you. But keep your warriors at home."

Degadoga scowled. He was pressed against the wall. He knew what had happened in the old days in the east when the Cherokees had fought against the United States. There were but few soldiers in the West, yet he knew that if he angered the United States enough, they would send more. He didn't want to push them far enough to find out the hard way.

But Major Bradford had mentioned compensation. Maybe, Degadoga thought, the government would actually pay the Cherokees for what the Osages had done. That would be good. He could always fight the Osages later. Still, he didn't want to seem to be backing down in front of the white men.

"And if I do as you say and the Ani-Wasasi attack my people while I sit still," he said, "what then?"

"I do not believe that the Osages will attack,". said Bradford. "They assured Governor Miller that they would not."

"But if they do, then what am I to do? Am I to sit on my hands and watch while my people are killed, then go to Washington and beg to be paid for the bodies?"

"If the Osages do attack," said Bradford, hesitantly, "Governor Miller has said that we will no longer interfere in your fighting with them."

Degadoga felt his soul leap with joy. It was much more than he had hoped to hear from the white man soldier. He knew in his heart that the Osages would commit another act of aggression against the Cherokees sooner or later, and when that time came, he would be free to do what he wanted. He had the word of the major himself, the major repeating the words of the governor. Outwardly, the old war chief maintained his dignity, but inside, he was gleefully shouting and dancing. He had won the debate.

"We'll do as my friend the governor asks," he said, pretending to be disappointed. "We'll keep ourselves at home, unless the Osages attack us first."

Major Bradford and his escort turned their horses and headed back to Fort Smith, the major fully believing that he had actually headed off the war. Degadoga, smiling, watched them go.

Degadoga went to see Captain Dutch to tell him what the major had said, and the two of them went together to see John Jolly. A council was called, and the decision was made to send a delegation to Washington to press their claims. After all, the suggestion had been made by an officer in the United States army. Walter Webber, also known as Watt, and two others were selected to make the journey and present their case to the president of the United States. But since they knew that there were likely to be arguments about who, between the Cherokees and the Osages, had stolen the most from the other, they also prepared claims for horses stolen from them by whites while they had been moving from the east. The three delegates packed clothes, food, weapons, and ammunition, loaded them all onto a flatboat and headed east.

★ ★ ★

Mad Buffalo did not care what his old father had said to the white man. He was tired of waiting to see whether or not the hated Cherokees would attack. He rounded up some like-minded young warriors, about four hundred, from his father's own town and from that of White Hair. They would attack the Cherokees in their own homes.

But Mad Buffalo and his followers had only bows and arrows, and he knew that the Cherokee men all had guns. He did not want to rush foolishly into this fight. He meant to win. He would take his time. He would go first to the white man's fort for guns and ammunition. Then he would attack the Cherokees, and the fight would be more even.

Clermont knew what his unruly son was doing. He had tried to stop him, but Mad Buffalo was headstrong. Clermont rushed to Union Mission to warn the white men there of the possible danger. He told them to gather in their livestock and keep themselves together for safety. He did not approve of his son's actions, and he did not want any whites to be hurt.

Mad Buffalo and his large war party

arrived on the bank of the Arkansas River just opposite Fort Smith. Across the river they could see the thirty-foot-high sandstone bluff at the juncture of the Arkansas and Poteau Rivers. Up on the bluff stood Fort Smith, a cluster of log buildings surrounded by a stockade of square timbers set closely together in the ground. Blockhouses stood tall at the two corners nearest the river. A few outbuildings were scattered around the periphery.

Mad Buffalo and three others crossed the river on a raft and went into the fort. Major Bradford was away, so Lieutenant Martin Scott came out to meet the Indians. A fresh-looking young officer, he was wearing fitted blue trousers with a yellow stripe down each leg, a darker blue jacket with a double row of brass buttons in the front, epaulets on the shoulders, and a high collar. He offered to shake hands with the four Osages, but they each stubbornly refused.

"We're hunting," said Mad Buffalo, "and we want to hunt on this side of the river. Can I bring my men across?"

Scott was not sure what to do. What a time for the major to be gone, he thought. He could see a large party of Indians on the other side of the river, enough to overwhelm the small force at the fort if they got themselves inside. And these four certainly did not seem friendly.

They had introduced themselves as Osage, and Scott knew that they were well out of their usual range. He also knew of the troubles between the Osage and the Cherokee, and these were close to the Cherokee settlements. He wasn't certain what was going on, but he was sure suspicious of their motives.

"I'll have to confer with my staff before I can give you an answer," he said. "While you wait you can be my guest in our mess."

"We didn't come to eat," said Mad Buffalo, looking around at the different buildings. "We came to hunt. We'll wait for you out here."

"Just as you please," said Scott. "Excuse me then. I'll return soon."

He hurried into the office of Reuben Lewis and found the agent already standing at his window studying the situation outside. Lewis looked over his shoulder as Scott stepped in through the door.

"We may have a situation on our hands, sir," said Scott. "I think I need your advice."

"We do have a situation on our hands," said Lewis. "That's Mad Buffalo out there. Clermont's son. What did he say?"

"He said he wants to bring his men over on this side of the river to hunt," said Scott. "There's about four hundred of them waiting over there, I'd say."

"They're not out hunting," said Lewis. "Come with me."

Lewis led the way to the governor's office. As Governor Miller was still in New Hampshire, Acting Governor Robert Crittenden was behind the desk. He looked up when the two men came into his office, and he could see right away that something was wrong.

"What is it?" he asked.

"Mad Buffalo is out there with three other Osage warriors," said Lewis. "There's another four hundred or so across the river. They want to come on this side to hunt, or so they say."

"They wouldn't shake hands," said Scott, "and they wouldn't eat. I'd say they're unfriendly."

Crittenden got up and walked over to his window to look out. "Yes," he said, "I see them. They seem to be studying the layout here."

"Sir," said Scott, "my guess is that they've come to attack the Cherokees, and they want to get into the fort to get their hands on some guns and ammunition. Sir, if they get in here among us, that many of them, I'm afraid they could take us."

"There are enough of them out there to do it," said Lewis. "That's certain."

"Lieutenant Scott," said Crittenden, "get back out there and tell Mad Buffalo to keep his men on the other side of the river. Tell him that if they try to cross, they'll be fired on."

"Yes sir," said Scott, and he hurried on out the door. Lewis and Crittenden both followed him, but at a more leisurely and dignified pace. By the time they caught up with Scott, Mad Buffalo and the other three Osages were stomping angrily back down toward the water's edge.

"What do you think they'll do?" asked Crittenden.

"I don't know, sir," said Scott. "He was pretty mad."

"Well," said Crittenden, "I think we should be ready for anything."

"Yes sir," said Scott, and he alerted the post for action. He ordered two six-pounders brought up and placed in position to fire at the riverbank below. Then, Crittenden and Lewis by his side, he watched as Mad Buffalo and the three others disembarked on the opposite bank. They could hear Mad Buffalo shouting, but of course, they could not understand what he said. While they watched, the Indians began dragging logs to the river's edge.

"What are they doing?" said Lewis.

In a few more moments, Scott answered the question.

"They're building rafts," he said. "About fifty of them. I'd say they mean to cross."

"Discourage them, Lieutenant," said Crittenden.

"Yes sir," said Scott, and he shouted an order at one of the cannon crews. A soldier touched a match to a fuse, and the gun belched flame. On the opposite shore, Osages shouted, screamed and ran into the woods as water and splinters flew into the air. Soon there were no more Indians to be seen across the river.

Furious at the failure of his plan, Mad Buffalo led what was left of his four hundred along the west bank of the Poteau River, where they encountered three Quapaw hunters. They killed them and scalped them and continued on their way. Some families of whites living along the river heard of the approach of the Indians and fled. When Mad Buffalo's band reached the abandoned homes, they went through them, taking anything that caught their fancy and smashing up the rest. They especially stole guns and horses. Then they came across three Delawares, and killed them for good measure.

News of the rampaging Osages traveled fast, and for miles around, white settlers and Cherokees were in a panic. Three different Cherokee settlements raised bands of warriors to fight the invading Osages. In other areas, the people all gathered themselves together in one house to defend themselves against attack.

The riders never found Mad Buffalo, and the attack on the Cherokee settlements never came. Mad Buffalo, having failed to secure the guns and ammunition he wanted, abandoned his plan of attack on the Cherokees and contented himself with killing the few unsuspecting men he encountered along the way and looting the several abandoned houses he came across. It was an inglorious end for the raid he had planned for his four hundred mounted men, but it gave Degadoga the opening he was wanting so badly.

12

Three hundred Cherokees, Delawares, Creeks, Choctaws, Shawnees, and a few white men were camped alongside the Arkansas River about fourteen miles from Fort Smith. Their leaders were Degadoga, Captain Dutch, and Thomas Graves, the white man who had become a Cherokee. It was an army moving west on its way to invade enemy territory on this early morning in late September. A heavy fog lay over the wet, green land when Major Bradford and his small military escort with two pack mules rode into the camp.

Degadoga invited the soldiers to dismount and sit around a small fire to talk with him. He gave them all tin cups filled with steaming coffee. "I told you," he said to Bradford, "that if you wanted to see me you would find me here. And so you see, here I am."

"Yes," said Bradford, a stern edge to his voice, "already on your way to war. You know that I wanted to see you before you had started such a movement."

"You wanted to try to talk me out of it again," said Degadoga. "I told you it was too late. The motion had already begun and could not be stopped or reversed."

"Degadoga," said Bradford, "my government does not want this war to continue."

"The last time we talked," said the old chief, "you told me that Governor Miller had said that if the Ani-Wasasi should attack us, you would no longer interfere. You remember that talk. They did attack us, and yet you are still trying to interfere. I can't keep it in my mind what your government wants of me."

Bradford sipped a little of the hot coffee. Then he heaved a sigh. The old fox is right, he thought, but I mustn't admit it.

"Chief Clermont did not condone the invasion that was led by his son, Mad Buffalo," said the major. "Chief Clermont is very sorry that it took place. He did his best to stop it. Now he is willing to agree to an armistice if you will also agree."

"What is this armistice?" asked Degadoga.

"Clermont will promise that no Osage war parties will go against the Cherokees for twenty days, if you promise not to send any Cherokees against them for the same period of time. At the end of that twenty days, we will all meet together once again

163

at Fort Smith and calmly talk among ourselves to resolve the differences between your two peoples."

"More treaty talk?" said Degadoga. "What's the point of more treaty talk? We've gone all over all of it before. There's nothing more to be said."

"There may be. It seems that there's been a major misunderstanding," said Bradford. He sipped more coffee from the tin cup in his hand. It was still hot, and it felt good in the cool, damp morning air. "Clermont says that when the Osage gave Lovely's Purchase to the United States, they gave the land alone. They did not give away the animals there, and your hunters have been killing his animals."

"That's Ani-Wasasi lies," said Degadoga. "What good is land without the animals that live on it? Who ever heard of giving land away and keeping the animals? He knew that you were getting that land for us to hunt on."

"If we meet and talk with him again," said Bradford, "perhaps we can straighten out this problem."

"It's foolish to talk with liars," said Degadoga. "Anyway, we have our own way to resolve differences, and right now we are on the way to do it." He shook his head.

"We don't want any more talks with those liars."

"We've lost more men than they have lost," said Dutch. "They have more of our horses than we have of theirs. For them, this would be a good time to stop the war, but not for us. When we come back, Major Bradford, when we've evened up the score, talk to us again about this armistice."

"I see that I'm not getting anywhere with you on this matter," said Major Bradford, "and I lack the authority to give you any direct orders. I do have authority, though, over these white men who are riding with you, and I order them to return to their homes immediately."

He was looking directly at Tom Graves, and Graves calmly returned the stare.

"Tom Graves is one of us," said Degadoga. "A Cherokee."

"Do you deny the fact that he's a white man?" asked Bradford.

"I don't deny anything," said Degadoga, "and I don't care what he was born. He has become a Cherokee man."

"What about the others then?" Bradford blustered. "Are you going to tell me that they're all Cherokees?"

"Well, Major," said Tom Graves, "I'll tell them that you want them all to go on home."

Choosing to accept that statement as a minor victory and to leave on that triumphant note, Bradford stood up, and the rest of the soldiers imitated his action immediately.

"We'll be going along then," he said. "Private Corbin."

"Yes sir?" said a skinny soldier, quickly stepping forward. He looked to be about sixteen years old.

"Bring up that gray mule."

"Yes sir."

Corbin ran to fetch the mule, while Bradford shook hands around the fire with the Cherokee leaders. His relationship with these people, the major considered, had developed into something strange, something that he himself could not quite understand. He gripped Degadoga's right hand and looked the old chief in the face. It was a hard face to read, and that unpleasant fact frustrated Bradford.

"I wish I could talk you out of this," he said, "but since I obviously cannot, I wish you well."

Private Corbin returned then, leading the mule.

"Unload that keg, Private," said Bradford.

"This keg, sir?" said Corbin. "It's powder, sir. Gunpowder."

"I didn't ask you what was in the keg, Private," said Bradford. "I know what's in the keg. I told you to unload it. That's all."

"Yes, sir." Corbin untied a knot to loosen a rope and lowered the heavy keg to the ground with a thump and a groan. Dusting off his hands, he straightened up.

"That's all, Private," said Bradford, and Corbin led the mule back to where the rest of the escort waited with their mounts. Bradford looked at Degadoga once again. "Since you insist on going ahead against my wishes," he said, glancing down at the powder keg, "you might as well take this along."

Having lived with the Osages in Clermont's Town for an all too brief but happy year with Wind in the Meadow, Dutch knew the Osage habits well. He knew their seasonal cycle of hunting and planting and warfare. He even knew the order and the times of their ceremonies. This time of year, he knew, they would not be at home in their towns. They would be out in hunting parties, men, women and children, trailing the buffalo herds, scattered over the prairies in isolated camps. Dutch had taken part in these Osage hunts, and he knew the well worn trails.

He knew the directions in which the hunters would travel, and he knew the places where they would make their camps.

At Dutch's suggestion, therefore, Degadoga divided the Cherokee army into four companies of seventy-five men each. One company would be commanded by Captain Dutch, a second by Tom Graves, a third by a warrior named Nofire, and the fourth by the old war chief himself. Dutch told them where the Osage hunting parties were likely to be found, and they split up, going in four different directions. Each company was on its own from there on. They would see each other again back home in the Cherokee settlements.

Captain Dutch led his company almost directly west, toward the Comanche country. He had been there before, to hunt with the Osages and to raid the Comanches with them. The tall prairie grass called his mind back to wild buffalo chases of his carefree days with Osage hunters, and the swells and the billows in the grass caused by the breeze wafting gently over the plain seemed to whisper to him the name of his lost love. But the lovely memories of his time with Wind in the Meadow were always interrupted by vivid images of the horror of what had followed. It was not possible for him to recall one without the other.

His emotions were in turmoil, a tumultuous confusion of sadness and pain and a deep, resentful anger bordering on uncontrollable rage. He wanted to sit alone in a quiet haven and weep for his losses. At the same time he wanted to wade in gore. He wanted to commit bloody mayhem and inspire carnage in the hearts of his followers. He wondered if any amount of blood could wash away the hurt and the hate in his soul, if there were enough Osage people to kill to satisfy his need for revenge.

As he rode at the head of his company, none of this inner chaos showed through to the outside world. Captain Dutch sat straight in the saddle. His face wore a calm expression, almost cold, and his eyes were ever alert. In general his appearance was that of a capable commander, in command of his troops, in command of the situation, and very much in command of himself.

The sun was low in the western sky, and the light was growing dim when Dutch's two scouts rode back to the column. They reported no enemy sightings. Another day or two, Dutch thought, and they would find them. He knew that they were somewhere nearby.

But night would be on them soon, and Dutch had his eye already on a grove of trees not far off to the northwest. He knew there was a stream there, and it would be a good place for a camp for the night.

He led the company there. They had dismounted and were in the process of unsaddling their horses. Dutch had already unfastened the cinch and was about to pull the saddle from his horse's back, when war cries split the air and an Osage arrow drove itself into the fork of his saddle, just below where his left hand gripped the horn.

"Ani-Wasasi!" someone shouted.

Dutch pulled his long rifle from its buckskin sheath and turned to fire. He had no trouble locating a target. The painted Osage warriors were everywhere among them. It was as if they had dropped from the sky. One was coming directly at him with a raised war club. Dutch fired, and the Osage collapsed with a bloody hole in his chest. Dutch dropped his rifle and pulled the two pistols out of his sash.

Guns were popping all around, and the smell of burnt powder filled the evening air. Each man, it seemed, was locked in mortal combat with another. Shouts were heard in three languages, Osage, Cherokee, and a little English, and the neighing and stamping of frightened horses added to the din and the confusion of battle.

Dutch saw an Osage at the far edge of the fray draw back his bowstring and release an arrow. Cocking his pistol as he raised it, Dutch fired. It was a long shot for a pistol, but the ball tore the flesh in the Osage's left shoulder, causing him to howl with pain and retreat. Dutch looked around. He had still one more shot.

Not far to his left, he saw an Osage warrior grappling close with John Smith. Dutch stepped over close and shoved the barrel of his pistol right up against the Osage's ribs and pulled the trigger. The man screamed and clutched at the fresh wound in his side. As he did, Smith bashed his head in with the butt of an empty pistol.

Dutch turned, frantic to locate another foe, but to his astonishment, there were none to be found. It was all over. The hated enemy was gone, and all was silent. The fight had been ferocious while it lasted. Dutch looked around. He found the bodies of two Cherokees, both killed by arrows, and he found a few of his men with powder burns on their faces or upper bodies. A few others had minor scrapes and cuts. None of the living were seriously hurt. There were five Osage warriors killed. Any wounded had managed to escape.

It had been a strange fight. Dutch had no idea where the enemy had come from nor how they had managed to get right in the midst of the Cherokees without being detected. The fight had ended as quickly as it had begun, and the enemy had vanished almost as mysteriously as they had appeared.

There had been seventy-five men with Dutch, and he was sure that there had been more Osages there. Seventy-five fiercely fighting a hundred hand to hand and only seven had been killed. Two on one side and five on the other. There were no wounded to speak of. No captives had been taken. No horses stolen. It was the oddest fight that he had ever known. Yet he could say that he had been victorious, for he had been surprised, and in spite of that, he had prevailed.

13

"Major Bradford," said Dr. Palmer, a meek little man in a frock coat, recently established in the Osage mission, "I feel strongly that I must speak on behalf of the poor Osages. They're afraid to come and speak for themselves, and even if they dared, they are scarcely capable of rendering themselves understandable in the English tongue.

"They are my charges, and, pitiful wretches though they be, they, like all of us, are the children of God. Like all children, they are eager to learn. They are empty vessels waiting to be filled with the Word of God.

"But how can I proceed with my necessary work on behalf of these miserable savages, when they are beset on all sides by a cruel and remorseless foe even more savage than they? I beg you, sir, to intercede.

"Of recent events, I can tell you the following. First, a band of Cherokees, one hundred or so, attacked a hunting camp of Osage while the men were all away. They killed or captured seventy and stole seventy horses.

"Following that bold and brilliant success against a company of helpless women and children, the murderous bandits found themselves bested when surprised by men. The Osages found them unsaddling their horses for the night and surprised them. In this fight between warriors, the Cherokees, though led by the monstrous Dutch, that bloodthirsty scourge of the prairies, were thoroughly whipped and routed, and two of their men were killed.

"Their bloodlust not yet satisfied, the vengeful Cherokees surprised yet another peaceful Osage hunting camp and fell on it in a rage while most of the men were away. The ten or twelve who had stayed behind to guard the camp were no match for the hundred Cherokees who swarmed over them like locusts. One hundred innocent women and children were killed or captured at this place, and, I have heard, some of the helpless captives were later most cruelly murdered for no reason whatsoever.

"I appeal to you as a representative of my government and as a God-fearing and justice-loving man, to do everything in your power and the power of the United States army to put an end to this senseless and immoral war and to bring to justice the murderers of innocent women and children and helpless old men.

"The Osages are in a pitiable state. They're starving and they're naked. In their ignorant state of savagery, they depend entirely on nature's bounty to provide for their basic needs, and the current hostility has kept them from the hunt. Their very survival depends upon your swift action."

Bradford held his head in his hands, his elbows resting on his desk. He had heard various versions of these stories before, and he had heard some others as well. One month following his meeting with Degadoga and the others, just before they had launched their invasion into the Osage country — one month later the first company of Cherokees had returned from the raid and ridden proudly into Fort Smith. Bradford had personally interviewed the leader of that detachment, the stout young Cherokee called Nofire.

"We killed forty Ani-Wasasi," Nofire had boasted. "We took thirty captive and we brought back seventy of their horses."

Nofire and his company had the captives and the horses with them. Bradford had seen them. So that much of the tale, he knew, was true. Nofire had not said whether the forty they had killed were men

175

or women. The captives had been mostly women and children.

Well, Bradford had written down the tale as told by Nofire. Now he wrote the Osage version, filtered as it had been through the mouth of the missionary. He also wrote the story of the second encounter as told by the Osages, and he couldn't help but wonder how the Osages had managed to declare themselves the victors.

They had come upon the Cherokees by surprise. They had been evenly matched, and yet they had only killed two. The Cherokees, on the other hand, had killed five of them. He shrugged. He wrote it down. His notes would name the source.

The third incident described involved the company led by the white man, Tom Graves, and it was that incident that bothered Bradford the most. He still had difficulties with Graves's identity. He could not accept that the man had become a Cherokee. Graves was a white man, and as such, Bradford believed, he should fall under the jurisdiction of the United States government's military authorities in the territory.

There was, of course, the issue of naturalization, if one could grant a savage tribe, or nation, the right to such a process. And the

Western Cherokee Nation did claim Tom Graves as one of its own. Graves spoke the language like a native and he had a Cherokee family. It was said that he'd been raised by the Cherokees from infancy.

Still it bothered Bradford that a white man had led the company of Cherokees that had done the most vicious damage to the Osages on this recent campaign.

The Cherokees had said that eighty of them met up with seventy-five Osages and killed or captured them all. There had been no casualties on the Cherokee side. Now Bradford wasn't even sure they were talking about the same incident. After all, Degadoga's company had been out there, too, and their activities were as yet unaccounted for.

The most damaging evidence against Graves, though, had come from the missionaries at Dwight, and they were the Cherokees' friends. According to a statement Bradford had received from Reverend Washburn, Graves and his company had surprised an Osage camp after the warriors had all gone off to fight some Pawnees. The Cherokee attackers had quickly overcome the dozen guards and then gone on to kill twenty-nine women and children and capture over ninety.

The figures didn't match with those in the Osage version of the tale. That much was clear to Bradford, and, had it not been for Graves, he would probably have written off the discrepancies in the different versions of the several incidents to the fact of the different points of view and let it go at that. After all, as Degadoga had reminded him, he had said, repeating the words of Governor Miller, that the government would not interfere with the Cherokees if the Osages attacked them again, and the Osages had invaded the Cherokee country after that statement was made. But then there was Graves.

Even Reverend Washburn had said that during a frenzied victory celebration back at the settlements, Tom Graves, in a drunken rage, had killed a helpless Osage captive and her child and thrown the bodies to the hogs. Bradford could not let that pass.

He conferred with Agent Lewis and with Governor Miller, who had recently returned from his trip to New Hampshire, and the three of them concurred. Tom Graves must be arrested and tried for murder.

Cephas Washburn looked out the window of his small, recently completed log house to see Chief John Jolly riding toward the mission. It was November, and there was snow on the ground. Washburn slung a cloak over his broad shoulders, pulled his hat down tight on his head, and hurried over to the door. Looking back over his shoulder, he spoke to his wife.

"I see John Jolly coming," he said. "I must go out and meet him."

"Run along, dear," she said, with a pleasant smile. "We'll be all right here."

Washburn ran outside to meet the chief. He stood there waiting, thick chested, a stern look on his square face. Washburn's face, under his short white hair, seemed always stern, even when his mood was otherwise pleasant.

"Chief Jolly," he called out cheerfully, "welcome. Please get down and come inside out of the cold."

"Thank you, Reverend," said Jolly, as he swung down out of the saddle. He wrapped the reins of his mount around a hitching post and stepped forward to shake the reverend's hand. "So how are things with you here?"

"My biggest news and happiest is that Mrs. Washburn has just one week ago presented me with a darling baby girl," Washburn said, beaming his pride.

179

"I'm glad to hear of it," said Jolly.

"Come," said Washburn. "Come with me. We are making progress on our kitchen and dining hall. I want to show you."

"Oh, good," said Jolly, and he walked with Washburn to the newest and largest structure on the mission grounds. "It's looking pretty good," he said.

"Thank you," said Washburn. "There's plenty of work yet to be done on the inside, but we do have the fireplace ready, and there's a fire in it even now to keep the workers warm. Perhaps there's coffee on. Come in, come in. Let's warm you up."

The long, low log building was mostly bare inside, but there was a bench in front of the fire. After greeting all the workers, Jolly sat on the bench with Washburn. One of the workers brought them each a cup of coffee.

"We'd be farther along with the buildings," said the missionary, "had it not been for the recent tragic events. I've done my best to console the families that live near us, and I've had to go to Fort Smith and talk with the authorities there. It's a terrible, terrible business."

"When will you build the school?" Jolly asked. "I'm anxious for my children to be learning."

Washburn was stunned by the chief's seeming quick dismissal of the serious problem of the Cherokee-Osage war and the resulting personal tragedies. He was never good at deception, and his face gave away his feelings.

Jolly smiled. "My friend," he said, "the best way to change these things is to get the people all educated, like the Cherokees back in the east. Like the white man. I want to see my children in school."

Washburn sighed with relief and shook his head as if he understood. "I too," he said, "and all of us here want to be teaching the children. That is our mission and our sole desire. In addition to the troubles, our people here have all been sick, and so our progress has been slow.

"We decided to build the dining hall and kitchen first, because we cannot teach children who are hungry and cold. As soon as this work is completed, we'll begin the school. Perhaps by the end of the year, it will be ready."

"Good," said the chief.

"There is another thing," said Washburn. "Not all of your people feel as you do. Some, I might say many, are not nearly so well disposed to us as you. It takes time to win them over. We must win the trust and the friendship of the parents in order to get them to bring us their children."

"I'll help in every way I can," said Jolly.

"Uh, by the way," said Washburn, "is it true what I heard? Has Tom Graves been arrested?"

"Yes," said Jolly. "They arrested him for murder. There's to be a trial at Little Rock in April."

Washburn shook his head in sadness and concern. "A terrible thing he did," he said. "The war is bad enough, but what he did has nothing to do with war. A wanton act of murder against the most helpless of victims, a woman and her child. And then to — Ah, I can't even bring myself to say the rest.

"But, my dear friend, I must say this. I cannot help but believe that there is more savageness in the whites among you than in the genuine Indians."

14

Degadoga had become an obsession to Washburn. Chief John Jolly and other prominent men among the Western Cherokees encouraged the missionary effort every way they could and helped in various ways, but Degadoga and his followers were just the opposite. They were stubborn and old fashioned, superstitious and warlike. They were lost souls, desperately in need of the Christian influence.

Occasionally Washburn would see Degadoga riding his horse along the road that passed the mission, and the old man would not even deign to look in his direction. Word came back to Washburn now and then of things the war chief had said, ridiculing the work of the missionaries to the other Indians.

Washburn wanted badly to meet Degadoga. He had even sent word to the old man to that effect. Of course, Degadoga had declined. He was not at all interested in meeting the missionary or any of his company, as he was absolutely opposed to their work.

One day, out making his rounds, Washburn rode up to the modest log home of Watt Webber. Webber had been friendly to him and had expressed interest in his work. The missionary had raised his clenched fist and was about to knock on the door, when it was opened from the inside. It startled him just a bit. Webber stood there bareheaded and, smiling, took Washburn by the hand.

"Reverend," he said. "Welcome. Come in."

Washburn was about to step into the house when he noticed, standing to one side, wrapping his blanket around his shoulders as if preparing to leave, old Degadoga himself. The missionary's heart thrilled. It must have been the hand of God, he decided, that brought him to this house at just this time. He was standing in the one doorway. If the old man wanted to get out, there was no other way. A broad smile spread across Washburn's face, and he held his eager hand out toward the war chief.

" 'Siyo, Degadoga," he said. "What a pleasure to make your acquaintance at last. I'm Reverend Cephas Washburn of Dwight Mission, at your service, sir."

There was no escape. With no other

184

choice, the old man put out his hand and allowed the missionary to take hold of it, but he looked away as he spoke.

"'*Siyo*," he said. "I'm just leaving."

Washburn then stepped aside and allowed the chief to pass through the door. It had been brief, but it had been a formal meeting, and Washburn could not have been more pleased. He sat at the head of Webber's table, at the invitation of Mrs. Webber, while she brought out the food.

"Ah, Colonel Webber," said the preacher, "what a happy coincidence that was just now. I've been wanting especially to make that man's acquaintance almost since my first arrival in your country, and now I've done it right here in your happy home."

"He wasn't very friendly to you," said Webber. "I don't think he likes what you're trying to do here."

"No, of course not," said Washburn. "I know he doesn't like it and probably doesn't like me. He's been deliberately avoiding me all this time, but here he could not. And so we have met, and now I'll find an opportunity some time to stop by his home for a visit."

That said, the reverend bowed his head, folded his hands, and asked a blessing over the food that Mrs. Webber had put on the table for his enjoyment. He had already discovered to his delight that with these Cherokees, one did not have to plan ahead to show up at their homes at mealtimes. No matter when he might stop by, they always put some food out for him.

It wasn't long before Washburn made his promised visit to Degadoga. He rode directly and purposefully to the war chief's house and slipped quickly up to the door before the old man had a chance to know who was coming or to run away and hide. Feeling almost mischievous, he rapped sharply on the door. A moment later, the door was pulled open from the inside just a crack, and Washburn could see the old man's eye looking out at him.

" *'Siyo,* Degadoga," Washburn said. He stood up tall and straight and smiled his broadest smile. "May I come in?"

Degadoga said nothing, but stepped back, pulling the door open and turning his back on the missionary at the same time. Seeming to ignore his uninvited guest, he walked farther into the room. Undaunted, Washburn stepped boldly in and closed the door behind him. He removed his hat and cloak, looked around for a place to put them, located an unused peg on the wall, and hung them there. He meant to stay.

"I was just in your neighborhood," he said, "and I thought I'd stop by for a visit. Now that we have met, I would like to be better acquainted with you. I hope you don't mind. Uh, may I sit down?" Degadoga, not looking back at Washburn, gestured toward a stool which stood next to a makeshift table of planks set across kegs. Washburn sat down.

"*Wado,*" he said.

Degadoga looked over his shoulder at the missionary and raised an eyebrow. When he turned around, he handed Washburn a gourd filled with cool water. Washburn took it and drank from it. It was wonderfully refreshing. Then Degadoga put a bowl on the table, and beside it a spoon carved from the horn of a buffalo.

"Go ahead and eat," he said.

Washburn picked up the spoon and ate until the *kanohena* was all gone from the bowl. He knew what the hominy dish was. He had eaten some before at other Cherokee homes, and he had found it to be — not too bad.

As Washburn pushed aside the empty bowl, Degadoga was just lighting his pipe.

He got it going well and handed it to Washburn, who took it and puffed several times before returning it. They passed it back and forth until the tobacco and sumac mixture in the bowl was completely burned out.

Then Degadoga set aside the pipe and reached across the table for Washburn's hand. "Now," he said, "we are friends forever, you and I."

"I am very glad of that," said Washburn, "for my object in being here is to be a friend to all of your people."

"Tell me about your object," said Degadoga.

"We mean to build a school and a church," said Washburn, "and teach the ways of civilization and the word of God to all who are willing to learn."

"You want to put the Indians in breeches," said Degadoga.

Washburn smiled. "Well, yes," he said. "That, too."

"We're friends now," said Degadoga, "but I can never agree with you on these things. We have our own ways, and your way seems to me to be useless. And I don't believe that the president of the United States agrees with you either."

"Whatever do you mean by that?" asked Washburn.

"He doesn't want us to be civilized."

"Why, what makes you say that?" Washburn asked.

"When we agreed to come out here from the east," said Degadoga, "he gave us each a blanket and a rifle. If he wanted us to become civilized, like white men, he should have given us a hoe and a spelling book.

"No. I can be your friend, but I don't agree with you and the breeches party of Indians, John Jolly and those others. I don't agree with you. Your way is all right for white men, I suppose, but it's no good for Indians."

"My friend," said Washburn, "come and visit me at the mission. Come whenever you like. Let me show you the things we're doing there."

Degadoga sat for a moment as if in deep thought. "Well," he said, "I might go there some time to visit with you."

It was only two days later when Degadoga, accompanied by Captain Dutch, showed up at Dwight. Washburn was astonished. He could think of nothing he wanted more than the friendship and support of this recalcitrant chief. No one, the reverend thought, was more influential among the more backward Cherokees than was Degadoga. If the old war chief could be convinced of the advantages of education and Christianity, of civilization, then almost everyone else would follow.

For it was becoming clear to Washburn that the Western Cherokees were divided into two camps: Degadoga and his hunters and warriors on one side, clinging stubbornly and tenaciously to the old ways, old beliefs, and old superstitions, and John Jolly and his more progressive supporters on the other, the "breeches Indians," as Degadoga scornfully called them. And Jolly was already a strong supporter of the mission work.

Washburn dropped what he was doing and rushed to greet Degadoga, smiling and holding out his hands. "My friend," he said. " 'Siyo. Welcome. I did not expect you so soon. I'm glad you came. And you, Captain Dutch, welcome."

" 'Siyo, Washburn," said Degadoga. "Well, how do you succeed in teaching the Indian boys to wear breeches?"

"We're making some progress," said Washburn. "Come inside and see the school."

Degadoga walked beside Washburn to the log school building. Dutch followed a short distance behind. Inside, Washburn proudly showed off the recently finished schoolroom, complete with its new supplies.

Degadoga walked over to a globe on its stand. "What kind of bird laid that egg?" he asked.

"Oh, that's not an egg," said Washburn. Dutch smiled at the missionary's serious response to the old man's facetious question. "It's a globe. It represents this earth we're standing on."

Washburn gave the globe a spin.

"You see?" he said. "This model shows us how the earth spins on its axis. It's a device to help us teach the children about the way the earth is made."

"You say the earth is like this?" asked Degadoga. "Round and spinning?"

"Yes. Of course," said Washburn.

"That's a lie," said Degadoga. "The water would all spill out."

"No, no," said Washburn. "You see, when a body, like the earth, spins rapidly enough and constantly, a force is created that holds the water in. It's called centrifugal force."

Degadoga muttered, looked studious and said nothing more. He seemed to dismiss the lie about the spinning earth. A moment later the three men left the schoolhouse.

"We might as well go on over to the

dining hall," said Washburn. "I want you to see it, and besides, it will be time to eat soon. I hope you'll join us."

On the way to the dining hall, they passed by a well. Degadoga stopped and spoke to Dutch in a low tone. Dutch walked toward the well. Curious, Washburn watched and waited while Dutch drew up a bucket of water, carried it over to Degadoga, and put it on the ground. The old chief bent over and lifted the bucket by the bail. He hefted it to test its weight. Then suddenly he swung the bucket in a wide circle. No water spilled. He put the bucket down and jerked his chin toward Washburn.

"He's right," he said to Dutch.

Just then someone rang a bell three times.

"Ah," said Washburn, "the food is ready. Let's go and eat."

"Yes," said Degadoga, "we'll eat with you, but I don't like your way. When you come to my cabin, I say to you, 'go and eat,' and there's always food there. You can eat whenever you please. But when I come to see you, I don't see any food. You say, 'It's time to eat,' when the bell rings. Then we all go to eat at one time, and if we don't go right then, I suppose the food will all be gone. I don't like your way."

It was later in the afternoon when Sequoyah came by. His young son Tessee was with him. Washburn welcomed them to Dwight Mission, and everyone shook hands all around.

"Sequoyah," said Degadoga, "did you bring this young man here to the reverend so he can learn how to wear breeches?"

"No," said Sequoyah. "I'll keep him with me."

"Degadoga refuses to admit that I'm teaching anything useful here," said Washburn. "He won't admit to seeing any usefulness even in learning to read and write."

"Not even in Cherokee?" said Sequoyah.

"In Cherokee?" said Washburn. "Oh, well, that would be good, but it would take years to develop a system for it, I'm afraid."

Degadoga gestured at Sequoyah. "This one thinks he can do it," he said, "but most of the Cherokees just think he's crazy."

"Some of them think I'm a witch," said Sequoyah, "but I can read and write our language."

"That's a lie," said Degadoga.

"Then do you read and write English?" Washburn asked.

"No," said Sequoyah, "but when I saw the scratches on paper and learned what they were for, I decided that if white men can read and write their talk, so can Cherokees."

"Well," said the missionary, "I don't know."

"Are you willing to put it to a test?" Sequoyah asked.

"What kind of test?" asked Washburn. Degadoga gave a grunt.

At Sequoyah's request, Washburn ran into the schoolhouse and returned a moment later with paper and pencils and handed them to Sequoyah.

"Tessee," said Sequoyah, "go into the schoolhouse with the reverend."

Degadoga looked at Washburn. "Well?" he said. Washburn led Tessee into the school.

Sequoyah looked at Degadoga. "Now," he said, "if you will tell me something, I can put your words down on this paper."

"I still think it's a lie," said Degadoga. "I'm like the others. I think you must be crazy."

Sequoyah began scratching little marks on the paper.

"What are you doing?" said Degadoga.

"I'm putting down your words."

"Ha," said Degadoga.

Sequoyah finished writing and handed the paper to Degadoga.

"Take it to Tessee," he said. "I'll stay here."

"Come on," said Dutch, and he and Degadoga went inside, leaving Sequoyah alone. In the schoolroom, the old chief handed the paper to Tessee and glared at him. Tessee looked at the paper. Then he started to read the Cherokee words out loud.

" 'I still think it's a lie,' " he read. " 'I'm like the others. I think you must be crazy.' "

Degadoga raised his right eyebrow a little. Otherwise he betrayed no immediate reaction.

Degadoga's next visit to the mission was not so casual. Dutch rode with him again, and again he was enthusiastically received by Washburn, but this time the old chief was stern and all business. He produced a letter he had received and handed it to Washburn.

"Can you read me this paper talk?" he asked.

"Why, yes. Of course," said Washburn. "I'll be happy to."

"It's white man's paper talk," said Degadoga.

Washburn held the letter out and started to read.

"It's from Major General Pendleton Gaines," he said. " 'Brother,' it says, 'I am directed by your Great Father, the president of the United States, to say to you that the war between your people and the Osage tribe of Indian must come to an instant close. You must bury the tomahawk and be at peace.' "

"Ha!" said Degadoga, and the force of his voice caused Washburn to flinch. "What is that? Read it again."

Washburn started over from the beginning. This time Degadoga did not stop him, and he read the letter through to the end. The rest called for a treaty conference to be held at Fort Smith and attended by all the Cherokee and Osage chiefs, Governor Miller, and others. Finished, Washburn handed the letter back to its owner.

Degadoga held it out in front of him and stared at it for a moment as if trying to read. Then he spat on it and threw it to the ground. He stamped it hard and ground it with his foot until it was torn to shreds. Without another word, he turned and walked away. Dutch followed. Washburn, with a worried look on his face, watched them mount their horses and slowly ride away. He hoped that this would not mean trouble.

Safely beyond the view of the white people at Dwight Mission, Degadoga hauled back on the reins of his mount and stopped. Dutch pulled up beside him. Degadoga stared ahead for a moment, then glanced at Dutch.

"Who is this Gaines?" he asked. "Do you know?"

"He's the army's next commander up from Bradford, I think," said Dutch. "Bradford gets his orders from Gaines."

"And so do we, it seems," said Degadoga.

"Will we attend this council then?" Dutch asked.

"No," said Degadoga. "I don't think so."

15

1822

With the enthusiastic endorsement of old Degadoga, Sequoyah made his writing system known to all the Western Cherokees, and in a very short time, many of them had mastered it. Then Sequoyah announced his intention to go back east for a visit and introduce the system there. He offered to carry letters back with him, and many of the people wrote to friends or relatives and gave the letters to Sequoyah.

"When I come back," he said, "maybe I'll be bringing letters that they wrote to you."

They gathered toward the end of July at Fort Smith. Fort Smith: U.S. agents, Osage chiefs and Cherokees. Degadoga and Dutch were not there. Governor Miller was there, but the Cherokees did not know the other white men present. The government had assigned them a new agent. His name was Brearly. Agent Lewis was gone. Major Bradford was gone, too. General Gaines had replaced him with Colonel Matthew Arbuckle, and he had sent four companies of soldiers along with the new commander of Fort Smith.

It was abundantly clear to the Cherokees that the government of the United States was not happy with the situation and had just about run out of patience with them. It was as if someone had said, if Bradford and Lewis can't get the job done, then we'll send in someone who can, along with sufficient military force to back them up.

Under intense pressure from Gaines, an armistice had been previously agreed upon, and for two months there had been no hostilities between the Cherokees and the Osages. Even Degadoga, though he had not himself agreed to the armistice, had not broken it. At the end of the period of armistice, a new treaty was to be signed whereby both parties would agree to a permanent peace. So they were met once again at Fort Smith.

One hundred fifty Osages came to the meeting. Their chiefs were Clermont and Mad Buffalo. Watt Webber and others came for the Cherokees. They had been selected as the official delegates in a council meeting of the Western Cherokee Nation. Representing the United States were Governor Miller, Colonel Arbuckle, Agent Brearly, and the Osage agent, Nathaniel Philbrook. As if to show the Indians just how badly the U.S. government wanted this treaty to be signed, General Gaines himself had come along to observe.

They talked about the captives once again. Clermont said that there could be no peace unless the captives were returned. He said their families missed them, and some cried constantly for their lost loved ones. As before, the Cherokees said that many of the captives did not want to be returned. Women had married Cherokee husbands, and children were in school.

At last though, after much discussion, Watt Webber, speaking for the Cherokees, said that all the captives would be returned. Then they talked about stolen horses, and Colonel Arbuckle said that they should call it even on both sides and forget about it. Reluctantly, both sides agreed.

"But we don't like it when the That Thing on Their Heads People and the Heavy Eyebrows kill our animals," said Clermont. "When we sold you Lovely's Purchase, we didn't sell the animals that live there. We need our animals. When we want meat to feed our hungry children, we have to hunt. When That Thing on Their Heads People or Heavy Eyebrows kill our animals, they're taking food away from our children.

"We don't know how to raise cattle and hogs the way the Heavy Eyebrows and the That Thing on Their Heads People do. When we want meat, we have to hunt."

"This is the third time Lovely's Purchase has been dealt with," said the governor, "and I believe that issue was settled long ago. It is impossible for us to have bought the land from you and not the animals on it. There is good hunting on the lands west and south of Lovely's Purchase. Let's hear no more of Lovely's Purchase."

Then they talked about their people who had been killed, and Arbuckle dealt with them as he had the horses. Enough have been killed on both sides, he told them. Instead of killing more, forget about it. Call it even and live in peace from here on out.

"Maybe we can set most of it aside for the sake of peace," said Clermont, "but we can never forget about Tom Graves. We want the That Thing on Their Heads People to give Tom Graves to us, or if not that, at least we want the United States to punish Graves for what he did."

Arbuckle turned to Miller for response to that specific issue. He was new in the area and did not know about Tom Graves.

"Tom Graves has been tried in a federal court," said Miller, "and, unfortunately, the court found that it had no jurisdiction over the incident. I'm afraid there's nothing more to be said about it now. No matter how any of us may feel, it's over and done. Now let's not keep bringing up things from the past. If you keep doing that, both sides can complain from now on, and we'll never get anything done. Let's talk about peace and the future."

Then Mad Buffalo got up to speak. His shaven head was adorned with a high red roach, and he held a blanket wrapped loosely around his torso, exposing his bare shoulders. On his back was slung a quiver that was full of arrows and also held his bow. He was tall and straight and he spoke with a clear and commanding voice.

"How can we talk of peace today?" he said. "What difference does it make what we here decide? The great war chief of the That Thing on Their Heads People has stayed at home. He must not be interested in what happens here. He doesn't care to show his face and speak with us. He is the one who must say yes to peace, or there will be no peace. He is the one who tells the warriors of the That Thing on Their Heads People when to ride. Without his voice, these talks mean nothing. Where is he, and where is his captain, Dutch?"

So nothing much was accomplished on that day beyond the airing of grievances. When the meeting was adjourned in the early evening, General Gaines approached a tired and frustrated Governor Miller.

"Who is this great war chief of the Cherokees?" he asked.

"The reference was to Degadoga, I believe," said Miller.

"Isn't he one of the chiefs to whom my letter was sent?"

"Yes, sir," said Miller. "He is."

"Then why isn't he here? Did he receive the letter?"

"I'm sure he did," said Miller.

"And he has chosen to ignore it," said the general. "Was there any truth in what the Osage said, that we're wasting our time here without the presence of this Cherokee war chief?"

"I'm afraid there may be a good deal of truth in it, General," said Miller. "Degadoga is an old warrior, and he hates the Osages. I've tried to talk to him myself, but there's just no getting through to him. His mind is set. He believes that all Osages are liars, and therefore there's no point in talking with them. He advocates a war of total extinction of the Osages."

"Well," said the general, "it seems that we must have him here. Tell me how to find him."

Early the following morning, Gaines set out for Dwight Mission with a small military escort. On his arrival there, he presented himself to Reverend Washburn, and told him his purpose. Washburn saw that the members of the escort were taken care of, then had Gaines brought into his house as his personal guest. He introduced the general to his wife and showed him his new daughter, but Gaines was anxious to get down to business.

"Can I have a message sent to this Degadoga right away?" he asked.

"Yes," said Washburn. "I believe we can send someone to him with your message. I believe that Brother John knows the way."

"Will Degadoga be able to read the message that I send?" Gaines asked.

"Brother John will read it to him," said Washburn.

"Good," said Gaines, and he wrote a brief note, signed it with a flourish and all

204

of his titles, and handed it to Washburn. "It's a simple demand for him to present himself to me here at your mission immediately," he said.

Washburn took the note and gave it to one of the workmen at the mission. Returning to the house, he informed the general that it was likely to take three hours to get the chief's response. The general settled down to wait.

Three hours later Brother John, the messenger, was back alone. Gaines scowled when he saw that his note had not been obeyed.

"What did he say?" he asked.

"He said that he was busy with important personal matters at home," said John, "and he did not think that he would come."

"Go back at once," said Gaines, in his best commanding voice, "and tell Degadoga that if he is not right here with me three hours from now, I will send an officer and a file of men to fetch him back in chains."

John sighed but made no more specific complaint. He left again, and Gaines waited yet another three hours for his return. Surely, he thought, the second message would do the trick. Could it be that the ignorant savage did not understand the significance of his rank? He wondered what was happening back at Fort Smith at the meeting. A day was being wasted. He was angry and impatient. He should have been on his way back to the council already with the stubborn war chief in tow.

At last Brother John returned, and he was still alone. It was all the general could do to suppress his rage and keep himself from running to meet the man. He retained his dignity, however, and stood waiting for the messenger to come to him.

"Well?" said the general. "Why has he not come this time?"

Brother John shrugged and looked at the ground to avoid the general's stern glare.

"I don't know, sir," he said. "He just said that he'd wait for the file of men."

Gaines was furious, but it was too late in the day to send another message. Peremptorily, he dismissed Brother John. He would have to think of another tactic. Clearly, this Degadoga was not a man who could be easily intimidated. He turned to Reverend Washburn.

"Do you know this Degadoga personally?" he asked.

"Yes," said Washburn. "I do. I'm proud to say that I think I can call him friend. I made it a very special point to get to know him. I consider him to be a most important person among the Cherokees. He's highly respected and therefore very influential."

"Yes. So I gather," said Gaines. "But he's also holding up some very important negotiations. And he's challenging the authority of the United States government and thumbing his nose at the might of the United States army. We can't have that. Is he so ignorant that he does not know the possible consequences of such a challenge?"

"He's a proud and obstinate man," said Washburn, "and no authority outside himself impresses him. Not even heavenly authority, I'm sad to say. Why, you should have seen the way in which he dealt with your recent letter."

"My letter?" said Gaines. "What do you mean?"

"You sent him a letter, did you not?"

"Yes, of course."

"Well, he brought it to me to read for him," said Washburn, "right after he received it, you know, and when I had done, he took it back, spat upon it, tossed it to the ground, and stamped upon it and ground it with his foot to shreds."

"He did?" said Gaines.

"He did, indeed," said Washburn. "I think he was mightily offended by its tone. You see, sir, he takes his position with his people very seriously, as much, I think, as you do yours. He's a hard man to move when his mind is set."

"Well, I'll move him," the general said. "I'll call on him personally first thing in the morning, and then we'll see if he will still refuse to attend the council. Stamp on my letter, will he? Grind it to shreds? I'll show him some authority the like of which he has never seen before."

Early the next morning Major General Gaines appeared to the Washburn household in the glory of his full-dress uniform, epaulets on his shoulders, shining medals on his chest, and a saber rattling at his side. He breakfasted with Reverend and Mrs. Washburn, eating everything that was put in front of him. The meal done, he dabbed at his lips with a napkin, thanked Mrs. Washburn kindly, pushed back his chair and stood up. He brushed off the front of his tunic and picked up his plumed cocked hat and set it firmly on his head. Washburn accompanied him out the door.

"Will you send along someone to show me the way?" asked Gaines.

"Of course."

"I'm going to call upon this stubborn chief in the character and uniform of a

208

major general of the United States army, and I'm going to tell him to take his Osage prisoners and instantly start with me to the council. And I will tell him further that if he refuses me still, I will hang him upon the nearest tree."

Gaines waited for Washburn's reaction to his speech, but the missionary made no comment. He did not even raise his eyebrows. Instead he stood silent and looked the other way. After a brief moment, the impatient general spoke again.

"You know him best," he said. "Do you think that approach will move him?"

Washburn sighed deeply and turned to face the general.

"I mean no disrespect to you or to your uniform," he said, "and I suppose you know your business best. I don't want to interfere or try to influence you in any way. But since you asked me, I will tell you what I think. I think that if you go to Degadoga's house in that manner and say to him what you have just said to me, the old man will laugh in your face."

Gaines stiffened and tightened his jaws. His face turned purple. He stood straight and silent for a nervous moment.

"Well," he said at last. "I don't like to have anyone laugh at me, and I especially wouldn't like to be laughed at by an Indian. I won't go to Degadoga's house at all. I shall go straight back to the council and see if we cannot conclude a peace without his presence there."

The peace was concluded on the ninth of August, with the Cherokee delegation having promised to return all of the Osage captives by the twenty-first of September. Both sides agreed to a complete cessation of hostilities, and they further agreed that if either side should break the peace, the United States army should punish the offender. The treaty was signed by the entire Cherokee delegation and by Clermont, and Mad Buffalo, with their marks, for the Osages.

When the Indians had all at last left the fort and headed for their homes, Gaines, Arbuckle, Miller, Brearly, and Philbrook sighed their collective relief and gave each other hearty congratulations. They had brought an end, so they thought, to the long, bitter, bloody, and difficult Cherokee-Osage war, a war that had come very near to destroying several prominent military and civilian careers. They were all very proud of themselves.

PART 2

Gone to Texas

16

1823

Dutch was riding toward his house. Up ahead, a woman walked along the side of the trail. She was carrying a basket under one arm. As he rode closer, she looked over her shoulder to see who was coming, and she stepped a little off the trail to get herself safely out of the horse's path. With that brief glance, Dutch recognized Susanna, the daughter of his nearest neighbor, Mary Miller, widow of Soldier, who had been killed by the Osages.

Riding up behind her like that, not knowing who she was, he had seen a young woman. Funny, he thought, that he had never seen her that way before. He had seen her only as a girl. He slowed the pace of his mount as he came alongside her.

" 'Siyo, Susanna," he said.

" 'Siyo, Tahchee."

"Climb up on my horse, and I'll give you a ride home."

She hesitated, looking at her basket, which was full of wild onions she'd been gathering. Dutch reached for it, and she let him take it. He held the basket and the reins in his left hand and offered her his right, at the same time removing his foot from the stirrup. She took his arm, stepped into the stirrup, and with his help, swung up behind the saddle. He gave her back the basket, clucked at his horse and moved on.

"How's your mother?" he said. He wasn't really interested in Mary Miller, but he had to have something to say.

"Oh," said Susanna, "she's all right. She works hard, but without my father, I guess it's difficult for her."

Susanna had one arm around Dutch's waist, and he could feel her breasts pressed against his back from time to time as they rode along. He had a thought, and he couldn't be sure if it was because he suddenly wanted to see more of this young woman or if he was feeling guilty at having neglected the widow of a friend.

"I'll bring her some fresh meat," he said. "Maybe that will help."

"That would be nice," she said.

When he saw the house ahead, he stopped. He almost embarrassed himself, for he didn't want to tell Susanna why he had stopped so far from her house. He wondered if she knew. In that short ride, he had decided that he wanted to have this woman for his wife, and if Mary Miller was to become his mother-in-law, he couldn't speak to Mary any more. It would be easiest to just avoid seeing her.

He gave Susanna a hand down. Standing in the road, she looked up at him and smiled, and he thought, how big and beautiful are her eyes.

"Thanks for the ride," she said.

"*Howa,*" he said. "I'll see you again in a few days with the meat I promised."

He rode to Degadoga's home and went inside. The old man gave him *kanohena* and coffee, and Dutch sat for a while and ate in silence.

"You know about the treaty that they signed," said Degadoga.

"Uhn," said Dutch. He was still eating.

"It was a foolish thing for them to do. A stupid thing. I'm ashamed of this Cherokee government of ours. You can't make a treaty with liars and expect them to keep it. Besides, we're just about to whip them once and for all. We could wipe them out. Why should we quit when everything is in our favor? We should press on."

Dutch shoved aside the bowl he had just

emptied. "John Jolly has wanted peace ever since he came out here," he said.

"I should have opposed John Jolly when they put him up for chief," said Degadoga. "It's my own fault. Well, I'm fed up with these breeches Cherokees. I think I'll go to Texas."

"With Bowles?" said Dutch.

"Yes. I'll go down there and find Bowles."

"Uncle," said Dutch, "I'll be gone for a few days. I'm going hunting. I promised the widow Miller some fresh meat."

Degadoga gave Dutch a slight leer and a nudge with his elbow. "Is it the widow you're interested in," he asked, "or the daughter?"

Dutch smiled and ducked his head. How does this old man always seem to know everything? he wondered. "Anyway," he said, "when I come back, I'll bring you something, too."

"Don't bother," said Degadoga. "I'll be gone to Texas."

Dutch looked up with the sudden realization that the old man was serious. He had been so caught up in his own thoughts that he hadn't paid attention. He had thought that Degadoga was just saying those things, just grumbling about the treaty.

"I was thinking that you might want to go along," Degadoga said.

Dutch dropped his head again. He thought about Susanna, what she looked like, the sound of her voice and what it had felt like to touch her.

"No," he said. "I don't think so. I think I'll stay here."

They had been hunting for several days, Tom Graves, his nephew Red Hawk, and thirteen other Cherokee men. It was a cold January and the buffalo were running in small herds throughout the country. The hunting was good. They were camped on the north fork of the Canadian River, well west of the area known as Lovely's Purchase.

It was early daylight, and one of the younger men was preparing to boil coffee for the camp. The fire was low, and they had used up most of the wood they had gathered previously. Red Hawk, being one of the younger hunters in the group, got up to fetch some more. He walked away from the camp and went into the woods.

He had not been gone long. He could not have been far from the rest of the hunters in the camp. A single rifle shot seemed to snap the brittle air. Graves was on his feet in an instant, his rifle in his hand.

"Red Hawk!" he cried, running into the woods toward the sound.

"Ani-Wasasi!" a hunter shouted. All of the men grabbed their weapons. Three followed Graves into the woods. The rest formed a ring around their camp, facing outward, waiting for any attack that might come.

Young Red Hawk was alone and probably in danger, and Graves, desperate to reach him and lend him a hand, crashed recklessly through the tangled underbrush of the thick forest like an angry bull. He stopped, momentarily disoriented.

"Red Hawk!" he cried.

A moment later a voice answered him, but it was not the voice of Red Hawk. "Tom!" it called. "Over here."

He followed the sound of the voice and found his companions, the three who had followed him into the woods, standing in a small clearing. They were looking down. He knew what they were looking at. He pushed his way forward, and though he was afraid to look, he did.

Red Hawk's body lay where it had fallen forward in the clearing. One rifle ball had torn a hole in his back just between the shoulder blades. He had fallen on the armload of wood he was carrying. Possibly he had heard the shot just before he felt the impact. But that was not the worst of it. The head was gone from the body.

Graves roared out his anguish and his ire and stalked around the clearing as if he were looking for someone or something to tear to pieces. Even his companions backed away to give him room. At last he stepped up close to the gory headless corpse and dropped to his knees beside it, weeping and wailing.

They searched, but they never found the head.

In the old days, Dutch's mother or one of her sisters would have approached Mary Miller to talk about the prospects of a marriage between the two clans. They would have made all the arrangements. At the same time they would have consulted a conjurer to find out whether or not the proposed match would be a good one.

Then if the conjurer's prediction was positive and the clan matrons all agreed, Dutch and Susanna would have approached each other in full view of the entire town population. She would have handed him a basket of corn, and he would have handed her a ham of venison. Then, wrapped together in one blanket, they would have walked into her house as man and wife.

But things were changing. It was partly because of the whites among them and all of the mixed marriages. Many of the old ways were falling by the wayside. The more pious among them, those that Degadoga called breeches Indians, were going to the missionaries to have a Christian marriage performed. Others, usually with the blessings of both families, simply moved into a home together, considered his not hers, another influence from the whites, and everyone knew that they were wed. Susanna moved into Dutch's cabin on the south side of the Arkansas River in the settlement of Dardanelle.

Degadoga did go to Texas, and sixty families went with him. John Jolly and the "breeches party" worried that the old war chief might do something to get them all in trouble. He had moved out from under their jurisdiction because he opposed the treaty with the Osages, and his feelings about the Osage war were widely known.

It was painfully clear that Degadoga was disgusted at the actions and attitudes of his own government, and he had therefore withdrawn himself from it. The question on everyone's mind, then, was whether or not he would continue to prosecute the war with the Osages from his new location.

John Jolly notified Colonel Arbuckle of Degadoga's move to Texas.

"We have nothing to say about his actions," Jolly said. "He left us, and he's on his own."

Watt Webber came to Dutch's house and brought the news. Some hunters had just come in from the west.

"He's riding up toward Clermont's Town," said Webber, "all the way from the Red River."

"Degadoga?" said Dutch.

"Who else?"

"How many men with him?"

"They said about nineteen."

Dutch tucked his pistols in his sash and went to get his long rifle down from its place above the mantle. The treaty didn't matter. It made no difference what John Jolly and the council might think, and Dutch wasn't even thinking about the feelings of the commander of Fort Smith or the governor of the territory. Degadoga was headed for Clermont's Town, now populated by maybe fifteen hundred Osages, with a band of nineteen men. And he would reach Clermont's Town at the end of a long and tiring ride for man and beast, if he reached it at all.

"He'll need some help," Dutch said.

17

Degadoga and his band rode hard, driving before them one hundred head of stolen Osage horses. Getting the horses had been easy, but the old man knew that Osage warriors would follow them. He had, in fact, counted on that. It was part of his plan, and he would be greatly disappointed if they did not follow.

Up ahead was a narrow gorge with high, rocky walls on either side. He had taken note of it on the trip north. The old man shouted orders as he rode. They drove the horses on ahead of them into the gorge, and then the men all fell behind the herd. At a command from Degadoga, all but one dismounted.

"Go on," said the war chief, and the mounted man drove their saddled horses on ahead the way the stolen herd had gone. "Come on now. Let's get up in the rocks," Degadoga called out to the others, and he and seventeen more Cherokees climbed up the rocky walls and hid themselves behind boulders and waited. They waited for the

Osages to come riding into their trap. The dust from the horse herd had not yet settled below.

Dutch's party of forty men saw the large horse herd coming out of the narrow gorge onto the prairie, and Dutch knew that it must be Degadoga with a stolen bunch from Clermont's Town. But when they rode closer, there was only one man to be seen with the herd. He was a young man, bare chested, turbanned, with long hair, and Dutch recognized him and called out to him by name.

"Ogala," he said, "where's Degadoga and the others?"

"They're waiting back there in the draw for the Ani-Wasasi to arrive," said Ogala. "What are you doing here, Tahchee?"

Dutch ignored the question and started into the south end of the ravine with forty Cherokees behind him. Just then, he heard the sound of shots ahead.

"Let's go," he shouted.

Degadoga was surprised that so many Osages had followed him to try to get their horses back. As they came riding into the trap he had laid, he saw them. There must have been sixty, at least, and he was waiting there to ambush them with only seventeen men.

Oh well, he thought, and he sighted in on the man in the lead. The others would wait for him to shoot first. He waited another moment and then he fired, and the man fell backward off his horse. Some of the Osages turned their mounts to retreat. Some headed for the sides of the gorge for cover. In their hurry and confusion, some of them ran into each other. The rest of the Cherokees fired their rifles, but most of them missed their marks. A few inflicted minor wounds.

Degadoga hurried to reload. Eighteen rifles had been fired, and then no more. The Osages would begin to figure out that there were not so many Cherokees up there. He and his men would have time this time to reload. They would be able to fire one more salvo, but then the Osages would rush them while they were reloading again. When that happened, the Cherokees would be overwhelmed by the Osage numbers. He hoped, at least, that Ogala would be able to drive the herd ahead alone. It was a difficult job for one man, but it was not impossible, and Degadoga did not want the Osages to get their horses back.

He raised his rifle and laid the barrel

across the rock in front of him, but the Osages he could see had moved too far back even for a rifle shot. The others had not showed themselves again. He wondered why.

Then one Osage in the bunch that had retreated to regroup shouted something and waved his arm. Others behind him began to shout, and down below, the ones who had hidden themselves came hurrying back out to join their comrades in retreat. What were they running from, Degadoga wondered. What could it be?

Some of the Cherokees fired at the Osages as they ran, but none of the bullets hit their targets. The behavior of the Osages puzzled Degadoga until at last he saw the band of Cherokees coming from the other direction through the passageway below. He stood up behind his rock to get a better look. Then he recognized their leader, and he smiled.

"Dutch!" he shouted. "Tahchee! Go get them for me!"

He came out from behind his rock and started carefully down the steep hillside, and the other members of his gang all started to descend as well. Down on the floor of the canyon, they stood and cheered and waved and shouted encouragement as Dutch and the others rode past them in pursuit of the Osages.

By the time Dutch rode out the north end of the gorge, he could see that the Osages had scattered and were much too far ahead for further pursuit. He called a halt, and he turned and led his party at an easy pace back into the natural passageway where Degadoga and the others were waiting. He reined in his mount and looked down at the old man standing there.

"They got away," he said.

" 'Siyo, Tahchee," said Degadoga, and he smiled and held out his hand for Dutch to shake.

" 'Siyo, Uncle," said Dutch. "You've come a long way from your new home in Texas."

"Ah," said the old man, "it's not so far to ride for so many fine horses."

"I saw your horses," said Dutch. "And you set a trap here with just these few men for all those Ani-Wasasi?"

Degadoga shrugged.

"You got here just in time," he said. "I knew you would be coming along."

Dutch smiled. The old man was incorrigible, he thought. He always has an answer. And what's more, he's always right.

"Get on behind me, Uncle," he said. "I'll

take you to your horses."

Agents Philbrook and Brearly were both sitting stiffly in Colonel Arbuckle's office at Fort Smith. Arbuckle was visibly agitated. He held a paper in his hand that he studied in silence for a moment.

"I thought we had this thing all settled," he said. "Like a fool, I really thought so."

"Yes, sir," said Brearly. "So did I. What else were we to think? The chiefs all signed the treaty."

"Not all the chiefs," said Arbuckle. "Not on both sides. And that's one of the problems. Clermont can't speak for all the Osage chiefs, and John Jolly can't speak for Degadoga."

"My Osages kept their word," said Philbrook. "Cherokees raided Clermont's Town and stole some horses. The Osages simply followed them to try to save their herd, and the Cherokees killed one of them."

"Those Cherokees," said Brearly, "were Degadoga's bunch. They rode up from Texas. They're out of our jurisdiction. Besides, the Osages killed a Cherokee hunter well before that raid."

"And Dutch took some men from Dardanelle and rode to the assistance of

227

Degadoga," said Arbuckle. "Let's not argue about who's responsible for what's going on. I've got a letter here from General Gaines, and he's very unhappy about the reports he's been receiving. It seems that after Degadoga's raid, the Osages killed another Cherokee at Chouteau's Trading Post on the Three Forks."

"Unfortunately, that's true," said Philbrook.

"They're not supposed to do that," said Arbuckle. "If someone violates the terms of the treaty, the injured party is supposed to let the army take care of it."

"I went to Clermont's Town," said Philbrook, "and asked Clermont to hand the murderer over to me for justice. He said that he would gladly give him over to me, but that he'd gone off somewhere on a buffalo hunt. I reminded him of the provisions of the treaty, and he assured me that he understood the terms perfectly and promised me that on the man's return, they would bring him in."

"And yet," said Arbuckle, "according to the reports received by General Gaines, a band of Osages made a raid on Degadoga's camp and stole ten horses even after that."

"In Spanish territory," said Philbrook, "outside our jurisdiction."

"It doesn't matter," said Arbuckle. "Cherokees pursued the Osages back up into Arkansas Territory, and a fight ensued in which one Osage was killed and several men were wounded on each side. The fight is being carried back into our jurisdiction, and it's only a matter of time before the Arkansas Cherokees get involved again. We've got to hold both sides to their promise. We can't afford to let this war get started up again.

"Mr. Philbrook, you've got to try again to apprehend the Osage who murdered the Cherokee. We can't let him go unpunished. The Osages will think that we don't mean business and they can do anything they please."

"I'll get him, Colonel," said Philbrook. "Clermont promised me."

Arbuckle stood up and walked over to the window. He leaned his hands upon the window frame and stared outside.

"Then there's this matter of Clermont's son," he said.

"Mad Buffalo," said Philbrook. "The killing of the white hunters."

"Yes."

"Clermont was very apologetic for that," said Philbrook. "He said that the Osages did not recognize the hunters as white men until it was too late. Even so, he said, he

229

did not approve of their actions, but he can't always control the young men."

Arbuckle turned back around to face Philbrook, a stern expression on his face.

"Those men must be turned over to me as well as the other one," he said. "When you next see Clermont, tell him so. And tell him this for me. Tell him that if he cannot control his young men, the United States army can. And will.

"Tell Clermont that I've been ordered to move my command west and establish a new post on the mouth of the Verdigris in the Three Forks area near Chouteau's post, and if he does not comply with my demands and turn over the murderers to us, I will be ready to launch an attack from my new position directly into the heart of his country."

Dutch stepped into his house with an armload of wood and kicked the door shut behind him. Susanna was cooking stew in a big pot over the fire in the fireplace, and the delicious aroma filled the small cabin. Dutch walked over near the fireplace and put the wood down on the floor. He put a couple of small logs onto the fire, then straightened up and moved around behind his young wife. He put his arms around her and pressed his cheek against hers. She stopped her stirring and leaned back against him to enjoy the moment.

"For a long time after my first wife was killed," he said, "I thought that I would never again enjoy life with another woman. Then you came along and showed me that I was wrong."

"I remember that *you* came along," she said. "I was walking down the trail with a basket of wild onions, and you came along and gave me a ride home."

Dutch chuckled softly in her ear. "That's right," he said, "and right then I knew that I must have you."

"So soon?" she said. "From that one ride?"

"So soon? I wonder that it took so long for me to see you."

"I had seen you before," she said. "I watched you for a long time."

"What were you thinking all that time?"

"I was wondering if you'd see me one day," she said. "And are you really happy with me now?"

"You know I am," he said. "With you, my life is perfect."

"Not perfect," she said.

"Nothing could be better."

"Perfect? Just the way it is?"

"Yes."

"Then how will you feel when my belly

starts to grow, and later when we have a new one in our house?"

Dutch stepped back. He put his hands on her shoulders and turned her around to face him.

"Are you telling me," he said, "that we will have one?"

She smiled and nodded, and then she lowered her head. Dutch took her chin gently in his hand and raised her face toward his. "Soon?" he asked.

Again she nodded.

"It's growing now," she said, and looking down again, she put her hands on her stomach. Dutch thought that he had never seen anyone so beautiful in all his life.

"Well," he said, "then I was wrong. Things are not yet perfect here with us, but they will be soon."

"The stew is made," she said. "Do you want some?"

"Yes," he said.

"Sit down," she said. "I'll get you some."

Dutch sat down and leaned his elbows on the table, resting his chin in his hands. He smiled softly. An *usti*. A little one. A baby in the house. *Agehyuja? Achuja?* A girl or boy, he wondered. Sifter or ballsticks? What will it be? Either way, he thought, would be just fine. If it's a girl, she'll grow up beautiful like her mother. If a boy, he'll be strong and brave and handsome. And girl or boy, it will have a very proud father.

Susanna stepped over to the table and put a bowl in front of him, and he looked up at her, still smiling.

"I'm very happy with this news," he said.

"Me, too," said Susanna, "especially now that I know you are. Now eat your stew. It's good and hot."

Dutch finished his meal, and he still felt as if he were drifting in a wonderful dream because of the news his wife had given him. He had a cup of coffee on the table in front of him, and Susanna poured one for herself and sat down across from him. Dutch picked up his cup and took a sip, breaking his reverie just a little. Then from outside came the sound of a number of approaching horses, and Dutch was suddenly alert.

He got up from his chair, took his rifle off the wall, and moved to the door. Hesitating only an instant to glance back at Susanna, he opened the door and stepped quickly outside. There must have been twenty mounted men in his yard, but he recognized the leader of the group at once, and he lowered his rifle and grinned.

"'*Siyo*," said Degadoga. "Guess who's come back home."

18

They sat outside in front of Dutch's house on tree stumps, on chairs, on logs, on makeshift plank benches, and on the ground. Some unsaddled their horses, threw the saddles on the ground and sat on them. Susanna had fed them all, and they sat and visited. It was good for old friends to be back together.

"Where are all your families?" asked Susanna.

"Oh, they're at home," said Ogala. "We all went back to our old houses."

"We had to chase some four-legged creatures out," said Degadoga, "but otherwise, everything's just about the way we left it."

"You weren't gone so long," said Dutch. "What made you leave Texas and come back here?"

"There were too few of us down there," said Degadoga. "Those Ani-Wasasi got bold and came riding right into our settlements. It's safer back up here where there are more of us. They've always been afraid to come into our settlements here."

"Did you see Bowles while you were down there in Texas?"

"I went to see him once," said Degadoga. "He's doing all right, and he asked us to join him, but there are too many Mexicans and white Texans down there where he lives. I don't like it. And I don't like the climate either. It's always hot, and the air is very damp. It's not good to breathe. Bowles is too far south."

"I'd like to go see him where he lives some time," said Dutch.

"So what's happening up here?" asked the old war chief.

"Arbuckle's moved the army post west of here," said Dutch, "over on the Three Forks where the three rivers come together. They call it Fort Gibson."

"Yes. I heard about that."

"It was because of the Ani-Wasasi," said Dutch. "They've been killing white men, I guess."

"That gives me a wonderful idea," said Degadoga. "Let's go see Arbuckle at his new soldier house and tell him that if he wants to punish the Ani-Wasasi for killing white men, we'll help him do the job."

"Okay."

"Let's go tomorrow."

★ ★ ★

Arbuckle looked up as the orderly stepped into his office.

"Excuse me, sir."

"Yes?"

"It's Captain Dutch, sir, the Cherokee, come to see you."

"Dutch? Well, I'll be damned. All right. Send him in."

The orderly hesitated, looking just a little nervous.

"Well?" said Arbuckle. "What is it?"

"He's brought someone else along with him, sir. Another Cherokee. An old man. I'm sorry, sir, I couldn't get the name. It was hard to understand."

Arbuckle wrinkled his brow in thought. "That's all right," he said. "I wonder who it could be. Bring them on in."

"Yes sir."

As the orderly stepped out the door, Arbuckle stood up and walked around his desk to meet his visitors. He raised his eyebrows in both surprise and recognition as Degadoga walked boldly into the room, followed by Dutch.

"Well, Degadoga," said the colonel. "It's been a while, hasn't it? And you've been busy during all that time. I don't know if I can say that it's good to see you. I should put you under arrest, you know."

"Arrest for what?" said the old man.

"Why, for raiding the Osages, of course. After the treaty was signed."

"I never signed that treaty. It was a no-good treaty, and I didn't even go to the meeting."

"It was signed by duly appointed representatives of your government," said the colonel, "and as such it is binding on all of the Western Cherokees."

"But I had gone to Texas," said Degadoga. "I wasn't part of that government any more."

"If you were a white man, Degadoga," said the colonel, "you'd have been a lawyer."

He held out his hand and Degadoga shook it. Then Arbuckle turned to Dutch.

"Welcome," he said, offering his hand again. "What can I do for you?"

"We heard the Ani-Wasasi have been killing white men," said Degadoga.

"Yes," said Arbuckle. "I'm afraid you heard right."

"We came to tell you that if you want to take your soldiers to punish that nation of liars, we will ride with you. We'll help."

"The United States army is perfectly capable of fighting its own battles," said Arbuckle.

"But we could make it easier," said

237

Degadoga. "We could bring one hundred men. And we know the Ani-Wasasi, where they live and how they fight."

"Degadoga," said Arbuckle, "the United States has been trying for years now to get you to stop killing Osages. Even if we were going to ride against them, which we are not, at least not yet, I could not allow you to ride along. No. Absolutely not."

"It seemed like a good idea to us," said Dutch.

"It would give you entirely too much pleasure," said the colonel. "I am glad you came by though, Captain Dutch. It will save me sending a message to Dardanelle. It has come to my attention that when you were ordered to move your settlements to the north side of the Arkansas River back in 1819, you ignored the order. You never moved. Captain Dutch, that order is still in effect, and you must move. If you fail to do so, the United States army will move you."

They stopped by a stream to rest their horses on the way back to Dardanelle. Dutch was furious at Arbuckle and, by extension, with the United States. He was thinking that he should have gone with Bowles in the first place, and he was wondering why Degadoga had bothered to come back. Texas was beginning to sound better to him all the time.

"I haven't killed any white men," said Dutch. "The Ani-Wasasi killed white men. We offered to help against them, and Arbuckle turned on me. If I were to kill a *yoneg,* I think it should be Arbuckle."

"That might be fun," said Degadoga, "but it probably wouldn't do you any good. Not in the long run."

"I'm not going to move to the north side of the river," said Dutch. "Even if I wanted to move to the north side of the river, I wouldn't do it now."

"What will you do then when the soldiers come to move you?" Degadoga asked. "Will you fight with them? I don't like to have to say it, but even we can't win a fight with the United States. We could win a battle or two maybe, sure, but in the end, they would beat us."

"Maybe I will move," said Dutch, "but I won't move where they tell me to go. I won't move to the north side of the river."

"Where will you go then?"

"I'll go where you went, maybe. I know why you said you came back, but I might go down there anyway. Let the Ani-Wasasi come at me. I'll be ready for them. Maybe you want to go back down there."

"No, I don't think so," said the old man, and Dutch thought, maybe the old war chief is at last getting tired after all these years of fighting. He is not as robust as he used to be.

"Maybe I'll go down to live with Bowles," said Dutch.

"I've got something else in mind," said Degadoga. "I didn't tell you yet the whole reason I came back."

Dutch didn't say anything to that. He just gave the old man a questioning look.

"Do you know what the United States is up to back in the east?" Degadoga asked him.

"Well, we get letters, ever since Sequoyah went back. I know that they're trying to talk all the Indians into moving west of the Mississippi River," said Dutch. "Is that what you mean?"

"Yes. That business. Think about it, Tahchee. All of the Indians out west. *All* of them. That's a lot of Indians. Lots of different tribes. Choctaw, Chickasaw, Creek, Seminole, Cherokee, Shawnee, Delaware, Oneida, Mohawk, Cayuga, Onondaga, Seneca, Wyandotte, Tuscarora, Catawba, Pamunkey, Chippewa, Menominee. And more. Lots of tribes. Lots of people."

"But most of the people back there don't

want to move," said Dutch.

"But they can be talked into moving with the right arguments, can't they? We moved, didn't we? I think that I'm going to give the United States a hand with this grand scheme of theirs. I'm going to volunteer to be their agent for this removal. I'm going to go traveling all around and see all the Indians everywhere. I'm going to tell them to just give in and go ahead and agree to move out here. Right away. Don't put it off any longer."

"You're going to help the United States?" said Dutch.

"Sure. Why not?"

"I'd rather fight the United States," said Dutch. "They told us to move out here where there are no white people. There are white people out here, more every year. Then after we move, they tell us to move again. How many times will they tell us to move?"

"If you want to fight the United States," said Degadoga, "that's okay, but why don't you wait to fight them until after all the Indians are out here together? They'll think that we're cooperating with them, but when we all get out here, then we'll kick all the white people back over to the east side of the big river. They want us west of it, we'll put them east of it. If they won't go, we'll kill them. We'll keep all the white people on the east side. How would that be?"

For a brief moment, Dutch's eyes gleamed, but then he frowned again. "It sounds good, Uncle," he said. "I like the sound of it, but I don't think that all the Indians will move, and even if they did, I don't believe they'll all agree on anything. Not ever. We'll keep on fighting each other, just the way we keep fighting the Ani-Wasasi."

"That will have to stop," said Degadoga. "I'll explain it to everyone. We'll have to all get together to drive the white men back east."

"You sound like Arbuckle," said Dutch. "I never thought I'd hear you say that our war with the Ani-Wasasi would have to stop."

"No," said the old man. "I didn't either, not until they had all been killed, but that was before I developed my grand scheme."

Nathaniel Philbrook rode boldly into the Osage country. He rode alone. He had been many times to Clermont's Town, as well as to some of the other towns, and he was personally acquainted with a number of the leading Osage men. When they had problems with the traders, with the Cherokees, or with the government, they came to him for help. He was their agent. He felt secure in their country.

His present mission, though, was a little risky, and he knew that. At the insistence of Colonel Arbuckle, he was going once more to Clermont to demand that the murderers of the white men be turned over to the United States for trial. This was to be the last demand. If Clermont refused or again delayed, the army would take up the matter.

Near the mouth of the Grand River, he turned his horse and waded into the stream to cross. He was rehearsing in his mind the speech he would deliver to Clermont upon reaching his destination. A rifle shot rang out. A ball thudded into Philbrook's back just between the shoulder blades.

He stiffened in the saddle. His last breath came out of his mouth as if someone had slapped him hard on the back. He relaxed and slumped forward, and his horse kept walking. Half way across the river, Philbrook's lifeless body slipped from the saddle and fell into the running water. When they found his horse, they thought that he had drowned. Weeks later, they found the body, and they saw the bullet hole in its back.

19

1825

Bowles put his long rifle aside as the lone rider he had been watching drew close enough for him to see clearly. It was not a white man coming. It was an Indian. The rider came closer, and Bowles thought, from the clothing, that it looked like a Cherokee riding in. He stood waiting, his hands on his hips, and then at last he recognized the rider and he grinned. It had been a long time.

"Tahchee," he said, as Dutch rode up into the yard. "It's good to see you, my old friend. Get down. Come on into my house and we'll eat."

"'Siyo," said Dutch. "I came to see how you live down here in this warm south country."

Dutch swung down out of the saddle, and Bowles turned to call out over his shoulder.

"John," he yelled. "John. Come out here."

A young man came out of the house.

"You remember my son?" Bowles said to Dutch. "John Bowles, my son. This is Captain Dutch."

"I remember John," said Dutch, "but not this big."

" *'Siyo*, Captain," said John.

"John," said Bowles, "take care of Dutch's horse, will you?"

"Yes, father."

John took the horse, and Bowles and Dutch went into the house, a log cabin much like the ones the Cherokees had built in Arkansas. They sat at a table of planks to eat. First they had *kanohena* and then some meat and beans and bread. When they had done with their meal, they sat with cups of coffee and talked.

"You rode a long way from Dardanelle," said Bowles.

"No," said Dutch. "Not so far. I rode from my new settlement. It's on the Red River. On this side."

"Ah," said Bowles, "so you're in Texas now."

"Yes. When they told us to move to the north side of the Arkansas River six years ago, remember? And you left to come down here. I didn't move. I stayed right there all this time. But recently the new

245

commander of the U.S. army there on the Three Forks said that if I didn't move, he'd come and move me with soldiers. I didn't want to move north of the river the way he told me to, so I left."

"Soldiers on the Three Forks?" said Bowles.

"They have a new post there," said Dutch. "It's called Fort Gibson. Arbuckle is the commanding officer's name."

"Ha," said Bowles. "Fort Gibson. Well, anyway, good for you for what you did. In Texas the U.S. can't tell you what to do. We have a good life here. We plant our crops. We hunt. We even have a lead mine, and we sell the lead in New Orleans."

"Texas belongs to Mexico," said Dutch, "but coming here to visit you, I saw white men."

"There are lots of white Texans," said Bowles. "They're all around us. More come every day. They want our land, too, because it's good land, but they can't get it. We had elections. Our new chief here is Richard Fields, and Richard has papers from Mexico City that give us this land to live on. When white men come to Texas, they have to get permission from Mexico before they can settle on land, just like we did. We already have the papers for this, so they can't have our land, no matter how badly they want it."

"Where we are," said Dutch, "on the Red River, no one has papers. No one has permission from anyone. They just go there and sit down and stay. That's the way I like it."

"So how do you live there?"

"Like you. Like always. We plant our crops, but we don't have a mine. We deal in horses."

"Buy and sell?"

"We sell," said Dutch, and he smiled.

"Osage horses?" said Bowles with a grin.

"Some Osage horses," said Dutch. "Some Comanche, some from other tribes. Tonkawa. We even get some horses from white men now and then."

"The war with the Ani-Wasasi goes on then?" asked Bowles.

"There's supposed to be a peace," said Dutch, "but it isn't working."

"Degadoga," said Bowles, "how is he?"

"He's traveling in the east. He means to form a great alliance of all Indians against the United States."

"For war?"

Dutch shrugged. "He says that the U.S. wants to kick all Indians west of the Mississippi River. And he says that he'll go along with that. He'll even help talk the Indians into moving, he says, but once that's done, once we're all on this side, then we'll kick all the whites back onto the east side of the Mississippi."

Bowles laughed out loud. "I hope he makes it work," he said. "I like it very much."

The two old friends sat silent for a moment. Bowles filled a pipe and lit it, then passed it to Dutch. "I'd like to steal some horses again," he said. "Down here, there are too many whites, and the Mexican army is around too much. We can't afford to make them mad at us. But I think about the old days sometimes, and I'd like to steal some horses again."

"From Osages?" asked Dutch.

Bowles chuckled. "That would be all right," he said, "but I think it would be even more fun to steal them from white men."

"Well," said Dutch, "when I go back to the Red River, you can ride along with me, if you like."

Degadoga and his new recruits, Spring Frog, Young Glass, the Witch, Tassell, Tah-lone, Young Duck, and John Drew rode on a Mississippi side-wheeler steamboat. None of them had ever ridden one before. They called it *tsiyu utana,* or big canoe. They rode it on the Mississippi River to a point southeast of St. Louis, Missouri, where the Kaskaskia River runs into the Mississippi.

There they disembarked for the night at the town of Kaskaskia in the state of Illinois. Kaskaskia, an old French settlement that had been taken from the French by the British and then by American revolutionary forces under the command of Colonel George Rogers Clark, was not much of a town. The accommodations would have been better at St. Louis.

But the Cherokees were traveling according to the schedule of the steamboat line at the expense of the United States government, for they were on a mission to the eastern Indians that suited the purposes of the United States. Not long before they landed they ate a meal on the boat, a lavish meal, paid for by the government: pheasant, rice, biscuits, potatoes, beans, and whiskey. Lots of whiskey.

When they settled into the inn at Kaskaskia, Degadoga was not feeling well. Right away, he took to his bed. Spring Frog was by his side.

"By morning," Degadoga said, "I won't

be here with you anymore. I'll know by then if my father was right or if Washburn is right. If I can figure out how to do it, I'll come back and tell you how it is on the other side.

"But you have to stick around for awhile yet, my friend, and I want you to carry on this work, this grand scheme of mine. I hope you'll do that."

In the morning, Degadoga was dead.

Alexander McNair, the new agent for the Osage Indians, walked into the office of Colonel Arbuckle at Fort Gibson. Arbuckle looked up at McNair anxiously.

"Is it over?" he said.

"Yes," said McNair, and he heaved a sigh. "I've just come from the trial. Mad Buffalo has been found guilty of murder and sentenced to hang."

"I've been trying to bring peace to this region," said Arbuckle, "but I didn't want it to end like this."

"You haven't yet received an answer to your letter to the president?" asked McNair.

"No," said Arbuckle, shaking his head. "Nothing."

"Do you think the president will grant the pardon you've requested?"

"I don't know, McNair," said Arbuckle. "I explained the situation out here as best I could. It doesn't help that the governor is in favor of the execution. I just don't think that our cause with the Osage will be served by killing this man. How did Mad Buffalo take the news?"

"He took it very well, I'd say," McNair answered. "He first declared his innocence, claiming that he had not even been with the others when the killings took place, but when he was declared guilty and sentenced to hang, he stood quite calm. He did object to the manner of his execution, saying that he wasn't afraid to die, but he didn't like to be hanged. He said that he would kill himself before the date of execution comes around."

"His only hope is the president," said Arbuckle.

"There's another matter we have to discuss while I'm here," said McNair. "The Osage chiefs are very angry that Mad Buffalo's going to hang and the government allows Dutch to run free. He's been back to the Osage towns several times. He steals horses and takes them down into Texas out of our reach. He's killed three Osage men during these recent raids."

"Dutch has removed himself from the

Western Cherokees," said Arbuckle, "and the Western Cherokee council has disenfranchised him. They passed a resolution saying that they have nothing more to do with him and are not responsible for any of his actions. He took himself down into Texas out of our jurisdiction, but he continues to raid up here in the Arkansas Territory.

"I understand that his settlement there in Texas consists of Kickapoos, Coushattas, Delawares, Shawnees, Creeks, Choctaws, and Caddos, as well as Cherokees. It's not an Indian tribe we're dealing with here, McNair. It's banditti, a group of outlaws. I'm placing a bounty of five hundred dollars on the head of Captain Dutch. Tell that to your Osages, McNair."

"Yes sir," said McNair. "Oh. I almost forgot. Did you hear the news from Illinois?"

"What news is that?" Arbuckle asked.

"Old Degadoga's dead. He died at Kaskaskia."

"Well," said Arbuckle. "That might make things a bit easier for us."

It was a cold early morning in northeast Texas. Dutch, Bowles, and two other Indians lay flat on the ground peering over a rise onto the small white-man town. There were a few cabins and there were many canvas tents. The people there were not farmers or stockmen. They were hunters.

A few of them were stirring around the camp. Most were still inside, probably asleep. Here and there small fires burned. On the near side of the camp, a large corral held maybe sixty horses.

Bowles nodded his head. "They look pretty good," he said.

"Are you ready then?" asked Dutch.

"Yes."

They backed a way down the hill, then stood and trotted to where their horses waited, along with another sixteen mounted Indians, Cherokees and others. They climbed into their saddles.

"Let's go," Dutch said.

Twenty mounted Indians rode hard over the hill and down to the corral. As two riders pulled down the pole gate, Dutch watched the town. A man came out of a tent, and Dutch fired off a round from one of his pistols. At the same time he let out a shrill whoop. The man ducked back into the tent, but other white men were coming out, and they came out armed.

Dutch glanced back toward the corral and saw that the other Indians had the horses on the run. A white man stepped out of a cabin door and fired a rifle shot, and Dutch heard the ball whistle as it sped by the side of his head. He turned and raised his other pistol, but the man had ducked back inside. By then white men were coming out of all the tents and cabins. He could hear them shouting at one another and at the horse thieves.

"They're getting the horses!"

"You goddamned horse thieves!"

"Shoot! Shoot!"

"They're Indians!"

And they did shoot, but the range was too much for their weapons. Dutch looked again at the herd, and his men were moving it out pretty well. He fired his other pistol back toward the tents, then turned his horse and raced after the others. There wouldn't be much pursuit, if any, he thought. There were only a few horses left for the entire settlement.

Back at Dutch's settlement the herd had been calmed down and Dutch and Bowles sat beneath a tree and smoked.

"That was a good raid," said Bowles. "I'm glad I came to visit you."

"And so am I," said Dutch.

"They're good horses, too," said Bowles.

"They're yours," said Dutch. "When you go home, take them with you."

"How many of them?" asked Bowles.

"All of them. I don't usually take horses from the white settlements near here," said Dutch. "But before long, someone will come around here looking. When they do, I'll just tell the truth. I'll say that I don't have their horses. Besides, I can get lots more from the Tonkawas and the Comanches."

"And from the Osages?" said Bowles.

"Yes," said Dutch, breaking into a slow smile. "Especially from the Osages."

Bowles took his horses and went home, and in just a few more days, a rider delivered a letter to Dutch. It was written in Cherokee, in the Sequoyan script, and it told him about the death of Degadoga.

20

1826

The raids continued back and forth between the Cherokees and the Osages. More and more, Osage raiders hit the newer Delaware settlements and the camps of white hunters as well. White settlers were alarmed. The Delawares, under their chief, Anderson, declared an all-out war of extermination against the Osages, and Colonel Arbuckle was fearful of a widespread Indian war, in the midst of which no one would be safe.

If war should happen, Arbuckle reported to General Gaines, six hundred to a thousand warriors easily could be involved on both sides, and there were but three hundred soldiers at Fort Gibson with which to try to enforce the peace and protect white settlers. And they were all infantry. The situation, he said, was desperate. Gaines took the report to heart and held four companies of cavalry in readiness to move into the Arkansas Territory.

★ ★ ★

Dutch and Susanna sat in straight-backed chairs that Dutch himself had made, in front of the log cabin he had built for them below the Red River, watching little William Dutch at play. Wili, two years old, was their delight. He ran just to be running. Now and then he stumbled and seemed to fall hard, but each time, he just got up to run some more.

Sometimes he would stop to study intently a bug he had spotted on the ground or to pick up a fallen leaf. Usually when he picked something up, he ran to one or the other of his proud parents to show what he had found. When he ran to them, he ran into them, and he ran hard, and when he brought them some object he had found, they always named it for him, and they always acted as if they found it every bit as interesting as did he. For everything was new to Wili. Every day of his short life was a new adventure, and so it was to Dutch and to Susanna, watching him.

They laughed together, watching him run on short legs, and they looked at each other and smiled their pride and pleasure. Dutch was happy. Life was everything it should be. Not even the continuing war with the Osages could lessen his joy. For it was just another part of life, the only kind of life he had ever known, and though he sometimes lost a friend or relative in a fight, he mourned the loss for a time and then set out to avenge the death. Things had always been that way.

And his heart did thrill at the chase, and a good fight gave his body a rush that caused his muscles to react, seemingly on their own, without any thought, and he had never been hurt in a fight. He was a warrior in the age-old tradition of the Cherokees, *Ani-yunwi-ya,* the Real People. He loved it, and he could think of nothing better in the future for his son.

One day Ogala, formerly of Degadoga's Texas settlement, came by, returning from a visit back to Arkansas.

"How is all your family back there?" Susanna asked.

"They're all doing well," said Ogala.

"That's good," she said. "I'm glad to hear it."

"Is there any news?" asked Dutch.

"Yes," said Ogala. "After all, Mad Buffalo won't hang. He's been set free. There at Fort Gibson, they got a letter from the president."

"A pardon?" said Dutch.

"I suppose," said Ogala. "They let him go home."

"The United States government expects us to live up to the terms of these treaties," said Dutch, "but it doesn't live up to them itself. The treaty said that if anyone on either side did wrong, we should not seek revenge, because the U.S. would punish that person. And so they have a trial and sentence him to hang, and so they get a pardon from the president and send him home again."

"Well," said Ogala, "they sent him home. That's all I know about that. But I have some other news that should interest you."

"Tell me, then," said Dutch.

"You have become an outlaw everywhere but here. Our own government has turned its back on you. The council has set you aside. You are no longer a citizen of the Western Cherokee Nation. They don't want to get in trouble because of what you do."

Dutch shrugged. "I set them aside," he said, "when I came down here. I'm glad that they did that. They were right. Now, just like you said, the army can't blame John Jolly and the others for anything I do."

But something in the tone of his voice and something in his eyes belied the words he spoke. Susanna saw it. Ogala may have seen it. Neither one said anything though, and Ogala continued with his report.

"And the army has made you an outlaw," he said. "Colonel Arbuckle's put up a big reward for you. Five hundred dollars, they said. You'd better be careful, my friend. Lots of men would risk their necks for that much money."

Dutch sat silent for a moment thinking about the things Ogala had told him. In spite of what he said, and even though he meant what he said, being set aside by the council hurt. It made him sad. He understood the action though, and he could live with it. But the rest of the news angered him, and he felt that it called for action.

"So Arbuckle wants my head, does he?" said Dutch. "I wonder, Ogala, do you suppose that Clermont has any horses left?"

They drove the horse herd east from Clermont's Town until they reached the old Osage Trace, and then they headed south. This time they had gotten away quickly and quietly. There had been no immediate pursuit. Of course, the Osages would eventually notice that the sixty horses were gone, and soon enough they would be following the trail, but Dutch thought that he and his gang would be so far ahead of them by then that it wouldn't matter much. Just in case, though, he had one rider fall well back and watch the trail. Two more were well out on the flanks, and one was up ahead.

They had crossed the Verdigris River and were headed for the Arkansas, west of Fort Gibson and Chouteau's Trading Post, when the rider from the eastern flank rode in.

"There's an Osage camp down by the fort," he said.

Dutch thought about the treaty, which, of course, he had not signed. He thought about the U.S. army's orders regarding Cherokee-Osage hostilities. He thought about the Western Cherokee Nation having set him aside, and he thought about the five hundred dollars Arbuckle had offered for his head.

"What are they doing?" Dutch asked.

"Nothing," said the rider. He shrugged. "They're just camped there."

"Where?"

"Across the river from the main gate."

"How many, would you say?"

"Six tipis. Twenty horses."

"Stay with the herd," Dutch said to the outrider. "Keep them moving. I'll catch up with you later."

He turned his horse and headed east. He angled off the main trails and the way was rough, through wooded hills and valleys, but he wanted to avoid being seen. Arriving at the top of a high hill covered with trees and brush, he stopped, facing east, dismounted and looked down. The Neosho River was down below, and Dutch could see Fort Gibson on the opposite bank.

Between the bottom of the hill he was standing on and the west bank of the river was a wide flat area, and there was the Osage camp.

Dutch thought that the camp was in a good spot for his purposes. It was across the river from and in full view of the fort. In a low-lying spot near the river, cleared of the natural growth of the canebrake and the forest, the fort was nothing more than a cluster of log buildings. No wall had been started, and toward the back of the cleared ground, a few buildings were still under construction. There were plenty of soldiers in view, some working, some milling about. At just that point, the river was not very wide. A good rifleman could hit his mark from the opposite shore.

Dutch studied the Osage camp. It was just as the outrider had described it. Six tipis were set up, and six small fires burned. At four of the fires women appeared to be cooking. He could see a couple of men walking around, a few more lounging on the ground. To his left, a small herd of horses grazed, twenty perhaps. Now he had to figure his own approach.

The way down the hill to the back of the camp was too steep and too cluttered with trees and brush to allow for a mounted attack from that direction, and if he were to go down on foot, he would have to have his horse somewhere handy for a quick escape. He decided that was not the way.

It would be better to ride into the camp. A man charging on horseback always throws a group of people into a panic. It takes a few seconds at least for even the most alert to assess the situation and respond. He decided on a horseback attack.

If he came at the camp from the north, he would have to contend with the twenty horses grazing there, and he would have a distance to travel after the Osages had spotted him. Coming from the south, the curve of the hill was not far from the camp. If he were to come racing around the curve, by the time they could react, he would be in their midst. He led his horse down the back side of the hill, the way he had come, mounted up again and rode around.

Dutch was at the curve. He could see a part of the fort across the river, but he could not see the camp. He knew it was not far ahead. A short hard ride. He took out his steel knife and held it in his right hand. Then he kicked his horse in the sides.

He came around the curve fast. His horse's hooves were pounding hard. He sounded the loud, shrill war cry of the Cherokees, a sound like the gobble of the wild turkey. The Osages in the camp heard the familiar and dreaded cry, heard the pounding hooves, looked up and saw the man and beast rushing toward them.

Women grabbed small children and ran for the trees. Men ran into tipis, perhaps to hide, perhaps to get weapons. One man was down by the water's edge, separated from the others in the camp. Dutch rode for him.

The man saw him coming and turned to run into the river, but Dutch was on him, right beside him. Dutch leaned to the right. With his left hand, he grabbed the Osage by the hair and pulled. At the same time he plunged the knife into the man's back. As the man went limp, Dutch pulled free the knife and reached around to make a cut just at the front of the scalp lock, and he gave a jerk with his left hand.

The scalp came loose, slinging blood in a high arc over Dutch's shoulder as the body fell into the stream. Dutch waved the bloody trophy over his head, and he could see a soldier on the other side of the river. "I'm Dutch!" he shouted. "Tahchee!"

A rifle shot sounded behind him, and he felt something like the scratch from a hot iron across his right cheek. He'd been shot. He was wounded, for the first time in his life. He turned his horse back toward the camp, and he saw the woman with the rifle. He'd been shot by an Osage woman.

He saw some men there, too, one at least with a rifle, a couple with bows and arrows. He screamed the war cry again and kicked his horse into a run headed directly back into the camp. Again the Osages scattered, and at the last second, he jerked the reins. His horse made a sharp turn, and he raced away, back around the curve of the hill, back the way he had come.

Safely away from Fort Gibson and the Osage camp, not yet caught up with his band of horse thieves and their herd, Dutch stopped to rest beside a small stream. He felt the scratch across his cheek. It stung. He thought about how close the shot had been, and he thought about who had fired it. An Osage woman. He smiled.

He unwrapped the turban from around his head, loosening his thick, shoulder-length hair, and leaned over the stream to drink and then to bathe his cheek. He felt good. So they thought they could tell him to stop killing Osages, did they? A bounty on his head? He showed them. In full sight of the soldiers at Fort Gibson, he had showed them what he thought of their orders and their bounty.

He wondered who the Osage woman was who shot him. He would like to know. One day, he thought, he would like to be able to congratulate her, for she had done what no man had ever been able to do. In over twenty years of fighting, no man had ever wounded Captain Dutch.

He leaned back against a tree for a moment musing and relaxing from the rush he felt in his veins. Then he rewrapped his turban, mounted his horse and started to ride. He should be able to catch up to the herd before nightfall.

21

1828

Thomas Graves, Sequoyah, and five others were in Washington. They had been selected by the Western Cherokee council as an official delegation to protest the organization of Lovely County by the territorial government of Arkansas. James Rogers had been sent along as official interpreter.

While Cherokees and Osages had been killing each other for years in squabbles over the land known as Lovely's Purchase, white squatters had moved in. Three thousand whites were there, and they had laid out three town sites. In order to accommodate them, the territorial government had designated the area a county.

A special council meeting had been called by Chief John Jolly to address this new development. The United States had secured Lovely's Purchase from the Osage Nation, he said, specifically for the use of the Cherokees. Now the territorial governor was making it into a county for the benefit of whites.

The assigned task of the delegates was to make sure that the government in Washington knew what was happening in Arkansas Territory and to talk them into putting a stop to it. So they went and they talked with congressmen and with presidential aides.

"That land was for us to hunt on," said Tom Graves. "We have three different treaties to prove it. We don't want to give it up to whites. We were even thinking about asking the government if some of us could live on it, not just hunt there."

And the government men suddenly saw a wonderful new opportunity as soon as they heard that plea. They said that there might be a way for them to take Lovely County back from the territorial government. If we were to draw a new boundary line, they said, north and south, to run just west of Fort Smith, then perhaps we could tell all the white people to stay east of that line.

You said that some of you wanted to move over onto Lovely's Purchase, the government men said. Why don't all of you move over there? If you would do that, they said, then we could move the white people out of there and take the county away from Arkansas Territory.

The delegation protested that not all of their people wanted to move over there, only a few of them, and the government men said, that's the only way we can do it, for there is also in Washington, right now, a delegation of white people from Arkansas wanting us to recognize the county and their right to live there. They know you're here, and they know why you're here. They're angry. They are our citizens, and they're demanding that we protect their rights and homes. We have to make a decision, one way or the other, right now while you are here.

Then the government men asked the delegates to sign a new treaty agreeing to make the move. The delegates talked among themselves for a moment or two. "We weren't authorized by the council to sign any treaties," Sequoyah said. "Just to tell them that we wanted those white people out of Lovely's Purchase."

Then the government men interrupted them. Well, they said, what is it going to be? If you refuse to sign the treaty agreeing to move across the new boundary line, then we are going to have to go along with the whites who are living on Lovely's Purchase and with the decision of the territorial government of Arkansas. "It must be one or the other?" asked Sequoyah. Yes, the government men said. It must be one or the other, and we must settle the matter now, while you are here. And so the delegates all signed a new treaty in the name of the Western Cherokee Nation, giving up all rights to the land that all of the Western Cherokees were living on, all except, of course, those who had gone to Texas, who had no rights at all.

Clermont sat in a straight chair across the big desk from Colonel Arbuckle in Arbuckle's office in Fort Gibson. He had a lit cigar in one hand and a tin cup full of steaming hot coffee in the other. He sat straight and proud. The leggings he wore were fringed with the scalps of his enemies. He sat bare chested, having allowed his blanket to fall over the back of the chair.

"Clermont," said Arbuckle, "I feel as if I'm saying the same thing to you over and again. This war between your people and the Cherokees has got to stop."

"It is the same thing over," said Clermont, "and so is my answer always the same. We want to live in peace. Do you think we want to fight the That Thing on Their Heads People with only our bows

270

and arrows, when all of them have rifles? But every time we think we have a peace, they steal some more of our horses or kill some more of our people. They kill the animals that belong to me, the animals that I need to feed my children."

"They tell me the same thing about you," said Arbuckle, ignoring the issue of the game animals. "What am I to believe? We know that some of your people killed Red Hawk, and that killing occurred after the last treaty had been signed. The Cherokees say that they must see the murderer brought to justice before they can lay down their weapons."

"You want me to turn one of my men over to the That Thing on Their Heads People?" asked Clermont.

"No," said the colonel. "Turn the murderer over to me, and he will be given a fair trial in a court of the United States."

Clermont thought about the trial of Mad Buffalo, the decision of the court, the sentence of death, and then the pardon from the president. Giving the man up to the United States didn't really seem like such a bad idea. Mad Buffalo had gone through the white man's system. The process had been a long and painful one, but he was alive, and he was at home.

"Maybe I'll bring this man to you," said Clermont, "when next I see him. He's gone out hunting buffalo, and I don't know where to find him. But if I bring him to you when he comes back home, then I want the That Thing on Their Heads People to give me Captain Dutch, the murderer of my people."

"Clermont," said Colonel Arbuckle, "I thought you understood. It's not possible for me to make Dutch a part of this bargain. Dutch is already declared an outlaw. If ever I get my hands on him, I'll see that he's brought to justice — in U.S. courts. But he's living in Texas now. My government cannot reach into Texas. Do you understand? If I can catch him in the Arkansas Territory, then I can arrest him. But in Texas, which is part of Mexico, he's beyond my reach, and he is no longer a part of the Western Cherokee Nation. They are not responsible for his actions. To them he's an outcast and a renegade. Do you understand what I'm telling you? He's an outlaw."

"If I give up the man who killed Red Hawk," said Clermont, puffing on his cigar, "then I should get Dutch in exchange."

When the delegates to Washington returned to their homes in the Western Cherokee Nation, two of the men, James

Rogers and Thomas Maw, were not with them. They had been hired by the United States government to go around the eastern Cherokee country and talk to people about the desirability of moving west. They had just acquired this new land known as Lovely's Purchase. The white people who lived there would be kicked out. The land was good. Hunting was good.

But back in Arkansas, no one was happy with the new agreement. The white people in Lovely's Purchase were furious and indignant. Imagine, being made to clear out of one's own home by one's own government to make room for Indians.

The Western Cherokees were angry at their own delegates. They had not been authorized to sell land, and no one wanted to have to move again. And what were the provisions of that treaty they had signed? There were incentives to entice eastern Cherokees to move west. There was not land enough in Lovely's Purchase even for all of the Western Cherokees, they said.

According to the treaty, Lovely's Purchase was to become a permanent home for the Cherokees. They would not be bothered again. Ha! They had heard promises like that one before. Words like permanent and forever seemed not to have the same meaning for the white men in Washington as they did for everyone else.

Then there was the matter of five hundred dollars to Sequoyah for making his alphabet, five hundred to James Rogers for the loss of a horse, and twelve hundred for Thomas Graves for suffering confinement on a false arrest. Many of the people thought that these figures sounded more like bribes.

"They went to Washington to tell them that we want the *yonegs* off of Lovely's Purchase, and they signed a treaty promising that we will all move our homes," said one.

"And for signing it," said another, "they got money."

And when the delegates arrived at their homes back in Arkansas, they found tall poles standing in their yards, poles from which their bodies might be hanged. They recognized these poles for what they were and left again, all but Thomas Graves and Sequoyah. So when the council met again, those two alone of all the Washington delegation showed up.

"When you elected me to go to Washington," Sequoyah said, "I did not want to go. But you voted, and you told me to go, and so I did. It was a long trip, and very tiring, and we were constantly surrounded by ugly white people staring at us. We had to eat strange food, and then we had to deal with those white men, those government men. We did our best, but it was hard. We had to make a choice. We couldn't ask you what to do. We were far away, and you were here. They told us that we could either sign the treaty or they would let the white people stay in Lovely's Purchase and call it a county. You sent us there to stop the county and get the white men out. What were we to do?

"I don't know why they put that money in there for me. I didn't even know about it. I can't read the white man's paper talk. You all know that. I did not take a bribe to sell our land. I signed the paper because they told me that it was the only way to save Lovely's Purchase for us. So kill me if you want to. That's all I have to say."

Then Thomas Graves got up to speak. The bulky white man who had been raised a Cherokee looked over the stern faces in the crowd. He thought that he would rather fight them than talk to them.

"I agree with everything Sequoyah said," he told them. "I didn't ask to be sent on that trip. But I went, and I did my best. We all did. If any of you had been there in my place, or in the place of any of the delegates, you'd have done the same thing we did.

"And they did put me in that prison when they had no right to do so. So if they want to pay me back for that, that's all right with me. But the twelve hundred dollars was not a bribe to get me to sign the paper. That's all I have to say, and if you don't like it, well, do what you will. But if you want to kill me, you'll have to fight me, and I'm not afraid of any man here."

A frowning, obviously dissatisfied Cherokee got up and asked to speak. "I think that we should have another meeting," he said, "and that meeting should be a trial. And we should try all of these delegates for betraying us while they were in Washington."

There followed much discussion. Some agreed with the dissatisfied speaker, and some defended the delegates, based on what Sequoyah and Graves had said to them earlier. At last, debate having subsided, Chief Jolly took the floor again. He looked worn and tired and old.

"What's done is done," he said. "I don't like this treaty any more than any of you do. I don't want to move, but I believe what Sequoyah and Tom Graves just told us. I believe that they thought they were doing the best they could for us. I don't know, but maybe it was the best that could be done.

"How would we like our homes here if

we were no longer allowed to go into Lovely's Purchase to hunt? If white people lived there? We would have whites on all sides. That is the choice they were given. If we are angry, it seems to me, it's the United States government we should be angry at and not our brothers who suffered hardships to do service for their people. And whatever we think of the treaty, we know the behavior of the United States from past experience. They will insist that it's legal, and that we live up to its terms. And according to those terms, we have one year in which to move our homes."

They argued the matter in the council for some time, but in the end they all agreed with Jolly that they had no choice. They would have to move. And at least the land known as Lovely's Purchase would at last be recognized as theirs. Of course, they knew, the Osages might have a different point of view on that issue.

No other meeting was set. No one was put on trial, and no one was killed. They reconciled themselves to the inevitable, and they made plans to move. Some went right away looking for home sites across the line. Others procrastinated. They had their crops to tend, and, after all, their deadline for moving was a year away.

22

1829

Leaving the homes they had built and the fields they had cleared, they traveled up the Arkansas River, past Fort Smith, east across the newly drawn imaginary line into their new territory. Sequoyah dropped off soon after crossing the line to establish his new home and a salt works at a beautiful spot beside Lee's Creek.

James Rogers and others went a little north of Sequoyah to a place called Skin Bayou to build their homes. Another group made a settlement at the mouth of the Sallisaw River on the north side of the Arkansas. Chief John Jolly settled on the east bank of the Illinois River about a mile above the Arkansas, and south of him on the opposite side of the Arkansas, Walter Webber made his home near a falls in the river. The settlement around him came to be known as Webber's Falls.

A council ground, called Tahlonteskee in

honor of John Jolly's departed brother and immediate past Western Cherokee chief, was set up near Jolly's home to serve as a national capital. A huge shelter was constructed there for meetings. Reverend Cephas Washburn, of course, abandoned the structures he and his staff had built and followed the Cherokees, re-establishing Dwight Mission along the military road that ran from Fort Smith to Fort Gibson.

While the Cherokees and the missionaries were busy moving in, the white squatters who had been living in Lovely's Purchase were grudgingly moving out. Giving up their town sites and carrying their recently established post office with them, most of them moved east, back across the new boundary line into the newly established Washington County, Arkansas Territory, to glare back across the line in anger and curse the government, the Cherokees, and all Indians in general.

The same year that the delegation from the Western Cherokee Nation had signed the treaty in Washington, twenty-five hundred Muskogee, or Creek, Indians, having been induced by agents of the United States to move west, had settled just south of the area known as Lovely's Purchase. So the

279

Western Cherokees had new and close neighbors, not only to their east, but also to their south. And the western prairie Indians, seeing their own boundaries closing in on them and pressures intensifying on the population of game on which they so desperately depended, grew more angry and more nervous.

At Clermont's Town the year was an especially sad one. Not only had the Cherokees been given the land known as Lovely's Purchase, land the Osages claimed they would never have sold to the United States had they known that it was for the use of their hated enemies, but Creeks and other eastern Indians were crowding in. The white population was growing around them, too. The Osages were forced to range farther to the west to hunt, and their conflicts with other western tribes grew more intense. Finally, adding to their other sorrows, their great leader, the beloved Clermont, died.

It was spring when the steamboat *Facility*, traveling the Arkansas River on its way to Fort Gibson from Nashville, Tennessee, made a stop at the mouth of the Illinois River to unload supplies destined for

Walter Webber's store at Webber's Falls, and to allow a distinguished passenger to disembark. The big white man with a strong, square jaw and an aquiline nose, dark, piercing eyes, and thick, short-cropped dark hair, was dressed like a riverboat gambler. People were gathered there watching this major event, and almost as soon as the man appeared, he was recognized. As soon as he was recognized, a runner hurried to the home of John Jolly with the news.

"Golanuh is here," he said. "Your son has come. The Raven arrived just now on the big boat."

Chief John Jolly quickly wrapped his head in a brightly colored turban and pulled on his equally colorful hunting jacket. He called out for a black slave to hitch a horse to his buggy. In a few moments, riding in the buggy driven by the slave, John Jolly rushed to meet Sam Houston, his adopted son, called by the Cherokees by the honorable war title, Golanuh, or the Raven. Jolly spotted Houston easily. Tall and powerfully built, the Raven was a striking and imposing figure in any crowd.

In the years since he had left the old chief to go out and make his own way in the world, Houston had accomplished enough for several lifetimes. Only thirty-six years old, he had risen in the ranks of the United States army to become a lieutenant by the age of twenty-one. He had then served as sub-agent to the Cherokees. He had resigned that position in 1818 and begun the study of law in Nashville. Admitted to the bar, he had set up his practice in Lebanon, Tennessee, and within five years had served as district attorney, adjutant general of the state, and major general of state troops.

Then, in 1823, Tennessee voters had sent Houston to Congress where he served two terms. In 1827, at the age of thirty-four, he was elected governor of the state of Tennessee by an overwhelming majority. It seemed there was no stopping his fast-rising star.

In January of 1829, the Tennessee governor married, but two months later he left his wife, resigned the governorship in the midst of a swirl of scandal, and boarded the *Facility*, headed west. He would never tell anyone what had gone wrong with his marriage. There on the banks of the Illinois River, the spring lush and green in the new Western Cherokee Nation, Houston and Jolly embraced and wept with joy at seeing one another again.

"Father," said Houston, speaking in the

Cherokee language, "it's good to see you again."

"It's good to see you, my son," said Jolly, "but what brings you out here so far from your duties?"

"I have no duties," said Houston. "I have nothing. I'm an exile."

"You have a home," said Jolly. "As long as I live, you have a home. Come with me."

Houston was amazed to see his old father's new home. It was not the rude cabin he had expected. The buggy pulled up in front of a beautiful home, built in the style of the southern plantations back in the old country.

"You've done well, Father," he said.

John Jolly smiled. "Come in," he said. "Welcome home, my son."

Jolly fed Houston, then sat with him to talk. "I heard you were the governor of Tennessee," he said.

"I was," said Houston, "but I resigned."

The old chief knew that there was much more to the tale, but he wouldn't press for the details. If the Raven wanted to tell him about it, he would in his own time.

"How are things for you here in the West?" Houston asked, changing the subject.

"The land is much more crowded with people than the government led us to believe," said Jolly, "and they send more out here almost every day. We have problems with the prairie Indians. They think that we've moved into their hunting grounds. They attack our hunters, and we have young men who want to go to war against them. I try to hold them back."

Houston sat back and thought for a moment. Politics and intrigue were his natural element. "Perhaps I can be of some help to you," he said.

John Jolly smiled. "Perhaps you can," he said. "I'm glad to have you back, my son."

Four Indians rode into Dutch's settlement in Texas, where they found Dutch at work in his yard splitting rails. Susanna was working in the house. Wili chased a brown puppy around the yard. A black hound started to bark, sensing the arrival of strangers. Dutch calmed him with a word. He set his ax in a tree stump and watched as the riders approached his house. As they rode in closer, he could see that they sat slumped and round shouldered in their saddles, and they wore long faces.

He invited them to dismount and sit in the yard, while he tended to their tired horses. Susanna came out of the house and brought them bowls of *kanohena* and cups of coffee. Soon Dutch rejoined them. They sat on plank benches at a plank table in the shade of a tall oak tree.

"We were hunting buffalo," said one of the men, a Cherokee. "There were seven of us. Six Cherokees and one Creek."

He gestured toward a man at the far end of the table who had said little and sat with his head down while the others talked. The man, the speaker told Dutch, was one of the recently arrived Creeks, and his home was just south of Fort Gibson.

"We had killed a cow," the speaker went on, "and we were skinning it, when riders suddenly came at us from over a hill. They were Tawakoni, I think. We tried to fight, but there were too many of them. Three of us were killed. We who are left just barely escaped.

"But when we knew that we were safe, we hid and watched the Tawakonis. They took the scalps of our friends, and then they tied ropes to their feet and dragged the bodies after them. We followed from a safe distance to see where they would go and what they would do.

"They dragged the bodies home with them, and then they set up stakes around their fire. They stripped the bodies naked and tied them, standing upright, to the poles. They left them there, scalped and naked, as if they were just standing and watching the scalp dance the Tawakonis did. It was like that still when we left to come here."

"It's good you came to me," said Dutch. "These deaths and this insult will be avenged. I promise you. Can you tell me, where is this town from here?"

They gave him all the details of their travel, where they had been hunting when they were attacked, which direction the attackers had ridden to go to their town, and finally the way the hunters had come from the town to find Dutch's settlement. They told him how long they had traveled.

"I know the town," he said. "It's Tawakoni all right, and it will suffer for what these men have done."

Dutch had fresh meat, and he gave it to them to take home with them. Their trip had turned out tragically enough. He didn't want them to have to return empty handed. But before they left, he sat down and wrote a letter, using the Sequoyan script. Finished, he blotted the ink, folded the letter, and sealed it with wax. Then he handed it to the one who led the group.

"Do you know John Smith?" he asked.

"Yes," said the young man. "He lives not far from me."

"Good," said Dutch. "Deliver this

letter to him for me."

"I will," said the other.

John Smith had just returned home from a council meeting he himself had called. Cherokees and Creeks, their new neighbors, had met at Bayou Menard, seven miles east of Fort Gibson. There they had made a war dance at night and talked the next day. John Smith had talked for war, and the young men had agreed with him. They meant to go to war against the Pawnees to their west who had been bothering their hunters.

The Cherokees treated the Creeks like little brothers at this meeting, for the Creeks were recent arrivals to this land, and the menace of the western Indians was new to them. The Western Cherokees had been involved in warfare over the hunting grounds for nearly twenty years.

"The United States told us," the Creeks said, "that if we would move out west, the white men wouldn't bother us anymore, and the hunting would be good. There's plenty of room and plenty of game for all, they told us. But now when we go out to hunt, these prairie Indians attack us. They kill our hunters."

There was discussion at the council about the way in which Colonel Arbuckle kept telling them not to fight because the United States army would punish the offenders of the peace. But when the prairie Indians attacked the Cherokee or Creek hunters, the army did nothing.

The young men at the council, both Cherokee and Creek, had just about all agreed to go with John Smith to attack the Pawnees, when Sam Houston, his hair grown out and braided into a long queue that hung down his back, stepped forward and asked to speak. He was dressed in yellow buckskin leggings and moccasins finely decorated with beads, and he wore a brilliantly embroidered white hunting jacket and a colorful and feathered turban. He had come, he told them, speaking in Cherokee, to bring the words of his father and their chief, John Jolly, because the old chief was sick and not able to attend the meeting in person. Their chief, the Raven told them, did not want them to go to war against the Pawnees or anybody else. Houston's speech was animated but decorous, in keeping with traditional Cherokee style, and it was effective. He talked them out of attacking the Pawnees.

Smith had gone home sulking, and he was still in a funk when a man came to his house bringing a letter.

"From Captain Dutch?" he said.

"Yes," said the carrier. "Some of us just came back from his house."

"In Texas?"

"Yes."

The letter carrier, who had been one of the hunting party, then told Smith the story of the encounter with the Tawakonis and how the Tawakonis had treated the bodies of the three slain Cherokee hunters.

Smith flew into a rage upon hearing that news. He stalked back and forth across the floor of his cabin. Shaking his fist, he railed against the Tawakonis, the Pawnees, the Comanches, the Osages, the United States army, and finally against Sam Houston and John Jolly for having so recently prevented his own planned war party from taking final shape and action.

At last, with nothing more to say, he grew quiet, if not calm, and he sat down to read the letter. Finished, he looked up and stared ahead, a faraway look in his eye. Pawnees in the north or Tawakonis in the south, it made little difference to John Smith. He was in a mood to fight the enemies of his people.

"He wants me to come down to him in Texas," he said, "and bring some men."

"I'll go with you," said the other. "Just tell me where and when we'll meet."

23

1830

Dutch stepped outside with empty hands to meet the heavily armed party of men who had ridden up close to the house. He was not alarmed at their approach. He knew who they were. He had been expecting them for some days and had even pitched a large canvas tent beside his house to accommodate them upon their arrival.

" '*Siyo*, Tahchee," called out the leader of the horsemen. "We've ridden a long way to be with you."

" '*Siyo*," said Dutch. "I've been waiting for you." He looked at the many guns, knives, and steel trade tomahawks in the band. "Are you thinking of something?" he asked with a wry smile on his face.

"We received your letter," said John Smith. "We're going to the grand prairies to take our revenge on those people who killed and humiliated our warriors."

"And I'll help," said Dutch. "You're

290

welcome to my home. Right now, get down and rest your horses and yourselves. We'll eat, and you can stay here for the night."

The following morning, Dutch, with nineteen men from his settlement, led Smith and the others fifteen miles west to the settlement of Boiling Mush, the grizzled old warrior recently elected chief of the Cherokees who lived along the Red River. There they danced the night away, singing and whooping, to the accompaniment of turtle-shell rattles. No one slept that night.

The next day was spent talking about the reasons for the gathering, the sad fate of the hunters at the hands of the Tawakoni, the insulting way in which the Tawakonis had treated the bodies, John Smith and the men who had ridden all the way down from the Arkansas River to help set things right, and the absolute necessity of taking massive revenge on the guilty Tawakonis. Almost everyone made a speech. That night they danced again, and the next morning, the war expedition was formally agreed on by everyone present, and approved by Boiling Mush. Dutch and his guests returned to his home.

Susanna and the other women busied

themselves preparing food for the men to take with them on the trail. They parched corn and pounded it into meal, which they then divided into equal shares, one for each warrior. Each share was put into a small bag of soft tanned deer hide, and the bags were distributed to the men.

Dutch shaved his head, leaving only a small tuft for a scalp lock, something with which to taunt the enemy. Take me if you can, it seemed to say. He made a headdress of short hawk feathers and painted half of each feather red, leaving the tips white, and he fastened the feathers to his scalp lock. Then he painted his head red.

Four nights running they danced. Dutch led the dance, going around the fire from east to north to west to south and back again to the eastern point from which he had begun. He moved in a slow stately manner, and right behind him came Boiling Mush, singing a war song. The wife of Boiling Mush followed, wearing turtle-shell rattles strapped to the calves of her legs and pounding out the rhythm of the dance. The other men who meant to fight followed her.

At a certain point in the dance, Dutch turned sharply and fell in behind the woman, leaving Boiling Mush at the head of the file. The song was a call to war, calling on all the young men to join in.

When the song came at last to an end, the men lined up abreast facing east. Each man held in his right hand a ceremonial red and black war club. One man sat with a drum just out of the dance area on the south side. The drummer started beating a steady rhythm, and then Boiling Mush began to sing. The men crouched and took a long step forward and then took another back again. After some time, Boiling Mush stopped singing.

"He! Ha! Li!" he cried.

And the dancing men answered him with a long and shrill war cry.

"Yeeee! Yeee!"

Then Boiling Mush started to sing the same song again, but at a faster pace, and this time when the men stepped forward, they swung their war clubs as if they were bashing in an enemy's skull. The song continued for some time, but eventually it changed again.

Now the men began to dance individually, milling around in any direction, breaking up the line in which they had been standing and dancing, striking unseen enemies at whim. When Boiling Mush stopped singing, the dancers also stopped, and they sounded out together four long, shrill war whoops.

They went through these same dances all four nights, all night long. On the morning following the fourth night of dancing, the warriors took up their weapons and their bags of corn meal and they headed west, Captain Dutch and John Smith in the lead. Men with horses rode. Others went on foot. Altogether, sixty-three warriors went out that day.

Susanna, standing in a group of women and children and older men, watched them go. Conflicting emotions battled in her breast. Like the others, she had felt outrage at the actions of the Tawakonis, and she thirsted for revenge. She was proud of her husband, the brave and famous Captain Dutch, and she longed to see him return victorious, for she basked in the glory of his honors. And yet she was afraid, for he was going into deadly combat, and what, she wondered in dread, would she do without him?

On a hillside overlooking the still sleeping Tawakoni village, Dutch and the other Cherokee warriors stripped to their breechcloths and moccasins. They applied fresh paint to their shaved heads and their grim faces. They had traveled ten days to reach this spot. Now it was time.

The village below contained perhaps fifty large grass houses, each house with a large arbor beside it. In the center of the village was a corral, crowded with fine horses. The whole was surrounded by cultivated fields on three sides and the Red River running quietly by on the north. A field of tall corn was on the south.

Dutch, with John Smith standing beside him, nodded toward the cornfield. "There will be our approach," he said, and John Smith nodded in agreement.

At a signal from Dutch, the warriors made their way quietly down the hillside and into the field of tall corn. Afoot or on horseback, they moved slowly and silently down the long, narrow rows between the tall, green stalks. They were just coming out of the corn on the other side of the field, very close to the houses, when they were seen.

A bare-breasted and tattooed Tawakoni woman, lighting her morning fire in front of her lodge, screamed the shrill alarm, and the Cherokees answered immediately with their hideous war cry, sounding like a huge flock of giant, angry wild turkeys.

As frantic Tawakoni men came running

out of their houses, Cherokee riflemen picked them off from the cornfield. Rifles emptied, the men laid them aside and took up other weapons, rushing wildly into the town. Dutch put his empty rifle down and ran, a pistol in each hand. Closer in, he fired the pistols, each ball finding a mark. He dropped the empty pistols then and pulled his war ax out.

John Smith swung his ax and split the skull of a Tawakoni man, then grabbed up a firebrand from a small fire and touched it to the grass house nearest him. The dry grass ignited quickly and easily, and the flames climbed fast. With the torch in his left hand and his ax in his right, Smith rushed from house to house, pausing only to swing his ax if someone tried to interfere.

Children cried in terror. Women screamed and ran with their children toward the river. Dogs barked. Confused and frightened horses neighed and stamped their hooves. The Tawakoni men armed themselves quickly as best they could. They fought back valiantly, but the early-morning surprise had worked too well.

Those who did not escape were killed. The entire village was consumed by flames. By midmorning it was all over. The air was thick with black smoke and heavy with the stench of death and burning grass and wood and flesh. And the triumphant Cherokees, driving several hundred newly acquired horses, waving fresh scalps and covered with blood, were headed home.

After ten more days of traveling, the tired and hungry Cherokee warriors were close to Dutch's settlement. Dutch sent a young man on a fast horse ahead to tell the people in the settlement that they were coming. He then had some others cut down a tall pine sapling. They trimmed the branches except for a tuft of green on the end, and stripped it of its bark.

They painted the pole red. Then they combed and painted red the Tawakoni scalps they had taken and tied them to the pole. At last they once more painted themselves — also red. They were ready to make their entrance to the settlement.

Singing a victory song and carrying the pole, they marched in among the people who were waiting, ready to receive them, and at the end of the song they gave out a number of whoops equal to the number of scalps that dangled from the pole.

Food was laid out ready to eat, and the returning warriors were hungry, having had nothing for the last twenty days but parched corn meal. Still, they did not rush upon the food. Each returning warrior first went to each individual waiting there to shake hands and to tell some tale about the battle. Men with switches kept the dogs away from the food while this was going on. At last they were allowed to eat, and each man ate until he could hold no more. The three hapless Cherokee hunters had been satisfactorily avenged.

24

1831

Having Sam Houston around proved to be a great benefit to the army in its efforts to promote peace among the various tribes. Houston was accepted as an Indian, having been adopted in his youth by Chief Jolly, and since his arrival in the West, the Western Cherokee council had formalized his citizenship in their nation.

In addition it was widely known, or at least assumed, even by the Osages, that Houston was a man of considerable experience and some influence with the government of the United States. He set himself up in business with a store not far from Fort Gibson, which he was calling Wigwam Neosho, and he married Diana, the daughter of Captain John Rogers, a white Cherokee citizen, and Jennie Due, a mixed-blood.

Houston had been used in an official capacity more than once by the Western Cherokee Nation, but he had also become chummy with the trader and friend to the Osages, Chouteau, and through him had written petitions to the government for the Osages. He seemed to get along with everyone, as long as they caught up with him while he was sober, for he was drinking heavily, still chafing from the scandal he had left behind in Tennessee.

It didn't take Colonel Arbuckle long, therefore, to seize the opportunity to make use of Houston as a peacemaker. And the time was right, the colonel thought, for the Osages were in a weakened condition. They had suffered great losses from a recent epidemic of cholera in their towns and were in a poor position to have to defend themselves from any invading forces. With the help of Houston and the cholera, a treaty was concluded between the Osages and the Creeks. From there, it was an easy step, a few days later, to get the Western Cherokees back to the table with the Osages. Chief Jolly, after all, had been seeking peace since his arrival in the West.

During the negotiations, the Cherokees claimed that the Osages owed them for thirteen horses. The Osages acknowledged the claim and agreed to pay. The Cherokees maintained that they were not responsible for the actions of any Cherokees living south of the Red River. The Osages agreed. The Cherokees also said that if the Cherokees living south of the Red River should decide to move back into the jurisdiction of the Western Cherokee Nation within twelve months of the date of the signing of the treaty and agree to abide by the terms of the treaty, both the Osage Nation and the United States government should forgive them for their past deeds. Amazingly, the Osages agreed. But if the Red River Cherokees should fail to make the move in the allotted time and refuse to agree to the terms of the treaty, the Osages were free to continue warfare against them. The Cherokees agreed to that. The treaty was signed.

They were still on the grounds at Fort Gibson when Chief John Jolly, recovered from his fever but still weak, approached John Smith from behind and touched him on the shoulder.

"I'd like to talk to you," the chief said.

"Of course," said Smith.

They walked together to where two unoccupied chairs sat on the walk just outside one of the buildings in the shade of the overhanging roof. They sat down side by side, their backs to the wall, looking out over the parade ground.

"I want to talk with you as chief," said Jolly, "on a matter of importance to all of our people."

Smith was guardedly curious. He wondered what the chief could want of him. He had never been involved in governmental affairs, no more than to cast his vote at election time, and sometimes he had not even come around for that.

"All right," he said.

"This treaty that we signed today," said Jolly, "is important to us all. We've had other treaties with the Osages, but we need to make this one work. We need to keep this peace. We've fought the Osages for too long already. Too many have been killed on both sides."

He paused a moment, hoping for agreement, but he got no reaction from Smith that he could read. He went on.

"Dutch and the others in Texas are a problem for us," he said. "As long as he remains down there, this peace will be uneasy."

"What about Bowles and the ones with him?" asked Smith.

"They're way south of here," said Jolly, "and they're not making any trouble for us now. Dutch is our only problem."

"But the treaty said that we're not responsible for his actions," said Smith.

"Yes, and that's easily said," Jolly answered. "But if Dutch should make another raid on the Osages, the Osages might simply say that Cherokees did it. They might not make any distinction between those in Texas and the rest of us."

Smith nodded his head slowly and murmured as if he understood.

"And if Dutch and the others are fighting Osages or anyone else, some of our people here are liable to go to help him," Jolly said. "That's happened before."

He knew, of course, that Smith had done exactly that on more than one occasion. Again he waited for response, but Smith sat silent.

"I need to have someone," Jolly continued, "who knows Dutch well to go to see him and talk him into moving back up here."

"He won't come back," said Smith. "The army made him an outlaw."

"No longer," said Jolly. "The treaty says that if he and the others come back within a year, all will be forgiven. The Osages signed the treaty and so did the United States. Now is the time for him to come back to us. Will you go and tell him?"

A long line of wagons was coming in

their direction. Horseback riders rode alongside the wagons, and a number of riderless horses and mules followed behind. Susanna stepped up beside Dutch in front of their cabin to watch the approach.

"Who could it be?" she asked.

"I don't know," said Dutch.

Soon one of the lead riders spurred his mount and moved out ahead. He came closer, and Dutch recognized him.

"It's John Smith," he said.

He wondered for a moment if Smith had come to Texas with all those other people and wagons to establish a new settlement, but then he noticed that the wagons did not appear to be loaded. Smith rode on up into the yard.

" '*Siyo*, Tahchee," he said.

" '*Siyo*," said Dutch. "Get down and tell us what's going on here."

Smith swung down out of his saddle. "We've come to move you home," he said.

Dutch and Susanna lay awake in bed that night. The visitors, forty men, were in canvas tents outside. Everyone had been fed, and Dutch and Smith had talked long into the evening.

"Will we go?" Susanna asked.

"I don't know," he said. "I haven't let

anyone tell me what to do in a long time now. Anyone but you."

"I don't tell you what to do," Susanna said.

Dutch smiled and held her close. "Maybe not," he said, "but when I know what it is you want, I do it, don't I?"

"Well —"

"So what do you think?"

"You want to know what I think?"

"Yes."

"About the move?"

"Yes."

"Well, they said the fighting with the Osages is over," she said.

"Except for me."

"Yes. And if we move back, then it will be over for all of us."

"I remember an old man," said Dutch. "He was a great war chief. He said that it's no good to make a treaty with the Osages, for they're a nation of liars."

"Times have changed," said Susanna. "And Chief Jolly sent John Smith and the others to bring you back."

"Am I so important?" Dutch asked.

"They must think that you are," she said. "*I* think you are."

"If we agree," Dutch said, "we'll have to start all over. We'll have to build a new house, clear fields."

"We've done it before, and John Smith said that he and all those others who came with him will help us. He said they'll build us a fine home, the kind that John Jolly has now. Like the house of a rich white man."

They laughed softly together at the thought of such a home.

"There's fighting all the time down here," she said, "with other Indians."

"Umm," said Dutch.

"Many of my relatives and my old friends are back there."

"You want to go," he said, "don't you?"

"I didn't say that."

"I think we'll go."

For several days they loaded wagons. It wasn't Dutch and his family alone that had to move. It was Dutch's settlement, all the families that had followed him to Texas, and they had furnishings in their homes as good as any to be found on the frontier. Much of it was homemade, but some had been purchased in New Orleans with money made from the sale of stolen horses.

Dutch and Susanna owned a large feather mattress, and a few other families had them as well. Pots and pans and dishes had been purchased and had to be carefully packed. Susanna and some of the other women had spinning wheels and looms.

But packing was not the biggest chore of the move, for the Cherokees also had herds of cattle and horses and hogs. The hogs were a special problem, for they were not kept in pens but allowed to run loose. If a hog's owner wanted to slaughter one of the beasts, he went out hunting, almost as if he were hunting a wild animal.

Some of the hogs were slaughtered and butchered, as were some beeves, for food for the long and slow trip north to the Canadian River. Everyone was busy.

When at last they were ready to go, John Smith took the point. Dutch rode horseback alongside the wagon with Susanna and Wili and their household goods. Outriders rode on both flanks. On the first day they reached the Red River and made a slow and tedious crossing. Then they camped for the night in the shadow of Fort Towson.

On the second day they traveled west on the old Pawnee Trail to the Kiamichi River. The rest of the day was taken up again in a crossing. They continued west for several days before coming to the bank of the Blue River just east of the juncture with the Texas Road. It was the long way around, but with the wagons, they had to keep to established roads as much as possible.

Headed northeast at last, the wagon train had first to recross the Blue River. From there they would be on dry land until they reached the Canadian near the new Western Cherokee settlements. With slow-moving wagons, cattle, horses, and hogs to drive, children to watch over, and well over a hundred people to feed, travel was slow. The supply of prepared food they had brought with them was soon gone, and along the way the men hunted and slaughtered more beeves and hogs.

Ninety-five days after John Smith had ridden into Dutch's yard south of the Red River, the wagon train of Cherokee families reached the south bank of the Canadian River. Dutch rode up beside John Smith.

"So," he said, "is this our land?"

"On the other side of the river it is," said Smith.

"Then we'll camp here tonight," said Dutch, "and cross in the morning."

After the next morning's crossing, people went out in all directions in search of homesites. In the rolling hills on the north side of the Canadian River, Dutch found a lush green spot beside a running stream, a natural clearing in a wooded valley.

"I like it here," he said.

"So do I," said Susanna.

Dutch lifted Wili down from the wagon seat to let him run and play. Then he looked around.

"Right over there," he said, indicating a spot near the creek. "That's where we'll build."

John Smith nodded his approval. "We'll build you a cabin," said Smith, "so you'll have shelter while we wait for the materials to build your house. You can stay with me until the cabin's up, if you like."

"*Wado,*" said Dutch, "but we'll stay here. I'll pitch my canvas tent. What do they call that creek there?"

John Smith gave a shrug. "I don't know," he said. "Since this is your new home, why don't we call it Dutch's Creek?"

PART 3

Death March: The Dodge Expedition

25

Fort Gibson, Indian Territory
Spring 1834

Catlin was anxious to get started. At first it had been interesting enough to be at Fort Gibson, established just ten years before. The soldiers of the recently formed First Regiment of United States Dragoons had a dashing appearance in their dress uniforms of dark blue jackets, light gray-blue trousers, and tall cockaded hats.

When the regiment mounted to parade, the men wearing their sabers on their left sides, each company rode horses all of one color: Company A was all on black, Company B on white, Company C on gray, and so on. It was a splendid sight for the romantic eye of an artist.

The horseback exercises had been exciting to watch, too, with the soldiers dressed in their battle fatigues, feigning saber attacks and other battle maneuvers, whooping and shouting in front of crowds of fascinated civilians, Indians as well as whites.

The popular and internationally acclaimed writer Washington Irving, returning to the United States after seventeen years in Europe, had spent some time at Fort Gibson just two years earlier during his own western tour. He was said to be writing a book on the subject of those adventures. The French-Osage scout, Pierre Beatte, who had scouted for the Irving expedition, was around Fort Gibson, and there was talk that he might be going along on this one, too.

In 1834, George Catlin was thirty-eight and no longer an impressionable youth, nor was he an eastern dandy out for his first taste of the wild west, although his tastefully decorated brand-new buckskins did seem rather fresh and pretty for the frontier, and his ear-flapped traveling cap was unique in his surroundings.

Born in 1796, in the Wyoming Valley of Pennsylvania, he had grown up in New York's Susquehanna Valley, canoeing, hunting, and fishing. At twenty-one he had studied law in Litchfield, Connecticut, and two years later he had been practicing in Lucerne, Pennsylvania. But he had discovered another interest.

In 1823, he sold his lawbooks and moved to Philadelphia, where he established himself as a portrait artist and was elected to the Philadelphia Academy of Art. He saw some Indians en route to Washington for treaty talks, and he managed to paint some of their portraits. That experience proved to be a turning point for him. He discovered what would become his major interest for the rest of his life. He also launched himself on a new career, his third. He told himself, Nothing short of the loss of my life shall prevent me from visiting their country and becoming their historian.

Always impulsive, Catlin abandoned his family in 1831 to head west. In St. Louis he met with Governor William Clark of Lewis and Clark fame, but by then superintendent of Indian affairs for the Western Tribes.

Clark took Catlin up the Mississippi River to Wisconsin Territory to observe a council of Sioux, Iowa, Missouri, Sauk, and Fox Indians. Catlin sketched in a frenzy and later went back to St. Louis to paint from his sketches. The following year he went up the Missouri River on the steamboat *Yellow Stone* to Fort Pierre, then traveled west from there. He painted

Sioux, Mandan, Assiniboine, Blackfeet, Cree, and Crow people.

So Catlin was not new to the west. Still, this was a new adventure, and he had not before met any Comanches. He had been glad to obtain permission to accompany this expedition of dragoons from Fort Gibson to the Comanche country. But he had by this time seen enough of the fort to satisfy him, and he was more than ready to be on the way west.

The soldiers had with them at the fort a Wichita girl about eighteen years old, and two Kiowas, a girl fourteen and her younger brother. These children had been captured by the Osages, and General Leavenworth, commander at Fort Gibson, thought that the return of the children to their families would be a good show of friendship to the Western Tribes. It would also provide an opportunity to enquire about the whereabouts of two missing whites, a Ranger Abbay and a boy named Martin, rumored to have vanished in the land of the Wichitas.

Unhappily, the Kiowa boy had been killed when a ram battered him into a fence post. Catlin had witnessed the horrible incident just after he finished sketching the boy and his sister. The child's death had saddened and depressed Catlin. The fort was beginning to pall, and the adventurous artist wanted desperately to be riding to meet the Comanches.

He was lounging in the shade with his sketch pad in idle hands, when he noticed a man he had not seen before. A striking figure, the man rode into the army post on the back of a black horse with three big, slack-jawed, black and tan dogs running alongside. No one challenged him as he rode through the gate, nor when he dismounted in front of the general's office and strode right in, leaving the horse and dogs without a glance back over his shoulder. He moved with confidence and authority, even, Catlin thought, with a little arrogance.

He was a tall man, Catlin noted, dressed almost entirely in buckskins. He wore moccasins on his feet, and his fringed leggings, or breeches, Catlin couldn't be sure because of the nearly knee-length jacket, were wrapped in colorful strips of cloth. The buckskin jacket, also fringed, almost covered the white shirt he wore underneath. The buckskins were further decorated with porcupine quills dyed red. A bright red woven sash was tied around his waist, and on his head was a turban of red, white, and blue patterned cloth, further decorated with feathers of various hues. Several long, loose strands of beads were slung around his neck, and draped over his shoulder to hang at his right side were a bandolier bag and a powder horn. He carried a long rifle casually in the crook of his left arm.

The man had the look, to the artist, of a frontier half-breed. His skin was olive, not too dark, and his features were sharp but smooth. His short-cropped hair, what could be seen of it under the turban, was brown and wavy. He wore a mustache, but it was thin and sparse. On his neck, on either side of his Adam's apple just under the jawbone, thin, sparse whiskers grew, Catlin figured, more from neglect than by design. All in all, the artist thought, a bold and dashing frontier type, and a rather handsome man at that.

The man had gone inside the office, and Catlin looked aside. He saw Jeff Davis, smart in his fresh uniform, walking toward him. Tall and thin with angular features, the young lieutenant had become his friend. Catlin stood up to greet the officer.

"Good morning, Jeff," he said.

"Good morning, George," said Davis, in his aristocratic southern drawl. He gestured toward the sketch pad. "Can't find any suitable subjects this morning?"

"As a matter of fact," said Catlin, "I just saw one. He rode in on that black horse over there."

"Oh," said Davis. "That's Captain Dutch."

"Captain Dutch?" said Catlin. "What is he? Tell me about him."

"Well, sir," said Davis, "he's just been hired by our general as a captain of scouts. He's supposed to raise up a company of scouts to lead us on our way into the Comanche country, keep us fed and bring us home safely again. They say that he's been all over that country for years and knows it as well as anyone except maybe a Comanche."

"He certainly looks up to the job," said Catlin.

"Oh, I'd say so," said Davis. "As long as he doesn't revert to his old ways."

Catlin cocked his head and looked Davis in the eyes.

"You're not going to leave it at that, are you?" he asked. "Are you going to tell me more?"

"Well, George," said Davis, leaning back against the stockade fence and staring ahead at the black horse across the way, "I don't know exactly where to start or what to tell you. Dutch is a legend around here. When a man gets to be legend, you know, half of what you hear about him is tall tales. At least half."

"Well, give it a try, will you?"

"All right," said Davis, with a sigh. "Well, he's a Cherokee."

Catlin nodded in agreement. "The turban, at least, is characteristic," he said. "I've seen them on the eastern Cherokees."

"Yes," said Davis.

"But the rest of his outfit looks more like that of a white frontiersman to me."

"These Western Cherokees are a strange mixture of types," said Davis. "There are some full-blood Indians among them, and there are even some pure whites. Tories, I expect, who stayed with the Cherokees after the revolution for their own safety. And there are a substantial number of mixed-bloods. They also have among them some people from other Indian tribes, mostly Delawares and Shawnees, I understand."

"So what is the legend of Captain Dutch?"

"He's a fearsome killer of Osages," said Davis. "They say that even Dutch himself doesn't know how many Osage scalps he's taken over the years. They say that you could empty out an entire village of Osages simply by shouting, 'Dutch! Dutch!'

"The army got the Cherokees and Osages to stop their war a few years back, but Dutch wouldn't stop killing Osages, so the army put a price on his head. To show what he thought about the situation, Dutch rode up here while a party of Osages was camped just outside the post, killed and scalped an Osage man, waved the scalp at the soldiers in defiance, and rode away."

"Do you mean to say that he was an outlaw?" asked Catlin.

"And not just to the United States," said Davis. "The Western Cherokee Nation, by act of council, ejected him from the tribe. It seems they didn't want to be held responsible for his actions."

"I don't understand," said Catlin. "If the man was outlawed and had a price on his head, then what is he doing here now? He rode in here like he owned the place and walked into the general's office like it was his own home."

Davis shrugged.

"Times change," he said. "There's peace again between the Osages and the Cherokees. The government's trying to get the rest of the Cherokees to move out here from the east, so we need to make room for them, them and the other eastern tribes. So we're sending expeditions out west to meet the tribes out there. We're supposed to try to obtain treaties with them to get them to move a little farther west and make more room here. That's the whole purpose of this little expedition we're about to embark on to the Comanches.

"Dutch and his followers know the Comanches and the other western tribes. They know the country. They speak the languages. The army needs them."

"And the reward?" Catlin asked.

"Oh, it's been rescinded," said Davis. "Captain Dutch is no longer an outlaw. Our government requires his services, so they've wiped his slate clean."

"What about his own government?" asked Catlin. "Have they taken him back into the fold?"

"Yes. He's back in good standing all the way around."

Catlin stared at the black horse and the three big dogs waiting patiently outside the general's office. He wondered how long the man Dutch would be inside.

"I'd like to meet this man," he said.

"Don't worry, George," said Davis. "I expect you'll have plenty of time to get acquainted on this trip."

26

Five hundred soldiers rode out of the fort on the fifteenth of June, headed west for the planned meeting with Comanches, Kiowas, and Wichitas. None of them, of course, knew just where they were going, not even the officers, among whom were Colonel Henry Dodge, Lieutenant Colonel Stephen Kearny, Captain Edwin Sumner, Captain Nathan Boone, son of the famous Dan'l, Lieutenant Jefferson Davis, and, of course, their general, Henry Leavenworth.

None of them knew just where they were going, and, therefore, leading the way were over thirty Indian scouts, headed by the forty-four-year-old Cherokee, Captain Dutch. Among others, Dutch had enlisted the young grandson of old John Chisholm, Jesse, a mixed-blood Cherokee said to have command of fourteen languages, and Pierre Beatte, a French-Osage and a veteran of the Washington Irving expedition. Sergeant McCloskey was assigned to watch over the Wichita and Kiowa girls.

Catlin watched the scouts, especially

Dutch, anxious for a chance to interview the legendary Cherokee frontiersman and former outlaw. The days of travel, though, were long, and Dutch seemed always to be busy or away from camp. There seemed, in fact, to be two camps each night, the Indian scouts building their own fires well away from those of the soldiers, and Catlin seemed to have been relegated to the care of the soldiers, primarily Jeff Davis.

In less than a week, they stopped at Camp Rendezvous, a temporary military base consisting of tents and a few hastily constructed log houses. They rested horses and men and restocked their supplies. The regimental surgeon ordered the return to Fort Gibson of twenty-three men who had become too ill to continue.

At last, Catlin found his opportunity to have a conversation with Captain Dutch. Dutch was standing in a small group of scouts talking in low tones in a language other than English. Then the group broke up, and Dutch turned and started walking directly toward Catlin. His intention almost certainly was to pass by the artist and go to one of the tents that stood behind him. But Catlin boldly stopped him.

"Captain Dutch," he said. "If I'm not interrupting anything pressing, I'd like to speak to you for a few moments."

Dutch gave the artist a quick look and, raising one eyebrow, said, "Let's sit in the shade and have a smoke." He led the way to the shaded side of one of the log structures and sat down in the dirt, leaning back against the wall. Catlin did likewise, and Dutch reached into the bandolier bag at his side for pipe and tobacco.

No fire was near, so Dutch, having filled his pipe bowl, laid his long rifle across his legs. He took a piece of char cloth out of his bag and fixed it under the frizzen, then pulled the trigger. The spark ignited one end of the char cloth. Then Dutch took the smoldering cloth and laid it down in the bowl of the pipe over the tobacco. He sucked on the stem and soon great puffs of smoke billowed around his head. With the tobacco well lit, he leaned his rifle against the wall by his left side, drew up his knees, and handed the pipe to Catlin.

"What's on your mind, Mr. Catlin?" he asked.

Catlin puffed on the pipe a few times, then handed it back to Dutch.

"Well, I've met some Cherokees in the east," he said, "but I confess to a great ignorance and curiosity about your Western Cherokee Nation."

"I see," said Dutch.

"Have you lived all your life out here?"

"My only memory of the old country is from the first five years of my life," said the scout. "I've been out here for thirty-nine years or so, I guess. I was brought west at age five by my mother and her brother, my Uncle Tom."

"Why?" asked Catlin. "Most of the country is under the impression that most Cherokees are very much attached to their homeland. Chief Ross and other Cherokees back east are working very hard, it seems to me, to avoid removal at all costs."

"You have your Whigs and Democrats," said Dutch, "and you have Baptists, Moravians, Presbyterians, and all manner of stripes of Christian, too. Do you expect all Cherokees then to have just one mind?"

Catlin flushed a little. "No," he said. "Of course not, but —"

"My mother and uncle," Dutch said, interrupting, "were convinced that life would be better for us out here. You know, there were some out here before us, and now and then one or two of them would go back east and tell about what it was like here. There would not be the constant pressure to move, and, as you know, that has only gotten worse in the old country. There would not be so many whites around us. Of course, they're flocking out here now, too, but still they're not as bad as they are back east. And the hunting, they believed, would be better. It was, and it still is."

"But there were other problems, weren't there?" Catlin asked. "The Osages —"

"When we first came out here," interrupted Dutch, "this land was claimed by the French, and the French welcomed us, partly, I believe, because they figured that we'd help them tame the wild Osages."

"Was that how the troubles between the Cherokees and Osages began?"

"No," said Dutch. "I wouldn't say so."

"Then how?"

Dutch handed the pipe back to Catlin after taking a last puff for himself.

"I have no doubt," he said, "that you'd get a very different tack on the tale from an Osage. But here goes. When we first settled on the Arkansas River, with the blessings of the French governor of Orleans, there were no other Indian towns anywhere near us, and we weren't looking for trouble with anyone. We built houses and planted crops. It wasn't long, though, before a band of wandering Osages killed two Cherokee men who were out hunting, and that's what set it off."

He took his pipe back from Catlin and sucked on the stem. The tobacco was burned out. He bent his leg and tapped the dottle out of the pipe, then put the pipe away in his bag. Taking hold of his long rifle, he stood up.

"I have to be off, Mr. Catlin," he said.

Catlin stood up and dusted off the seat of his britches.

"Certainly," he said. "Thank you for your time. I'd like to visit with you some more, at your convenience, of course."

"We'll do it," said Dutch, offering his hand. Catlin took it in his own and held it for a moment.

"Yes," he said. "Thank you."

On the twenty-first of June, the regiment, led by Dutch and Jesse Chisholm, and short twenty-three dragoons, rode out of Camp Rendezvous and headed for the Washita River. Only a few hours away from the camp, one of the supply wagons lost its left rear wheel, and several hours were taken up in making the repairs. They moved on, but the going was rough. Each time they crossed a stream, several men had to dismount and heave on each wagon to help get it up the bank and on dry land again. More wagons broke down and more time was taken up with repairs.

The days were hot and still. The bodies and the clothing of the men were caked with sweat-soaked prairie dust and the vicious prairie flies were thick and bothersome.

Then, on the east bank of Little River, at its confluence with the Canadian, they met up with Lieutenant Theophilus Holmes and a company of the Seventh Infantry. Holmes's company was busy constructing a log fort on the site to house two companies of soldiers. It was being called Camp Canadian, for the Canadian River nearby. After a short rest, the expedition pulled out of Camp Canadian on June twenty-fifth, this time leaving behind twenty-seven sick men. They crossed the Canadian River and headed southwest.

They had been riding for about ten hours after crossing the river, when Dutch saw the Osages. Lined up on the horizon ahead, they were sitting on their horses, watching the approach of the expedition. Dutch reined in his mount and held up a hand to call a halt. Then he looked back over his shoulder and waved for Jesse Chisholm to come up beside him.

"Osage," said Chisholm.

"Yeah," said Dutch. "Five hundred, would you say?"

"I'd say six. You think it's trouble?"

"No," said Dutch. "I don't think so, but you can never tell with the damned Osage. It looks to me like a big buffalo hunting party. I've gone out with them like that. That's what I think it is. Get Pierre up here, and you ride on back there and tell the general what we've run into."

Chisholm rode back toward the main column, slowing down as he passed by Pierre Beatte to give him the message. Beatte hurried to Dutch's side. His bearded face was framed by long hair that fell over his shoulders. He wore a wide-brimmed hat decorated with the feathers of a red-tailed hawk. His buckskin suit was worn and had a greasy look.

"What do you think, Pierre?" Dutch asked.

"Osage hunting buffalo," said Beatte.

"Will they cause us any trouble?"

"No," said Beatte. "Why should they? The Osages are at peace, both with the United States and with you Cherokees. *Non?* No trouble."

"Ride on out there and talk to them, Pierre, will you?"

"Sure, *Capitaine*," said Beatte, "but what do you want me to say?"

"Tell them who we are and ask who they

are to begin with," said Dutch. "Then see if their leader, whoever he might be, will ride out and meet with us."

"Halfway between, huh?"

"Sure," said Dutch. "Halfway."

Beatte rode toward the Osages. He was about halfway across when Chisholm returned to Dutch's side. General Leavenworth, sitting straight in his saddle, was riding with him. A little white hair showed under his plumed, tricorner chapeau, and he wore a wide yellow sash across his chest. At his waist, which was no longer slim, the sash was tucked into a wide, red and yellow striped belt from which his saber dangled on his left side. Even out on the hot prairie, his white mustache was ever neatly waxed.

"Dutch," said the general, "what do we have here?"

Dutch gestured toward the Osages up ahead. "Osage buffalo hunters," he said. "That's what we think. I sent Pierre over there to talk to them. He's Osage himself. Half anyway."

Just about then, Pierre Beatte started riding back toward Dutch's position with one of the Osages riding along beside him. Then the Osage stopped suddenly, seemed to study the group ahead of him, said something back over his shoulder, and two more Osages rode out to accompany him. Then the three Osages and Beatte rode together toward where Dutch and the others waited.

"General?" said Dutch.

"Let's go," said Leavenworth, and he, Dutch, and Chisholm rode toward the other group. Just about midway, and within a few feet of the others, they stopped. Dutch looked at the Osage leader and thought how times had changed, how his own life had changed. A few short years ago, he would have killed this man without a thought. Briefly, he recalled Wind in the Meadow, and he wondered if the changes were, after all, for the good.

The Osage gave Dutch a haughty look. He was wearing buckskin leggings with a breechcloth and moccasins. He wore no shirt. Several strings of glass beads hung from his neck, around which he had tied a bright red scarf. His slit ears were tied with pieces of yarn, also strung with beads. His head was shaved except for a topknot or scalp lock that had been done up into two long braids. One was hanging down his back, the other had fallen over his shoulder and dangled in front of his chest. On top of his shaven head he wore a red roach of porcupine quills. He carried a bow, and slung across his back was a large quiver of arrows.

"This is Chief Black Dog of the Osage," said Beatte. Then he spoke to Black Dog in Osage, introducing the others. When Black Dog heard the name of Dutch, he stiffened, and his eyes narrowed.

"I know of Dutch," he said.

"Then you should also know that I speak your language," said Dutch, speaking in Osage.

Black Dog looked directly at Dutch. He waited, as if searching for just the right words to use. "Yes," he said, "and I know that you are a great killer of my people."

"Yes," said Dutch. "I have been. But today we're at peace, the Osages and the Cherokees, and I'm now working for the United States army."

"What is the army doing out here so far?" Black Dog asked. "These are my hunting grounds."

Leavenworth looked at Jesse Chisholm. "What's going on?" the general asked in a near whisper, and Chisholm began to translate the conversation for him.

"We're going farther west, way out to meet the Comanches," Dutch said, still speaking Osage.

"Why do you want to meet the Comanches?" Black Dog asked. "The Comanches are my enemies. I killed a Comanche just the other day."

"Well," said Dutch, "the Cherokees used to be your enemies, and look at us now, talking here like old friends. The army wants to make friends with all people and wants us all to be at peace with each other. We're just going out there to talk."

"Will you talk to the Comanches about my people?"

Dutch looked toward Leavenworth just as Chisholm translated Black Dog's last question.

"Tell him," said Leavenworth, "that peace between the Comanches and the Osages will be among the things we discuss with the Comanches."

Dutch repeated the general's statement in Osage.

"I don't think that there will be peace between the Comanches and the Osages," said Black Dog.

Dutch shrugged.

"I'm afraid you might get lost out there in the West," said Black Dog. "I think you need these two young Osage men to ride along with you as guides."

He indicated the two Osages who had ridden out with him and waited patiently and quietly by his side.

"Thank you," said Dutch. "We can use them." He looked at the two new scouts. "Ride with Pierre," he said, speaking to them in their own language.

"Go then," said Black Dog. "Go meet the Comanches. I'm going to hunt buffalo," and without another word, he turned his horse and rode hard back toward the main group of Osage buffalo hunters. Beatte led the two new Osage scouts back to the main group of scouts. Leavenworth looked at Dutch.

"We didn't need two more scouts," he said. "Especially two men that you don't know."

Dutch smiled. "No, we don't, General," he said. "Black Dog left these men with us as his spies. Later on, they'll tell him everything we do from here on out, all along the way. He wouldn't believe anything we told him about it. That's why he thinks he needs them to go along with us."

"Spies," said Leavenworth. He heaved an exasperated sigh and looked back toward the two intruding Osages.

Dutch shrugged. "We ain't got nothing to hide on this trip, have we, General?" he asked.

Leavenworth turned back toward Dutch

and, frowning, looked him in the eye. "No, Captain," he said. "No, we have not."

He wheeled his horse around and kicked it into a gallop, riding toward the waiting soldiers back behind the scouts.

27

Captain Dutch, Jesse Chisholm, Pierre Beatte, the two Osage scouts contributed by Black Dog, Lieutenant Jefferson Davis, and George Catlin, the artist, rode over the top of a small hill. Below them they saw the buffalo herd. It was a small herd, somehow separated from the larger one, the one the Osage hunters were following. Dutch had suggested a hunt. The opportunity was there. If they waited until they needed meat, there might not be any to be had. Out in the prairie, it was always smart to take advantage of an opportunity when it was afforded. Leavenworth agreed and ordered his men to establish a camp.

"We'll ride down easy," said Dutch. "Get as close as we can without spooking them. When they start to run, then kick up your mounts. Try to get right up close alongside one before you shoot. Then aim just behind his shoulder. You all ready then?"

He received affirmative answers from everyone, so he nudged his black horse forward. The seven riders moved slowly down the slope toward the unsuspecting herd. Toward the bottom of the hill, Dutch, Chisholm, and Beatte turned their mounts to swing around to the far side of the herd.

A big bull raised his shaggy head and snorted, and the entire herd started to move almost at once. Dutch's black horse started to run after them. Catlin's reaction was slower. He saw Dutch, Chisholm, and Beatte start to race after the herd, and just as he was about to react, he heard Jeff Davis behind him.

"Let's go, George!" the lieutenant shouted, and they were off. Even then, the horse underneath him reacted faster than did its rider. The first thing that Catlin noticed was that the speed provided instant relief from the pesky prairie flies. The second thing he noticed was that the dust from the thundering herd was thick and almost choking.

He was the last rider, but even so he had no trouble catching up with the herd. Dutch had selected a good buffalo horse for him to ride, and Catlin knew enough to let the seasoned horse take over and do the job it knew so well. Soon he found himself running hard alongside a healthy cow. He pointed his rifle just behind the shoulder, as he had been instructed to do, and tried to hold it steady, but he was jouncing so in the saddle that the rifle barrel seemed to point at the ground one instant and up into the sky the next. At last, as the barrel was about to race by its target on its way up again, he fired. To Catlin's amazement, the unfortunate cow crashed head first into the hard prairie.

The rest continued moving, and Catlin felt as if he were riding a living ground swell that would not stop even for death. No one had any control over it, not Dutch, nor Chisholm, nor Beatte, nor Davis, nor the buffalo themselves — certainly not himself. And there was no way to get off. The only thing that he or any one else could do was be sure to keep his seat.

He tried to reload his rifle, but he spilled his powder. He tried again. At last he got the job done, and he ran up beside another beast. He shot again, and his second buffalo was down and dead. Then suddenly it was all over, more quickly even than it had begun. Catlin wasn't sure how it had come to an end. He was not at all conscious of having reined in his buffalo horse. It seemed the swell had simply passed him and eased him off the edge as it went by.

The riders stopped and the surviving buffalo raced off into the distance. His head still reeling with the motion, Catlin turned in the saddle to look behind, and he saw the trail of buffalo they had killed strung out behind him along the prairie. The distance they had covered amazed him, as did the number of dead animals. He had killed two of them himself, and he had fumbled badly reloading. He knew that each of the scouts must have done much better than that. The flies began to swarm around him once again, and he turned his horse to ride back toward the camp.

The traveling was done for that day. The dragoons had made a camp, and much of the remaining daylight was taken up with the butchering of the slaughtered buffalo. Catlin was spared that chore, as were the other hunters. Several of the scouts, though, who had not taken part in the hunt were kept busy for several long hours. They took a wagon with them in which to load the hides and meat.

The prairie flies returned in greater numbers and with more vigor, it seemed, than before. Smudge pots were set around the camp and among the picketed livestock to keep the flies from biting beasts and men to death; although the weather was warm, the safest place to be was near a fire.

Once he had settled down for a while and rested himself from the chase, Catlin was grateful for the gift of the unexpected leisure hours. Because of the time required for the butchering, they were camped much earlier in the day than usual. The artist unpacked his sketch pad, pen, and ink, and opened the pad to a clean sheet. Jeff Davis walked over and sat down beside him.

"Time for a little sketching?" he asked.

"It's the first chance I've had," said Catlin.

"We have been pushing it pretty hard," said Davis. "Are you recovered from the hunt?"

"I think so," said Catlin. "But tomorrow morning will probably tell. It was exciting, but I felt like a clumsy oaf trying to load a rifle at a full gallop."

"It's a tricky business at best," said Davis. "These old scouts have had a lot of practice. You didn't do badly, George. You got two nice kills."

"Thanks," said Catlin, giving a casual shrug.

Just then Captain Dutch came walking toward the two men, his long rifle resting easily in the crook of his right arm. "You two managing to keep the flies off?" he said.

"They're not too bad close in to the fires," said Davis, swatting a bold one away from his face.

"Captain Dutch," said Catlin, "would it be asking too much of you to just stand there for a moment? I'd like to do a sketch. It won't take long."

Dutch shifted his rifle, taking it in his left hand by the end of the barrel and resting the butt on the ground.

"You want me to pose?" he said.

"Yes, if you don't mind."

"Well," said Dutch with a smile, "I don't reckon I mind. I've never had my portrait done before. How's this?"

"That's fine," said Catlin. "Just fine." He was already at work, making quick, sure lines with his pen, looking from Dutch to his pad and back again.

"I don't believe this will qualify as a por-trait," he said. "It will just be a quick sketch. When I get back to my studio, I'll use the sketch to develop a portrait in water colors."

The sketch was coming along nicely, and Catlin was pleased, for he had been wanting to do this since that first day he had laid eyes on Dutch back at Fort Gibson. The stance was good, relaxed, yet proud. The details of clothing and the rifle were probably actually more than he would need for the portrait, but the sketch itself would provide a good record of Dutch's overall appearance. He had just about decided that he would only do a bust for the actual portrait.

"You told me, I believe," said Catlin, "that you've been in the West since you were a child."

"We came out in 'ninety-five," said Dutch. "I couldn't yet lift a rifle."

"Of course," said the artist, not looking up from his work, "Fort Gibson wasn't here in those days. Had Fort Smith been established?"

"This territory was all French back then," said Dutch.

"Oh, yes, of course," said Catlin. "I knew that. A foolish question. The United States could not have established a fort until after 1803."

"Cantonment Smith was started up in 1817, I believe," said Davis, "toward the end of the year."

"I'd say so," said Dutch.

"So you would have been how old?" Catlin asked the scout.

"Oh, twenty-six or seven, I'd guess," said Dutch. "Thereabouts."

Catlin glanced up at Dutch and made a

few more quick strokes with his pen. Davis continued to watch, fascinated, over the artist's shoulder.

"Then you can well remember when there was no military presence out here at all," said Catlin. "What must it have been like to live out here in those days?"

"It was wild and free," said Dutch, "and I miss those days."

"But there was no authority," said Davis. "No law and order to count on for the safety and security of your families."

"We had our laws," said Dutch. "And we had the means of enforcing the law as well."

"You're referring, of course, to the government of your Western Cherokee Nation," Catlin said.

"That I am," said Dutch. "We had our government established, and it worked pretty well as long as no one interfered with it from outside."

"Like the Osages?" Catlin asked.

"Like the United States," corrected Dutch.

"I see," said Catlin.

Davis cleared his throat.

"But you were a small nation," said Catlin, "and you were surrounded by a great many warlike tribes."

"We had our fights with the Osages and

other western tribes," said Dutch. "No one paid much attention to them until the missionaries came out here. But things really began to heat up around 1815, '16, somewhere around there, after your government got Lovely's Purchase away from the Osages for the use of the Cherokees and shoved the Osages a little further west. Comanches got into the fight then, as did other tribes out west. Any time anyone makes a move, he pushes on someone else.

"And then the whites were coming in, too, from all sides, hunting where they had no right to be. It was then the government decided that it ought to have a military post out here, to put a lid on things, I guess. So they set up Cantonment Smith. It wasn't too long after that they decided they needed another one, a little farther west, and Fort Gibson was created. We came out here in the first place to get away from all that, but it's caught up with us now."

Catlin put down his pen and held the pad at arm's length away from himself to study what he had done.

"That's a fine likeness," said Davis.

"Is it done?" asked Dutch.

"Yes," said Catlin. "I think it's done, for now at least."

He turned the pad for Dutch to see, as the scout broke his pose and stepped forward. Dutch squatted and took the pad out of Catlin's hands. He smiled with pride as he perused his image in ink.

"Do you approve?" Catlin asked him.

"Well," said Dutch, "I got nothing to compare it to. It's the only one I ever seen, but I sure do like it. Yes sir."

28

Riding well in advance of the main body of the expedition, Dutch was the first to see the army camp up ahead. He could tell that it was a fort in the early stages of construction, and he knew from its location on the river that it was the planned Fort Washita. Colonel Dodge had said that they would come across it.

They were springing up all over the place, Dutch thought, these new army posts. He could remember a time when there were none. Then they had established Fort Smith in 1817, and from that time on they seemed to come like flies: Fort Gibson and Fort Towson, both in 1824, Fort Coffee in 1834, and now Fort Washita, the same year. It seemed they couldn't build them fast enough.

He indulged in a little nostalgia for the old days, which now seemed to him to have been absolutely wild and free. How many years are left, he asked himself, before the white men are all around us the way they are back east? How long before

347

the greedy arms of the insatiable United States are wrapped around us in a crushing hug?

But Dutch knew that Fort Washita would be a pleasant sight for the miserable soldiers behind him, especially those who were suffering the most from the strange sickness that had unexpectedly blasted them out there on the scorching prairie. Merciless and indiscriminate, the debilitating scourge had settled itself in enlisted men and officers alike. It had also stricken some of the scouts, and it was even attacking horses and mules.

It brought with it a burning fever and nausea, leaving its victims racked with pain and exhausted from severe stomach cramps and periodic fits of vomiting. Once they at last rode into the beginnings of Fort Washita, many of the sick men literally fell out of their saddles. Even General Leavenworth was down. Some thought that it might be cholera, but no one was sure. Captain Dutch and Jesse Chisholm seemed to have escaped the sickness.

"Maybe we're immune," said Jesse.

"I doubt it," said Dutch. "We've just been riding well out away from the others. If we hang around too close here at the fort, it might get us, too."

Dutch turned his horse around to ride back out.

"Where're you going now?" said Jesse.

"I'm just going out to take a look at the river," said Dutch. "We'll be needing to cross it soon enough."

Jesse glanced around quickly at the sick men in the camp.

"I hurt all over," he heard one say.

"I think I'm going to die," another moaned.

Jesse whipped his mount around and rode fast after Dutch.

When the command rode out again a few days later, they left behind them seventy-five horses and mules, forty-five enlisted men, and three officers, including the general, none of them fit to continue. Colonel Dodge had assumed command of the expedition. Many of the men continuing were also sick, but they could still function. They weren't as bad off as the ones they had left behind. At least, not yet.

The Washita River was deep and swift. They had to cross it on rafts, and building the rafts, together with the crossing, took all day. Two horses were swept away and drowned in the red, relentless current. Exhausted, the expedition camped on the other side of the river that night. Jeff Davis and George

Catlin were now sick, and Jesse Chisholm admitted to Dutch that even he was not feeling too well.

For the next week they traveled west. More men and animals developed symptoms of the ailment each day. Catlin began to think that he had joined a death march and that the very air had been poisoned by some mysterious and malignant enemy.

Then, as if the sickness alone weren't misery enough, they ran out of coffee, then bread. The talk was more and more of food and of the luxuries that they had left behind, of bread and beans and sweet potatoes, of cakes and pies, of coffee and milk and wine, of hot baths and soft beds.

Then they came at last to a wide, green valley crossed here and there by streams of clear, fresh, running water and populated by small herds of buffalo and wild horses. Dutch took some of the more hardy of the scouts out with him to get fresh meat.

Riding toward one of the small herds of bison in the valley, he saw a dozen mounted Indians on a distant ridge, but he kept to the business at hand. He and the other scouts killed a few of the shaggy beasts and butchered them.

Later, sitting by a small fire in their camp, fresh buffalo meat sizzling on a spit,

Dutch spoke to Colonel Dodge. "We had some company out there today," he said.

"Who was it?" asked the colonel.

Dutch shook his head. "We didn't get close enough to tell," he said. "They just watched us from a ridge. Maybe Pawnee. I ain't sure."

"Comanche," said one of the Osage scouts Black Dog had left behind.

Dutch shrugged. "He says Comanche," he repeated to Dodge. "Maybe he's right."

"Well," said the colonel, "that's who we came out here to see."

They filled up their bellies that day on buffalo meat and water, for that was all they had.

"Oh, for a cup of coffee," said Jeff Davis.

"Hot and steaming," said Catlin. "With sugar to sweeten it. Oh, for a chunk of bread."

"Fresh from the oven," said Davis, "hot and buttered."

They rested in the valley for a day and a night, and most of the sick men began to feel a little better. It was early morning when they saw the riders coming toward their camp. Colonel Dodge ordered his staff officers to mount up with him, and with Dutch and Jesse Chisholm along, they rode out to meet their visitors. Lieutenant

Davis was carrying a white flag.

"The Osage was right, Colonel," said Dutch, as the two groups of riders drew closer together. "They're Comanches."

"Good," said Dodge. "Can you talk to them?"

"Not in their language," said Dutch, "but maybe Jesse can try a little Spanish on them."

"By all means," said Dodge.

They stopped riding, and so did the other party.

"Jesse?" said Dutch.

Jesse Chisholm didn't wait for further instructions from the colonel. *"Buenos dias, amigos,"* he said. *"¿Cómo están ustedes?"*

"Tell them who we are," said Dodge, "and tell them that we're on a friendly mission."

Jesse carried on a brief conversation in Spanish with the Comanches, then turned back toward the colonel.

"They say that we're welcome," he said. "They're Comanches. Their village is not far from here, and they've invited us to follow them over there."

"Thank them for us," said Dodge, "and tell them that we'll be pleased and honored to visit at their village."

It was a short ride, and when they

topped a rise and looked down on another wide and peaceful valley, they could see along the bank of a river, a vast expanse of several hundred tipis. A herd of three thousand horses grazed nearby. Children played and women worked.

Catlin was nearly overcome with the sight. In spite of the sickness that troubled him, he could not restrain himself. While the rest of the column rode on down into the village, he stayed behind. The scene below had stirred his artist's blood, and he did not want to lose the feeling that he had upon first sighting it. He dismounted and unpacked his sketching materials.

Some of the Comanches who had led the expedition to their village stayed behind to watch what he was doing. Everyone else rode down the hill and into the village, where their arrival was heralded as a major event. Curious villagers flocked around to get a closer look at the white soldiers, the first that these Comanches had ever seen.

After much handshaking and many introductions, accomplished in Spanish through Jesse, the Comanches spread a sumptuous feast for their unexpected but nonetheless welcome visitors. The scouts and soldiers, who had had nothing but meat to eat for days, welcomed the variety of food that the Comanche women placed before them.

"It's not exactly what I would order in a restaurant in New Orleans," said Davis, "but it's a welcome sight."

"It certainly is," said Dodge. "I never thought that I'd be sitting down to an Indian meal with so much relish."

The feasting done, young Comanche men put on a wild exhibition for their guests, riding their horses at breakneck speed, hanging off their sides and standing on their backs. They reached down to swoop up objects from the ground as they raced by, and they engaged in mock horseback battles.

Catlin, who had finished his sketching and come down into the village to join the others, leaned over to speak to Jeff Davis.

"They're like centaurs," he said. "Each man is like a part of his horse. On foot, they seem to me to be just a bit clumsy and awkward, but mounted, they become half man, half horse, the very personification of grace."

"Yes," said Davis. "This is a most impressive demonstration. I hate to say it, but they put the U.S. cavalry to shame."

When the entertainment was over, the Comanches began to barter with the scouts and soldiers. Some members of the expedition had tobacco, blankets, and butcher knives they were willing to part with. They had not really come for purposes of trade, but the Comanches were still interested in what they had. And what the Comanches had most of all to trade was horses. Jesse Chisholm watched for a while with fascination. Then he walked over to stand beside Dutch.

"Do you see what's happening here?" he asked.

"The trading?" Dutch said.

"Yes. I think I'll go into the trading business. These Comanches are trading a horse for just four dollars' worth of stuff. The horses — any one of them will sell back at Fort Smith for eighty. Maybe more."

"I'd say as much as one hundred," said Dutch. "The Comanches raise good horses."

"That's a pretty good profit from a four-dollar swap," said Jesse. "Wouldn't you say?"

"Your profit would be even higher," said Dutch with a wry smile, "if you were to just steal the horses."

Eventually Colonel Dodge called an end to the day. He had Lieutenant Davis get the men together and back into formation, and he had Jesse tell the Comanches in Spanish that the soldiers would make a camp for the night a little way down from the village, along the banks of the stream. Then they rode away.

In camp that night, Dodge noted that while some of the men seemed to be feeling much better, others were still suffering considerably from symptoms of the mysterious illness and perhaps even getting worse. It was clear that they were not free of the dreaded disease.

They rested a few days and visited some more with the Comanches, giving and receiving pledges of friendship, and when the expedition at last rode out of the valley, headed more south than west, a Comanche from the village rode along with them as guide. Jesse said that the man was leading them to a Wichita town a few days' ride from there.

They had only been out a day, when Dodge noticed that some of the soldiers seemed ready to fall out of their saddles. He sent for Captain Dutch who was scouting ahead.

"Some of these men can't go any farther,"

he said, when Dutch came back to join him. "We have to stop somewhere soon and make a sick camp. Find us a suitable spot, will you?"

"You're going to leave the sick behind?" Dutch asked.

"Yes," said Dodge. "Along with enough well men to take care of them. I have no choice. They'll be dying in their saddles."

Dutch selected a place beside a stream with a grove of trees nearby, and Dodge ordered the men to set up tents and to begin cutting trees for logs with which to build a breastworks. Dutch made the scouts work alongside the soldiers, cutting and trimming the logs and setting them in place. Catlin even pitched in, as did Black Dog's two donated Osage scouts.

The work took the rest of the day, and the entire expeditionary force spent the night there at the sick camp. Making his count, Dodge found that nearly forty men were far too ill to continue on the way, and he selected another thirty to stay behind with them. He had already left a good many behind with the ailing General Leavenworth at Fort Washita, so when the more or less able-bodied rode out with him the next morning, there were fewer than two hundred.

29

The Comanche guide led Dodge's expedition through the foothills of the Wichita Mountains. It was a rugged ride. Near the north fork of the Red River, they spotted a lone Indian.

"Wichita," said the Comanche.

"Let's talk to him and ask him the way to his village," said Dodge. "He could accompany us there."

Dutch, Jesse Chisholm, and the Comanche rode toward the Wichita. The man saw them coming and started to run.

"Stop him!" shouted Dodge.

The three horsemen whipped up their mounts and raced after the man on foot. Glancing over his shoulder, he saw them coming faster. He was a good runner, but he knew that he could not outrun the horses. He veered to his left and headed for a steep, rocky hillside. Dutch whipped up his big black stallion and burst out ahead of the other two riders.

The man had started up the hillside. He had not gone far. He would have made an easy target for a pistol shot, but the goal was to talk with the man, not kill him. Dutch knew that he couldn't dismount and catch the Wichita on foot. He made a quick decision, turned his horse sharply and urged him up the hill.

There was no trail, no easy way to go. The hillside was covered with large, sharp rocks, and the paths around the large rocks were covered with smaller, often loose stones, so the footing was treacherous. The black horse valiantly stabbed at the loose footing, slipping here and there, regaining his hold and lurching forward. Dutch came up beside the man, but the black horse kept going a few more lurches. When he was far enough ahead, Dutch guided his mount over to the right to block the man's route.

The man looked up at the rider on the big, black stallion blocking his path. He hesitated, shot a quick glance over his shoulder at the two other riders below. Dutch's horse slipped a little, then regained his footing. The Wichita, thinking to take advantage of Dutch's brief distraction, started to move quickly to his right, and Dutch whipped out a pistol and fired a shot. The ball hit a rock in front of the man and he stopped.

Quickly, Dutch shoved the empty pistol back in his sash and pulled out the loaded one. He pointed it in the direction of the Wichita. He wanted to tell the man that they only wanted to talk to him, but he did not know a word of the Wichita language, and with one hand filled with a pistol and the other holding the reins of a horse with unsure footing, sign talk was out of the question.

He gestured with his pistol for the man to go back down the hill. After a moment's consideration, the man did. Dutch started his big horse slowly and carefully back down. Once again beside the other two scouts, the Wichita standing uncertainly before them, Dutch spoke to the Comanche.

"Do you speak his language?" he asked.

The Comanche shook his head.

"Well," said Dutch, "maybe he knows yours. Try it."

The Comanche said something that got no response from the Wichita. Dutch put his pistol away and dismounted. He stepped toward the man, not too close, and he started to make signs. We mean you no harm, he signed. We stopped you to talk. Walk back with us.

The Wichita looked suspicious, but he seemed not to have much choice in the matter, so he walked along with the other three men to where Colonel Dodge waited with the column. There, with more sign talk, Dutch gave the man a rudimentary understanding of the peaceful mission of the expedition.

"Ask him to take us to his village," said Dodge, and Dutch asked. The man thought about it for a moment, then agreed. With a Wichita guide to the Wichita village, the Comanche said that he felt he was no longer needed. Dodge thanked him, and the Comanche turned around and headed home. Dodge had a horse brought forward for the Wichita, and they started to move again.

Catlin had seen the large earth lodges of the Mandans in the far north. He had seen northeastern wigwams. He had seen the semi-cylindrical skin-and-bark-covered houses of the Osages, and he had seen large villages of conical, skin-covered lodges, sometimes known as tipis. But nothing he had previously seen prepared him for the sight of the large Wichita town of grass houses. There must be at least two hundred of them, he thought.

Situated on a riverbank with hills rising sharply behind them, the houses were nei-ther domes nor cones. They reminded the artist of nothing so much as large beehives. They were beautifully constructed, and Catlin was anxious to get a closer look to see how they were put together.

"Captain Dutch," said Dodge, "tell that man to go into his village and tell the others that we have come in peace. We mean no harm. We only want to visit."

Dutch made some signs. The man hesitated. He looked at Dodge, who smiled and made a gesture indicating that he was free to go. The Wichita turned and bolted for his town. Catlin broke out his sketch pad and started to work on a rendition of the town.

In a short while, when the released Wichita guide did not reappear from the town, Dodge began to get nervous. He allowed the troopers behind him to dismount and relax, but he kept Lieutenant Davis, Dutch, and Chisholm close by his side and watched the town. Catlin finished his sketch and put away his materials and still the man did not return. No one had come out of the town to greet them.

"Captain Dutch," said Dodge, "what do you think? Why haven't they come out?"

"It's hard to say, Colonel," said Dutch. "Maybe they don't trust us. Maybe they're afraid. Could be they're just having a long discussion to decide what to do."

"Do you think they might be hostile?"

Dutch shrugged.

"Lieutenant Davis," said the colonel, "have the men fix bayonets. Just in case."

"Yes sir," said Davis.

Just then a large party of Wichita men came riding out of the town. They carried lances and other weapons, and they rode fast toward the soldiers. Dodge braced himself for battle and ordered the men to mount up and be ready. Then about halfway from the village to where the soldiers waited, the mounted warriors stopped. They pranced their horses and shook their lances.

"They ain't going to attack, Colonel," said Dutch. "They just want to show their strength. Jesse, let's go."

Dutch and Chisholm rode toward the Wichitas, and as they drew closer, two of the Wichitas rode out to meet them.

"Try some Caddo on them, Jess," said Dutch.

Chisholm spoke and was answered. "He talks it," he told Dutch.

"Good. Tell him we're on a peaceful mission," said Dutch. "Tell him we'd like to camp right here, and later we'd like to talk with them."

Chisholm carried on a brief conversation in Caddo with the Wichita man who spoke the language, then turned back to Dutch.

"Okay," he said. "We can make camp here."

The Wichitas turned abruptly and rode back toward their town. Dutch and Chisholm rode back to Dodge with the news.

When the expedition's camp was set up, people started coming out of the Wichita town. Bare-breasted and tattooed women carried baskets and bowls of food, and the soldiers ate greedily. They were especially grateful for the fresh watermelons and plums. Catlin was fascinated by the geometric designs on the faces, arms, and breasts of the women.

Men from the town brought goods to trade, and, as with the Comanches, a lively barter was engaged in until the soldiers and scouts ran out of things to trade. Then a group of Comanches arrived, led by the very one who had been the expedition's guide. They joined in the festivities.

Somehow, in the midst of this action, Dodge was able to communicate, through Chisholm, that he would like to have a talk with the chief of the Wichita town and with the Comanches. It was arranged.

Dodge, Dutch, Davis, and Jesse Chisholm were invited into the town, where they were conducted to a grass house, the home of the chief. Inside, the introductions were made. The meeting was slow and tedious, for no one on the army's side could speak the language of the Wichitas, and only Jesse Chisholm could speak Caddo, which only a few of the Wichitas spoke. Everything everyone said had to be translated.

Dodge said that he was there to establish peace between the United States and the prairie tribes, and Captain Dutch was along to do the same for the eastern Indians. The Wichita chief, Wetarasharo, had short-cropped black hair. Two eagle feathers were fixed to the back of his head. He wore leggings and moccasins but no shirt. A buffalo robe was wrapped around his body and over one shoulder in the style of a Roman toga. He nodded his head and muttered but made no commitments.

During a lull in the proceedings, Colonel Dodge spoke up. "Where are Ranger Abbay and the Martin boy?" he asked.

After the translation, the answer came back. "He said that Indians south of the Red River got Abbay and killed him," Chisholm explained. "But they've got the Martin boy right here in this town."

"Tell him," said Dodge, "that we would like to have him back, and tell him about the girl."

He waited again for translations, looking from Wetarasharo to Chisholm and back again. At last Chisholm turned to him to speak.

"He wants to come to our camp in the morning for a council," said Chisholm.

"What's wrong with right now?" Dodge asked, his voice belligerent.

"Colonel," said Dutch, "we got a promising response. Don't press it."

Dodge took a deep breath and straightened himself.

"Tell him," he said, "that we'll be looking forward to it, and thank him for his hospitality."

They gathered the next morning in front of Dodge's tent: Dodge; Davis; Wetarasharo; Dutch; Chisholm; Beatte, representing the Osages; George Bullet, representing the Delawares; and other important men of the Wichitas and the Comanches.

Wetarasharo presented the Martin boy to Dodge. The boy stepped timidly toward the colonel, who took him by the shoulders and looked into his eyes.

"Are you all right, my boy?" he asked.

"Yes sir," young Martin answered, in a weak voice.

"Good," said Dodge. "You'll be going home now. Right now, I want you to go with Sergeant McCloskey. He'll take good care of you." Dodge straightened up. "McCloskey," he called.

"Yes sir."

"Take the lad along, will you? We have more to do here." Then he called over his shoulder again to someone inside his tent. "Bring the girl out now."

A soldier stepped out of the tent, holding the Wichita girl by her arm. He led her to Dodge's side. Wetarasharo and the other Wichita men present came to their feet, eyes wide and mouths dropping open. They spoke in astonished voices. Dodge gave the girl a gentle shove toward Wetarasharo. She started slowly, then ran to him, and he threw his arms around her. Then, in turn, each of the men hugged her. In the background, the excited voices of Wichita women could be heard. Wetarasharo spoke to the girl, gesturing toward the women, and she ran to them.

"I think we've got off to a good start here, Colonel," said Dutch.

Then Colonel Dodge spoke to the entire assembly through the interpretive voice of

Jesse Chisholm. A Caddo-speaking Wichita, in turn, put the words into the Wichita language. It was a slow process, but Dodge's words seemed to be well received.

He told them that he wanted peace between his people and theirs. He said that was the purpose of his visit. He hoped that the return of these children to their rightful homes was but one step in that direction. He also said that Captain Dutch, Pierre Beatte, and George Bullet had come along representing the eastern tribes, and they, too, would speak of peace among their people and the Wichitas and the Comanches.

Wetarasharo's response was predictable. He thanked Dodge for the return of the girl. It had made him and all of his people very happy, he said. He was glad that he had been able to preserve the life of the white boy and return him to his people. Finally, he said, he had no greater desire than to live in peace and harmony with the whites. It was Dutch's turn to speak. He looked at Pierre Beatte, the Osage, and he thought of all the many Osages he had killed and the many Cherokees they had killed. He thought about his first wife, long ago. He stood up, and when he spoke, he spoke in Cherokee, relying on Jesse Chisholm to repeat his words in Caddo. Then the Caddo was, of course, translated into Wichita, so Dutch's words were never heard in English. Dodge chafed a bit, wondering what his chief of scouts was saying.

"My friends," said Dutch, "I represent the Western Cherokee Nation. Our nation is split because of pressures in our eastern homeland from too many whites living there. The United States wants to make room for its own people, and they are trying to make all the eastern tribes move west. We can no longer fight the white men. There are too many of them. And so we move.

"And then we have conflicts with those of you who lived here first. My people, the Western Cherokees, fought for many years with the Ani-Wasasi, the people of my friend Beatte who sits right here among us. Perhaps I killed his uncle. Or he killed mine.

"Now we have peace between us, but it took many years to achieve, and it cost many lives on both sides. We come to you to seek peace between all our people, now, before any trouble starts. Why should we wait for war to make a peace?"

Beatte spoke next and then Bullet, each

echoing the sentiments expressed by Dutch. Wetarasharo was about to speak again, when they heard a commotion in the camp. Everyone in the circle of the council stood up to look.

"What's going on?" asked Dodge.

"Some Kiowas are riding in," said Chisholm.

30

The meeting broke up abruptly and unceremoniously at the surprise arrival of the nearly thirty heavily armed Kiowas. Wetarasharo and a few other Wichita men stepped to the edge of the crowd to meet the Kiowas as they rode up close to the camp and stopped sharply, scattering dust over those who were standing nearest them. It was a movement calculated to intimidate. The Kiowas seemed to be in a belligerent mood, and it made Dodge nervous.

"It's all right, Colonel," said Chisholm. "I think the Kiowas and the Wichitas are friendly enough with each other. This bunch is just showing off because we're here."

Wetarasharo held up a hand and called out a greeting. The translating process was tedious and complicated, but eventually the Wichita chief got across to the Kiowas that the U.S. soldiers were visiting on a mission of peace, and that they were accompanied by representatives from several of the eastern tribes.

The Kiowas were all still mounted, all had full quivers of arrows, and all had bows that were tightly strung and ready to use. Suddenly the Kiowas became visibly and audibly agitated. They talked to each other and to Wetarasharo in angry voices, as they sat astride their prancing mounts.

"Captain Dutch," said Dodge, "this looks dangerous."

"Yeah," said Dutch. "It looks like something's wrong."

"Well," said Dodge, "I'd feel much better if I knew what they were talking about. Can you find out what's going on over there?"

Dutch turned immediately to Jesse Chisholm, who was still standing close by.

"Jess," he said, "can you tell what they're saying?"

"I don't understand them," said Chisholm, "but I'll find someone who does. I'll have to use the Caddo."

He strolled casually over to one of the Wichitas, one he already knew could speak the Caddo language, and he had a brief conversation with the man. Then he returned to Dutch's side.

"It seems the Kiowas heard that we have Osages with us," he said. "They say that some Osages wiped out a whole village of

Kiowas a few months back. Killed a bunch of women and kids. What's even worse, the Osages got away with the Kiowas sacred medicine bundle. This bunch is out for some Osage blood, and they ain't going to take kindly to anyone who travels with the Osages, either."

"Where do the Wichitas stand on this issue?" Dodge asked.

"Wetarasharo's being real careful," said Chisholm. "He just keeps telling them that this is a peace talk and we're his guests."

"I should have the men get ready for a fight," said Dodge.

"That might start one," said Dutch.

"Sure enough," said Chisholm.

"Then we've got to do something to defuse this situation," said Dodge. "We can't just stand here and wait for them to decide to start shooting arrows at us."

"We've got that little Kiowa girl with us," said Dutch. "Why don't you bring her on out?"

"Yes. Good idea," said Dodge, and he looked back over his shoulder. "Sergeant McCloskey," he called out.

McCloskey came running to stand in front of the colonel. "Yes sir?"

"McCloskey, get the Kiowa girl and bring her here to me, right away."

"Yes sir," said McCloskey, and he was off like a shot.

Dodge turned immediately to Chisholm. "Can you insinuate yourself into this conversation between Wetarasharo and the Kiowas?" he asked.

"I reckon," said Chisholm. "The Kiowas are mostly talking among themselves right now anyhow."

"Tell them that we want to talk with them," said Dodge. "Tell them that we're glad to see them. Say that we were looking for them, because we have something to give them. Quickly now."

Chisholm approached Wetarasharo and spoke to the chief in Caddo in a low voice. The Wichita chief listened, nodded, then called out in a loud voice to the leader of the Kiowa party. The Kiowas quieted down, looked at him, and listened to what he had to say. Then they talked among themselves some more, and just then McCloskey returned to Dodge's side with the Kiowa girl.

The Kiowa leader shot a glance at Dodge, started to look away, then looked back again quickly at the girl standing there. His face registered astonishment. His eyes opened wide, and his mouth fell open. Then he called out something, jumped down from his horse's back and

374

rushed toward the girl.

Dodge stepped aside, braced for anything that might happen, but the man went straight to the girl and embraced her lovingly. In a voice that was choked with tears, he talked to her for what seemed a long time, then turned to Wetarasharo and said something. The Wichita answered him and gestured with his chin toward Dodge. When the Kiowa then straightened up and approached Dodge directly, the colonel noticed that tears were streaming down the man's face. Dodge was doubly taken aback when the Kiowa, fierce looking just a moment before, threw his arms around him and wept on his shoulder, sobbing out loud unashamedly.

Wetarasharo spoke to Jesse Chisholm in Caddo, as the other Kiowas, quiet now, dismounted. Chisholm walked back over to the colonel's side. The one Kiowa still held Dodge in a close embrace, still wept. Dodge looked tense and nervous, even embarrassed. Out of the side of his mouth, he spoke to Chisholm.

"What the hell's going on here?" he asked.

"It's a small world, Colonel," said Chisholm. "The little girl's his niece. He thought he'd never see her again."

"Well, I'll be damned," said Dodge.

The Kiowas, of course, were saddened by the news of the death of the boy, but they had long ago given up both children for dead. Therefore, they were so grateful for the return of the girl that they forgave the presence of Osages among the troops and refrained from any violence or threats. They joined in the council, and the uncle of the girl expressed his undying gratitude over and over again, occasionally to renewed weeping. He pledged eternal friendship, if not to the United States, at least to Colonel Dodge.

A few days later, Dodge decided that it was time to begin the return trip. At his request, a few of the Kiowas, Wichitas, and Comanches rode with them. But the sickness was not defeated. It rode along with them as well.

Jesse Chisholm was not feeling well now, and Catlin had gotten worse. He could no longer sit a horse. Several of the soldiers looked as if they would pass out at any moment. It was late July, and the heat was brutal on the open, dusty plains. The biting prairie flies were back as well.

Along the way, they picked up the men they had left at the sick camp. A few had died. Some who had been well had contracted the mysterious illness while tending the sick. They moved on toward Fort Washita. Catlin was riding in a supply wagon almost delirious with fever.

When they reached the banks of the Canadian River, they camped again. Horses and men needed rest. Dodge thought a few days leisure there would do them all some good, but he also wanted desperately to get back to Fort Gibson as quickly as possible. Most of his men, he thought, needed to be in the hospital. He was still trying to decide what he should do, when a soldier came riding into the camp from the east. Dodge stepped out to meet him with Lieutenant Davis by his side. The trooper dismounted and gave Dodge a snappy salute.

"Corporal Blevins," he said, "from Fort Washita, sir."

"What are you doing out here, Corporal?" said Dodge, returning the salute.

"I'm a courier, sir, with a message for you."

"Well," said Dodge, "let's have it."

"I'm afraid it's bad news, sir," said Blevins. "General Leavenworth is dead. So are Lieutenant McClure and fifteen of your troopers. From the sickness, sir. Some of our men are down with it, too."

"Oh God," said Dodge, turning his back to the courier. He thought of all the others under his command who were suffering from the same mysterious malady and wondered how many more would die, how many would survive. He took a deep breath, straightened himself, and turned back to Blevins. "You've had a long ride, Corporal," he said. "Would you like something to eat? I'm afraid we have no coffee."

"Yes sir," said the corporal. "Thank you sir."

"Lieutenant Davis," said Dodge, "would you see that the corporal is taken care of? Have McCloskey tend to it."

"Yes sir," said Davis. "Come with me, Corporal."

Blevins started to follow Davis, hesitated, and turned back to Dodge.

"Sir?"

"What is it, Corporal?" said Dodge.

"About the general, sir."

"Yes?"

"He got up out of his sick bed. He was awful sick, but he said that he needed to be with the expedition. He said that he needed to be with you and the western Indians. Nobody could talk him out of it. He mounted up and would have ridden out all by himself, but our commanding officer, when he saw he couldn't stop him, sent a squad to ride along with him. Well, they brought him back later. They had ridden about fifty miles, they said, before he just fell out of the saddle, dead. I thought you'd want to know."

"Yes, Corporal," said Dodge. "Thank you."

As Davis led Blevins over to one of the small fires, Dodge turned and looked over the camp. He recalled the day they had ridden out of Fort Gibson, five hundred strong in clean and gaudy uniforms, with General Leavenworth at the head of the column. They could have been riding in a parade in the nation's capital.

And look at us now, he thought. Ragged, sick, and miserable. Down to less than half strength, and not one battle fought. Correction. One battle fought. Still under way. A battle with an unseen enemy, a horrible and unidentified sickness. A battle with the summer heat and with the flies. A battle we seem to be losing. My God, the expedition has turned into a death march.

Davis came walking back over to the place where Dodge was standing in a kind of reverie.

"The corporal's eating, sir," he said.

"What?" said Dodge.

"The corporal, sir," said Davis. "He's being taken care of."

"Oh," said Dodge. "Yes. Thank you, Lieutenant."

"It's too bad about the general," said Davis. "He was a good officer."

"Yes," said Dodge.

"At least he died in the saddle. I think that he'd have preferred it that way."

"Yes," said Dodge. "In the saddle. Doing his goddamned duty."

31

The remainder of the trip back to Fort Gibson for what was left of the Dodge expedition was slow and torturous. Most of the men were sick by then, and even Dutch had begun to feel some of the distressing symptoms. The late July and early August heat was oppressive, and it was intensified by heavy humidity. The prairie flies were like a plague unto themselves.

At their last stop at Fort Washita they left behind more men who were unable to continue farther along the way. Dodge wondered how many would be left when they finally made it back to Fort Gibson. He even found himself wondering if any would make it back to Fort Gibson.

George Catlin wondered, too. He wondered about himself. He was no coward afraid to face death, but there was so much yet to be done, and there were, of course, his notes and his sketches from the present trip to worry about. If he should die along the way, he asked himself, who would take charge of his papers? What would become of them?

"Dutch," said Jesse Chisholm, riding up alongside the chief of scouts, "I guess you were right. We ain't immune to this damn thing, whatever it is. I feel awful."

"Hang on, Jess," said Dutch. "We'll make it home. Don't give in. If you once give in to it, that's when it'll get you."

He didn't bother telling Chisholm that he too was feeling miserable. There was no point in that. Everyone was suffering. He kept it to himself and rode on.

The post surgeon at Washita had done all that he could for the ailing, and Dodge, as soon as he felt the horses had rested enough, had ordered the march to resume. He couldn't help feeling that he needed to hurry back to escape the mysterious and deadly disease of the western prairies. If they lingered too long, his mind told him, they would all die.

And so they left Fort Washita, a ragged and weary lot. Their bones and muscles ached as they climbed painfully into their saddles or crawled pitifully into baggage wagons. They were feverish, and their heads ached. Stomachs roiled and bowels were loose. They groaned and they grumbled. Yet they rode on.

Tempers were short among the men who had the strength remaining to indulge themselves in losing them. Officers talked of resigning their commissions, and enlisted men talked of desertion. Everyone cursed the army and the western plains. Yet they went on.

One day seemed like the day before, except that the men felt worse with each passing day. They lost count of the number of days they had been traveling. They no longer knew the day of the month. Then they no longer knew the month. They knew only that it was blazing hot and miserably humid, that they felt sick unto death, and that Fort Gibson was nowhere in sight. Most of the men thought that they would never see Fort Gibson again.

And then, to their amazement, they saw it. At first, some of them did not believe their eyes. Miraculously, they had made it. All who had managed to ride, walk, or crawl away from Fort Washita made it back to Fort Gibson.

But it was a bedraggled, wretched looking lot that rode into the fort. The people, military and civilian, who were gathered inside the walls of the fort could scarcely believe that this was the same company that had ridden out so grandly only a short time ago. It was now the fifteenth of August. They had been gone for exactly two months.

When Dodge halted the troops inside the walls, men fell off their horses' backs. Many of the men were taken directly to the post hospital, and when the beds there were full, others were put to bed in their own quarters. Almost immediately, some of the sick began to die.

Colonel Arbuckle, after a quick report from Dodge, met briefly with the leaders of the western tribes who had accompanied the pitiful command on its return trip and asked that they stay to take part in a general council to be held beginning on the second of September. They all agreed. Messages were then sent to the Cherokees, Creeks, Choctaws, and Senecas, all eastern Indians recently moved into the country, asking them to send representatives. And a message was sent to the Osages.

George Catlin struggled to secure his gear behind a saddle on a big bay horse. He was weak and dizzy with fever. Dutch and Jesse Chisholm saw him and walked over to help.

"Are you planning a trip, Mr. Catlin?" asked Dutch.

"Yes," said Catlin. "I am."

"Well now, I ain't no doctor," said Chisholm, "but you don't seem to me to be in fit condition to go riding."

"Perhaps not," said Catlin. "Nevertheless, I'm going."

Chisholm shrugged. "Suit yourself," he said.

"Yesterday," said Catlin, "I heard the funeral dirge played outside my window eight times. Eight times in one day. Each day is worse than the one before. I'm convinced that if I stay here in my sick bed, I'll die here."

"Where you heading?" Chisholm asked.

"St. Louis," said Catlin.

"That's a long ride for a man to make alone," said Dutch. "Especially a sick man."

"If I don't make it," said Catlin, "at least I won't have died here in this charnel house."

"Well," said Dutch, "I don't blame you. I think I'd do the same thing. Do you have everything you need?"

"Yes," said Catlin. "I think so."

"Well," said Dutch, "good luck on your journey, Mr. Catlin."

"And the best of luck to you, Captain Dutch."

Catlin and Dutch shook hands, and then the weary artist turned to face Chisholm and shake his hand.

"I hope you reach St. Louis safe and sound," said Chisholm. "It's been a real pleasure getting to know you."

"Same here," said Catlin. "Don't let this damnable scourge get you. Either of you."

He climbed onto the back of his horse with some difficulty and rode toward the gate without looking back. Dutch and Chisholm stood watching him go.

"That fellow sure can draw," said Chisholm.

"Jess," said Dutch, "he's got the right idea. Getting away from here, I mean. I think I'll head for home myself. You want to ride out with me?"

"Well," said Chisholm, "I'd like to, but the colonel asked me to stick around to interpret for the big council coming up. I guess I'll stick."

"How're you feeling?" Dutch asked.

"A bit weak yet," said Chisholm, "but I think I'll get by. Like you said, I just ain't going to give in to it."

"All right," said Dutch. "Be seeing you then."

The gathering on the second of September was impressive. Dodge had brought back with him from the west Wichitas, Kiowas, and one Comanche. Representing the eastern tribes, immigrant tribes as they were being called, were Civil John and Totolis of the Senecas, Mushalatubbee of the Choctaws, Roley McIntosh and Benjamin Perryman of the Creeks, and Jesse Chisholm and James Rogers of the Cherokees.

A son of old Clermont, known as Young Clermont, or sometimes Clermont the Third, was there for the Osages, along with Pierre Beatte, the veteran scout and interpreter. The United States was well represented, first of all by Colonel Arbuckle and Colonel Dodge for the military. Major F. W. Armstrong, superintendent of Indian affairs was also there, as was Montford Stokes, newly appointed agent for the Western Cherokees.

The meeting had barely gotten under way when Young Clermont insisted on being heard.

"Why did you ask me here," he said, "to take part in a meeting with all my enemies? I am surrounded by enemies."

"We want you to make peace with your enemies," said Colonel Dodge. "For that reason we have brought you all together here to talk."

"If you make treaties with your old enemies," said Major Armstrong, "and with the United States at the same time, you will all be under the protection of the United States government. We want to talk about a peace that will be good for all of us."

Young Clermont sat down, but the expression on his face did not indicate that his question had been satisfactorily answered. Speeches were made for a good part of the day, and then the chiefs of the different tribes shook hands with one another. Some of them embraced. The meeting was adjourned until the next morning to give everyone time to think over the things that had been discussed.

Early the second day, Young Clermont complained again. He was getting bad looks from the Kiowas present, he said, and he could tell that the Kiowas had bad feelings for him. He didn't like that. It made him uncomfortable.

Dodge recalled the tense moment in the Wichita town when the visiting Kiowas had discovered the presence of Osages. The reason for the tension then was that the Osages had wiped out an entire Kiowa town some months before, and Dodge was certain that the same ugly episode fully explained the present feelings. He thought that Young Clermont shouldn't be surprised at the looks he was getting from the Kiowas, but he kept that thought to himself, and he and Major Armstrong had Clermont and the Kiowa chief shake hands again. Reluctantly, they did. Still the Kiowa looked and still Young Clermont scowled.

Montford Stokes, seventy-four years old, was getting tired. He had little patience any more for these petty squabbles. Squinting in the bright sunlight, he heaved a sigh, removed his spectacles, and wiped them with a cloth. As he was putting them back on, a ray of sunlight caught one lens and sent a flash of light across the crowd. Stokes, still squinting, looked out at the Indians gathered there. He was anxious for the day to be done.

Several long and solemn speeches were made that day by representatives of the various tribes, all protesting that they wanted peace. Then came the Kiowas' turn, and their chief got up to speak.

"Like everyone else here," he said, "we Kiowas want peace with everyone. We want to be friends with everyone, but we especially want peace with the Osages. That's why we came here. Why then are there so few Osages present here?"

Colonel Dodge quickly assured the

Kiowa that he had invited the Osages by reading aloud a copy of the letter Colonel Arbuckle had sent, and Pierre Beatte explained that the Osages were suffering from an epidemic of cholera. As a result, he said, not many could make the journey. Then Young Clermont got up to speak again.

"So you want to make peace with the Osages," he said. "That's fine. And you're worried that I'm the only one here. But there are many bands of your people, and some of those other bands, some of the ones who are not here, may not want to be our friends, and you can't speak for those who are not here. You only speak for yourself, for your one band.

"But look at me. You may see among the Osages many great chiefs, but look upon me and behold the great chief of all the Osages. When my people are informed that Clermont has shaken hands with you, it will be enough."

On the third day they smoked the pipe together and made more speeches, and the meeting was at last concluded. Everyone had made assurances of peace and friendship, but when the western Indians started home again, riding together, some of them fell ill. A few days later, on the trail, some died.

"The white men did this to us," one of their number said. "They had among them one old man who put something over his eyes and looked at us. One time when he looked, I saw the poison shoot out from his eyes toward us."

And that was the result of Dodge's peace expedition to the western tribes.

The general grumpiness on the part of the survivors of the sickly expedition lingered on for a while. A few resignations were tendered, and some men did actually desert. Lieutenant Jeff Davis was in an extended foul mood, and one rainy morning when reveille was sounded, he did not bother to get out of bed. Later in the day, Major Mason, Davis's immediate superior officer, who had not suffered the Dodge expedition, sent for Davis. Davis reported to the major's office.

"You sent for me, sir?"

"Yes, Lieutenant," said Mason. "You were not at roll call this morning. I should like to know why."

"Because I was not out of my tent," said Davis.

"I beg your pardon," said Mason.

"I was not out of my tent," said Davis. "The regulations require that when it is

391

raining, the rolls shall be called in quarters by chiefs in squads."

"Mr. Davis," said Mason, "you know it is my order that all officers of this command attend the reveille roll call of their respective companies."

"Hum," said Davis, turning sharply on his heel and walking out of the major's office.

"Hum?" said Mason. "Hum? Mr. Davis, come back here at once." But Davis was already gone. "Mr. Davis," shouted Mason. "Come back here immediately. Hum? I'm not accustomed to such insubordination. Come back here. Consider yourself under arrest. Hum, indeed."

At the insistence of Major Mason, a court martial was later held at Fort Gibson, and the finding was that Davis was in fact guilty of doing exactly what Mason had accused him of doing; however, the court found no criminality in the actions. Shortly thereafter Davis submitted his resignation from the army and returned to his home in Kentucky.

PART 4

The
Statesman

32

1839

The Western Cherokees were gathered at their council ground at Tahlonteskee, named for their former chief. Eastern Chief John Ross had called a meeting at Illinois Campground of both governments, the Cherokee Nation and the Western Cherokee Nation, with an eye toward a union of the two. Everyone knew what that meant. Ross meant to do away with the government of the Western Cherokees by absorbing it into the other.

The chiefs of the Western Cherokees had refused to attend. Instead they had called their own meeting at their own council ground. A few hundred attended, but they heard that over two thousand were at the other place. The Western Cherokees had met to elect a third chief. And they talked about the problem that was facing them in the aftermath of the infamous Trail of Tears.

The Western Cherokees had decided years earlier, because of the situation with the Osages at the time and the very real possibility of untimely death that might leave them without a leader, that instead of only one deputy or vice-chief, they should have two. That way they would always have a chief. If anything happened to the chief, the second chief would take his place, and the third chief would move into the second position. Then they would elect a new third chief. It was a sensible precaution born of violent times.

The troubles with the Osages had passed, but the times were nonetheless uneasy. In 1835, representatives of the United States government had signed a treaty with some Eastern Cherokees at a place called New Echota in Georgia. The signers of the treaty had not been authorized by the government of the Cherokee Nation, were not official representatives of the Cherokee Nation in any way, but the U.S. agents had been more than willing to accept any Cherokee signatures. And the United States Senate had ratified the treaty just as if the signers had been elected officials or delegates with official appointments.

The treaty called for total removal,

signing over to the United States all Cherokee lands east of the Mississippi River in exchange for lands out west, and agreeing that all Eastern Cherokees would move west. Headed by old Major Ridge, the signers and their families and followers had been known as the Ridge Party. The signing of the treaty had almost immediately given them a new name. They had become known as the Treaty Party.

The members of the Treaty Party, having done the deed, moved to the west voluntarily, where they were welcomed by the Western Cherokees. They, in turn, assured the Western Cherokees that they would live peaceably under the government of the Western Cherokee Nation and abide by its laws.

But the majority of Cherokees, some sixteen thousand strong, had remained in the east under the leadership of Principal Chief John Ross, and they had refused to move. They had insisted that the Treaty of New Echota was fraudulent and illegal, and they had taken their case all the way to the Supreme Court of the United States, and they had won.

But President Andrew Jackson, in open defiance of the Supreme Court of the United States, had ordered the army to round the Cherokees up and move them west anyway. And that miserable job had been accomplished.

Driven from their homes at bayonet point and placed in stockade prisons for a time, they had been marched west in thirteen waves over what had become known as the Trail of Tears. The trip had taken the different groups anywhere from three to five months to complete, and the travelers had suffered mightily from heat, from sickness, from hunger, from cold, from exposure, from exhaustion. No one knew for certain how many died along the way, but estimates ranged from sixteen hundred to four thousand. The weakest, the very young and the very old, suffered the most. Only a few Cherokees remained in their ancient homelands in the east, fugitives hiding out in the hills.

Fort Gibson had been the end of the trail, and Dutch had been there to witness the arrival of some of the detachments. A wretched lot, they had been ragged, weary, sick, and demoralized. Dutch had spent all but the first five years of his life in the West, but these were his people, too. He knew it, and he felt their misery as if it were his own.

But the misery had not ended at Fort

Gibson, at the end of the trail. The Trail of Tears had brought a whole new set of problems to the Western Cherokee Nation. Some had been anticipated and some had not.

Even though hundreds, perhaps thousands, had died along the trail, many thousands more had survived. They needed food and shelter and other supplies. They needed homesites and new homes. The logistical problems were enormous. The Western Cherokees had been protesting for some years to the U.S. government that there was not enough land for them all. So the Treaty of New Echota had provided for more land out west beyond the former Lovely's Purchase that the Western Cherokees already held. Still, some thought, it would not be enough.

Feelings were bad between the majority, known now as the Ross Party — those who had suffered the long forced march — and the Treaty Party. The majority blamed the Treaty Party even more, it seemed, than they blamed the United States. Only recently the three main members of the Treaty Party had been killed.

Major Ridge had been shot from ambush while riding down a road. His son, John Ridge, had been dragged from his sick bed and stabbed to death in front of his helpless wife and child. Elias Boudinot had been enticed away from where he was working on a house with a tale of a sick neighbor who needed his help. Then, in a dark lane, he had been attacked by several men, stabbed, and hacked to death.

Members of the Treaty Party and Colonel Arbuckle at Fort Gibson believed that John Ross himself was responsible for the deeds, which they considered brutal murders. Some members of the Ross Party believed the killings to have been justified, for the Cherokee Nation had passed a law forbidding the sale of Cherokee land. These men had violated that law, and the penalty was death. Still, there had been no trial and no formal sentence had been passed.

Then there was the problem of two Cherokee governments, a problem, it seemed, that no one had anticipated. The Western Cherokee Nation had existed on its own since Bowles had led his followers into Missouri in 1794, and the Western Cherokees did not intend to give it up. They had never considered such a thing. They had instead assumed that following their forced removal the new arrivals would simply settle down under the existing government in their new home. But

Principal Chief John Ross of the Cherokee Nation had other thoughts, and the removal treaty had spelled out other terms.

In Ross's opinion, there was but one government for the Cherokees, the Cherokee Nation, and when the majority of Cherokees had been forced west, he insisted, the government had moved with them. The treaty seemed to back him up. So the meetings had been called, one by each government, and only a few miles apart.

John Jolly was dead. In his place the Western Cherokees had elected John Brown, a fiery-spirited young man. While the meeting of the Old Settlers was in progress at Tahlonteskee, Sequoyah arrived late. He had come from the other meeting, and he brought with him a letter that he read to the crowd.

" 'We, the Old Settlers, are here in council with the late immigrants,' " he read, " 'and we want you to come up without delay, that we may talk matters over like friends and brothers. These people are here in great multitudes, and they are perfectly friendly toward us. They have said over and over again that they will be glad to see you, and we have full confidence that they will receive you with all friendship. There is no drinking here to disturb the peace, though there are upward of two thousand people on the ground. We send you these few lines as friends, and we want you to come on without delay, and bring as many of the Old Settlers as are with you, and we have no doubt that we can have all things amicably and satisfactorily settled.' "

Whether it was the influence of Sequoyah or some other reason, no one ever knew, but a few of the people gathered there returned with Sequoyah to Illinois Campground. Among them was second chief, John Looney. As soon as he was out of sight, he was removed from office, and Third Chief John Rogers was elevated to the second spot. An election was called for then and there to fill the newly vacant third chief position. Dutch was then elected.

He thought about the difficult times ahead, and he fell inadequate to the role that had been thrust upon him. Dutch was a fighter, and he wasn't at all sure that the present situation called for a man like him. He had always stood ready to fight any enemy of the Cherokees, but if a fight was coming now, it would be Cherokees killing Cherokees, and he didn't want to think of that.

He longed for a leader like Degadoga, or old Chief Jolly who had died just the previous year. Even Jolly's adopted son, the white man Houston, would have been a welcome sight to Dutch's eyes, but Houston had gone to Texas back in 1832. These men, Dutch thought, were great leaders, skillful politicians, even shrewd negotiators, and in critical times such as these, they are what is needed, not an old fighter and a scout. But there were none like them around. The times had changed.

Dutch thought for a time about going back to Texas and joining Bowles down there. Sam Houston had become an important man in Texas almost as soon as he had arrived, and he had been responsible for the signing of a treaty between the rebel Texans and Bowles. They had fought a revolution for independence from Mexico and had won, and Sam Houston was the President of the new Republic of Texas.

Then word came again from the other gathering. The messenger said that the Cherokee Nation had passed a law that said that the two Cherokee governments had become one body politic under the name of the Cherokee Nation and that John Ross was the chief. They said that this had been done with the approval of the Old Settlers.

"Sequoyah and John Looney?" said Chief Brown. "Our government is here, and we did not agree. Their act of union is illegal, and we refuse to recognize it."

Soon after the arrival of that news, a delegation arrived from the other meeting.

"We were sent to invite you to come over and join us at Illinois Campground," said one of the men, but before anyone else could answer, a tall, brawny Cherokee of mixed blood stepped forward. He had two pistols in the sash around his waist, and several other armed men stood right behind him. He pulled his pistols out and cocked them, and so did a few of his followers.

"We're not going to your meeting," he said. "We don't recognize your act of union. It's illegal. Get out of here, and tell John Ross that if he sends anyone else this way, they might get hurt. Tell him Tom Starr said so."

Dutch watched as the delegates from the other camp hurried away. He was glad to see them leave so quickly and to get away unharmed. He asked himself what he would have done had Tom Starr and his friends actually resorted to violence, and he could not answer the question.

He was a Western Cherokee and so was Starr. But then, the others were also Cherokee. It seemed to Dutch that there were two fights taking place, and they had gotten mixed together. The Old Settlers and the Treaty Party had been lumped together as opponents of the John Ross government.

Dutch wasn't at all sure that he liked being identified with the Treaty Party. He was sure that he didn't want to kill any Cherokees because of what they had done. He didn't want to give up his government. He didn't want to back down on that issue, but he hoped that it would never come to a fight.

He wondered if even his loyalty to the government of the Western Cherokee Nation was reason enough for him to be involved, for he remembered the time when he had turned his back on them and gone to Texas. They had also turned their backs on him when Arbuckle had declared him an outlaw.

Dutch, newly elected third chief of the Western Cherokee Nation, was thinking about the irony of his position when someone came with more news from the other meeting. The John Ross council had declared the three assassinated men from the Treaty Party to have been outlaws, and they had granted amnesty to the unnamed killers. They had also set up eight auxiliary police companies made up of volunteers, each with a captain and a lieutenant. They had declared the removal treaty to be null and void, reasserted their ownership of the old country back east, and called for the remaining treaty signers to surrender themselves for trial and punishment.

"They further intend to enforce their new laws on all of us," the messenger said.

That message resolved the argument Dutch had been having with himself. His independent nature asserted itself. No one, he thought, tells Captain Dutch what to do.

33

1840

Having been appointed agent for the Western Cherokees, Montford Stokes, following the removal, found himself agent for all Cherokees who were recognized by the United States government. He decided that he would have to get involved in the controversy that was threatening to erupt into violence at any moment. He went to see John Ross at Rose Cottage, his opulent home in Park Hill, just a few miles from the capitol at Tahlequah.

At the end of the mile-and-a-half-long rose-bush-bordered driveway, the new two-story white house stood on a slight rise, with a commanding view of the countryside. Stokes's carriage was met at the end of the driveway by a black slave, who took charge of it, and yet another slave met him at the front door of the plantation-style home.

As he was ushered into the parlor, he saw Ross there. The chief stood when he entered.

They sat together in the comfortable parlor on beautiful imported chairs, and tea was served them from a silver tea set by a black slave.

"Now," said Ross, "what can I do for you, Mr. Stokes?"

"Chief Ross," said Stokes, "I want to co-operate with you to do everything we can to avoid violence. I won't presume to try to tell you what to do, but I have known the Western Cherokees for some time now, and some of them confide in me from time to time. I think I have some suggestions that might help."

"I'll gladly listen to any suggestions," said Ross. "I desire nothing more than peace and prosperity for my people."

"Your government made many enemies among the other camp when it declared all the signers of the treaty to be outlaws," said Stokes. "If that one act could be re-scinded, I believe that it would go a long way toward reconciling the opposition to your government. They are afraid that you mean to kill them all."

Ross wrinkled his brow and looked thoughtful for a moment. He murmured and sipped his tea. "Anything else?" he asked.

"If Western Cherokees could have a few

significant elective positions in the government," said Stokes, "they would see that you don't intend to leave them out."

"You don't expect me to falsify election results, I hope," said Ross.

"No sir. Of course not," said Stokes. "But a simple recommendation from you carries much weight with your people. You could make endorsements. And elections are coming up right away, are they not?"

Seventeen hundred Cherokees gathered at their newly designated capital of Tahlequah, where a square had been laid out and a huge shelter had been erected for meetings. Around the square were a few log cabins. They had gathered there for the meeting and elections, and at the urging of Chief Ross, the decree of outlawry on the treaty signers was rescinded. John Ross did endorse for elective offices some candidates who represented the Western Cherokees.

When the votes were tallied, Ross had been re-elected principal chief. His deputy chief was Joseph Vann, a Western Cherokee. And three Western Cherokees had been elected to the six-position executive council: John Looney, Aaron Price, and Dutch. Dutch refused to serve.

Instead, he attended a council of Western Cherokees in Fort Gibson, where they reaffirmed the sovereignty of the Western Cherokee Nation and sent a delegation to Washington to plead their case. Dutch was a member of that delegation. Stokes sent letters to Washington, urging the secretary of war and others to work out a compromise, explaining that the situation was tense and volatile. Soon after that, Stokes was removed from office, and the whole Cherokee matter was turned over to Colonel Arbuckle.

The delegation returned home, having accomplished nothing, and Arbuckle set up a meeting at Fort Gibson of a delegation from each of the rival Cherokee governments. The meeting was held, but nothing was accomplished. Arbuckle was transferred.

Dutch was at his home, a large plantation-style house on Dutch's Creek, trying to put the troubles out of his mind. Wili, tall and straight now, was sixteen years old, a handsome young man, and he and Dutch were working together training a beautiful young spotted pony.

"She'll make a good one for some high-society lady down in New Orleans," Dutch said.

Looking over his father's shoulder, Wili noticed some movement in the distance. He squinted his eyes and watched for a moment. "Father," he said, "some riders are coming."

Dutch handed the rope he'd been holding to his son and walked over to the fence. He leaned his arms on the top rail and watched while three mounted men rode slowly toward his house. As they drew closer, he could see some others coming up behind them. Some rode, others walked. Then he saw that there were women and children among them, and they looked ragged and weary.

Wili stepped up beside him. "Who could they be?" he asked.

Dutch knew that there could be no more people coming from the east. The Trail of Tears was done, but these people approaching his home reminded him of those others he had seen. He leaned over to duck between the rails of the fence and walked out to meet the first rider. Dutch reached up to halt the horse. The rider looked as if he were about to fall out of the saddle. He was a young man, and he somehow looked familiar to Dutch.

"John?" said Dutch. "John Bowles?"

" *'Siyo,* Tahchee," said the young man.

411

"My father has been killed. Others, too. The rest of us have been driven out of Texas."

Dutch looked behind John Bowles, and he could see a line of people straggling toward him.

"Wili," he called over his shoulder, "go get your mother. Then ride to our nearest neighbors and get them to come and help."

When the refugees from Texas had been fed, given some new clothes, had some wounds tended to, and had time to rest in comfort, Dutch found young John Bowles. He would have been handsome, Dutch thought, but he was worn and haggard with a sad, defeated look about him. He seemed old for his years.

"Tell me what happened," said Dutch. "I thought your father had a treaty with Sam Houston."

A smirk passed over John's young face as he reached inside his shirt to produce a bloodstained tin canister. He held it out toward Dutch.

"I have it here," he said.

Dutch opened the canister and removed a paper, also bloodstained. He studied it a moment, then set paper and canister aside.

"After we helped them win their war, the white people of Texas turned against us," said John. "They even turned against Sam Houston. They said our treaty was no good. They said that we signed it before the war with Mexico was won and so there wasn't really a government of Texas yet to sign a treaty with us.

"Then they had another election, and because Houston had taken our side, they elected another man and kicked Houston out. They elected a man named Lamar. He called us Houston's pet Indians, and he said that he would determine the boundaries of Texas with the sword.

"He accused us of planning to join the Mexicans in a war against Texas and sent us a letter telling us to get out of Texas. He sent two companies of soldiers to watch us.

"You knew my father. There was only one way he would answer such a threat. He told the soldier chief that he was ready to fight them if that was what they wanted. They backed off.

"Then a man named Reagan came with three other men to our house. Father took them down beside the spring to sit and talk with them. They had brought another letter from Lamar. In this letter he said that we could never stay in Texas as a separate nation, and he said again that our treaty was no good. He said that Father made a bad mistake in threatening the army.

"He said that we should stay in our houses and be quiet until the Texas government could decide how best to move us up here where the rest of the Cherokees have been settled by the United States.

"Father listened to the words of the letter, and then told the men that he would have to talk to the other chiefs. He asked them to come back in ten days, and they said they would.

"They came back in ten days and Father took them to the spring again. He said, 'My young men want to fight. They believe that we can whip the Texans. So do I, but it would take ten long, bloody years of fighting. I don't want to go to war, but I will lead the young men if that's what they want, for I have led my people since 1794, and I won't stop now.

" 'Your new president is listening to lies about me,' he told them, 'or else he is telling the lies himself. I have not been making plans with the Mexicans. Also I have a treaty to this land. It was made between me and Sam Houston, and I believe that it is good.

" 'I am an old man,' he said, 'eighty-three years old, and I am not afraid to die.

I don't have many more years left to me anyway, but I worry about the welfare of my wives and children.'

"Those men went away to tell the president what Father said, I guess, and in a few more days, he had another letter. This was from a different man, but he said that he was appointed by the president. He said that we had to get out of Texas. He said that they would pay us for our houses and our crops if we would leave voluntarily, and he said that Father should come to see him in so many days. If not, he said, we would be attacked.

"Then the Texas government sent more soldiers to watch over us, and they asked for another talk, and Father consented to talk with them some more. The first day they talked and he listened. That evening he talked with all our people, and on the second day of the meeting, Father talked to the white men. He said that we would move, but he asked for three months' time. They said three months was too long. Even then he agreed.

"They met a third day, and the white men brought a paper for him to sign. They wanted us to give up our gunlocks and they said that soldiers would accompany us all the way to the Red River. Then Father got angry.

415

" 'You should have said these things before,' he told them. 'We came into this country without soldiers and we can leave the same way. We don't want to ride out of Texas like prisoners. And why should we give up our gunlocks? My young men will never agree to do that.'

"He told them that he would not sign their treaty. The next day we packed up and left our camp, and the Texas army followed us. Then they attacked. They killed eighteen of our young men in a fight, and the rest of us ran away. It was night by then, and the fight was ended.

"We were moving out. We were leaving Texas the way they wanted us to do, but we had not signed their paper, and we had not given up our gunlocks, and we had left without telling them that we were leaving, because we did not want soldiers riding along with us. So they attacked us.

"That next morning, they caught up with us again and they attacked again and we fought back. We fought for a long time, and many of our men were killed. The battlefield was covered with blood.

"Many of our men had run away, and I looked and saw my father on his horse. He was almost alone out there on the battlefield. He had his sword in his right hand, waving it over his head. It was the sword that Sam Houston had given him. He was shouting to us to retreat, for we were being badly beaten.

"There was no need for him to shout. Almost all of us had already run away. They shot his horse, several times. It was his favorite horse, a sorrel with a blazed face and four white feet. It was a beautiful horse, but at last it fell, and when it did, Father went rolling on the ground.

"But then, Captain Dutch, as old as he was, even after a fall like that, he got up to his feet. My father. He was there alone, and he was wearing the vest and sash that Houston had given him. He had a soldier's hat on his head, and he still held onto the sword.

"Then a white man rode up behind him and shot him in the back. He staggered and fell and then he sat up. He was sitting there on the ground, facing the soldiers. That man Reagan was there with the soldiers. I saw him then. He ran toward my father, but another man was running at him from the other side.

"The other man held out a pistol pointed at my father's head, and I heard Reagan shout, 'Captain, don't shoot him,' but just then the other man fired his pistol right into my father's head. He put the pistol right up to my father's head before he pulled the trigger. He killed him, and then he took the sword out of his hand.

"Then, while I watched from hiding, they took his scalp. They stripped off his clothes and started to cut up his body, and I looked away. I could not watch any longer."

John Bowles sat silent for a long moment, but no tears ran down his cheeks. Dutch wondered if young John had already cried enough or if he had not yet been able to cry. He thought about the hated Texans. White Texans, he thought, were worse than the whites in Arkansas. He thought a moment about revenge, but he knew that it was a futile thought. There was nothing to be done, nothing other than to provide for the living. He put a hand on John's shoulder.

"Your father was a great man," he said, "a great warrior and a great chief. This news saddens us all. We will all mourn his passing. We will all miss him very much. And remember this. He died a warrior on the field of battle. That's a thing that cannot be said of most men his age."

John took a deep breath and let it slowly out. "*Wado*," he said. "There's more to tell.

Our second chief was also killed, and altogether about a hundred of our men. Maybe more. In the night someone slipped out onto the battlefield and found the treaty, which my father always carried with him, and brought it back to me. We headed north for the Red River, and all the way we knew that they were following us, but they didn't catch us again. We never saw them after that.

"But when at last we reached the Red River and we saw that we were almost out of Texas, almost safely away from them, some white hunters came riding by and saw us, and as we were crossing the Red, they fired at us and killed four more. Then we got across, and we came here to you."

Dutch stood up facing John Bowles, and John, his tale told, also stood. Dutch embraced him and held him close for a moment. "Rest here," he said, "as long as you like. When you're ready, you and all the others, we'll help you locate and build your homes. Here you have only friends."

34

1848

It was mid October, and an early frost was on the ground. A council meeting had been called, and as an elected representative from the Canadian District of the Cherokee Nation, Dutch would have to attend. He decided to ride the big white stallion he and Wili had been working with. The long ride, he thought, would put the final touches on the training.

Dutch was fifty-eight years old, still active, and still spry for his age. His hair was showing gray, and the wrinkles in his face were deepening. His body had thickened a little, but not much. He was active enough with his horses to keep him healthy. In the years since his return from Texas, he had developed a thriving plantation there on Dutch's Creek, and some considered him to be a wealthy man.

In his household, in addition to his wife and son, he supported a sister-in-law and a

420

niece. No longer a warrior, he had become a prosperous, responsible citizen and a respected elder statesman, and he had recently admitted to himself that he rather enjoyed the role. The times really had changed.

The Western Cherokee Nation, with certain Treaty Party members as allies and often as instigators, had struggled mightily to maintain its existence up until 1846, and Dutch had stuck stubbornly with it right up until the bitter end.

Led by the recalcitrant Tom Starr, a certain faction had indeed resorted to violence, killing members of the Ross Party, perhaps in retaliation for the killings of the once-outlawed treaty signers, perhaps simply in resistance to the attempts of the Cherokee Nation to absorb the Old Settlers' government. John Ross had offered rewards of one thousand dollars each for Tom Starr and his brothers Ellis and Bean.

The years from 1842 to 1846 had been especially bad, so violent that it might easily have been said that a Cherokee civil war was in progress. Many had been killed on both sides, and many, especially Treaty Party members, had sought sanctuary across the line in Arkansas, now a state in the union. There were some who claimed that the politics was nothing more than an excuse for certain lawless elements to engage in open banditry. In the refugee camps in Arkansas, they said, there were many who were not refugees at all, but merely loafers taking advantage of the situation to live off of federal government handouts.

In spite of his own violent background, and in spite of his prominent political involvement in the conflict between the two Cherokee governments, Dutch had managed to keep himself well away from any of the actual fighting. Perhaps his age had something to do with it, but he doubted it.

He fancied that given the right cause, he could still engage an enemy and give him a good battle. He remembered with fondness and admiration old Degadoga and old Bowles, both fighters to the end. But neither of them had fought against other Cherokees, and Dutch would not do that either.

He always suspected that the violence had been the real reason Sequoyah had gone to Mexico in 1842. The venerable Cherokee scholar said that he wanted to find those Cherokees who had moved down there some years before. The ones who had accompanied him had come back later and said that Sequoyah had indeed accomplished his mission, but that the trip had been too much for him, and, sadly, he had died down there.

But Dutch had stayed, and he had gone twice with delegations to Washington to demand a separate nation for the Old Settlers and Treaty Party members, and right up until the end, the president of the United States and members of Congress had seemed inclined to go along with the plan. A bill had actually been introduced in the U.S. Congress to divide the Cherokee lands between the two warring governments.

Anticipating the failure of the bill, some of the Old Settlers sent a delegation to Mexico in search of a new place to live, but nothing came of that. Besides, everyone really thought that the bill would pass easily into law. But somehow, at the last moment it seemed, John Ross, lobbying in Washington, managed to thwart it. The bill was defeated in 1846.

Then, with the idea of two Cherokee nations put finally to rest, the new treaty that Ross had been advocating was drawn up and signed between the United States and the Cherokee Nation. The new treaty said that the land in the west that had been assigned to the Cherokees belonged to all Cherokees in common, and it promised that a patent for the land would be issued in the name of the Cherokee Nation. All party distinctions among the Cherokees were to be obliterated, and a general amnesty was declared. And just like that, the Western Cherokee Nation was no more.

Dutch had accepted the new situation calmly. He knew when a battle was over, and when the Cherokee Nation divided itself into voting districts, he was elected to the national council from his home Canadian District. This time, he did not refuse to serve.

He packed his saddlebags and a bedroll for traveling, pulled on his winter coat made from a heavy, colorful trade blanket, and put an arm around his wife.

"I'm just about ready to go," he said.

"Are you sure you packed everything you need?" she asked.

"Yes," he said. "I'm sure. You worry too much about me. Don't you think I can take care of myself?"

"Some ways you can't," she said.

"Ha," he said. "I'll be all right."

He released her and turned toward the door. To his left, on a shelf on the wall, a black silk stovepipe hat stood gathering dust. It was adorned with one white ostrich feather. Dutch reached for the hat and set it jauntily on his head. He looked at Susanna, and she laughed. He took off the hat and put it back on the shelf, recalling the conference five years earlier in Tahlequah.

It had been a large gathering, perhaps the largest Indian gathering ever in these parts. Chief John Ross had sent invitations out to all the tribes to meet in Tahlequah to establish peace and friendship. Dutch had attended the gathering, and he had visited with many old friends and many old enemies, as well, and one night, wearing the high hat he had obtained on one of his visits to Washington, he had led a dance of all the tribes.

He took a wide-brimmed hat with a low crown from a peg on the wall by the door and put it on. Then he picked up his saddlebags and blanket roll and went out the door. Susanna stood for a moment in the doorway watching him walk toward the corral.

"Be careful," she called after him.

Looking back over his shoulder, he smiled at her. He walked on to the corral where Wili had just finished saddling Lightning, the big white stallion they had been working with so much. Dutch loved the strong and spirited horse, and he and Wili had spent long hours together training it to ride.

"He'll bring a good price," Dutch had said more than once while they worked with the white horse in the corral, and then recently he had changed his tune.

"We might just hang onto this one," he said, and he had even given the horse a name, a thing he seldom did. He called it Lightning.

Dutch dropped his saddlebags over the top rail of the corral fence as Wili led the big horse over to him. He laid the blanket roll across the saddle seat, picked up the saddlebags and put them in place. Wili helped him tie them down. The big white horse was anxious to get moving. It stamped and fidgeted and blew cloudlike puffs of breath out into the cold air. It was hard for the two men to hold him still. Dutch moved the blanket roll back behind the saddle and tied it on.

Wili shook his head. "I don't know if he's ready yet for this," he said. "You sure you don't want me to switch the saddle over to that black one?"

"No," said Dutch. "By the time we've gone all the way to Tahlequah together,

Lightning will be ready for the missionary ladies to ride to church. Take care of things at home while I'm gone."

"I will," said Wili. "Don't worry about anything here."

Dutch took the reins in his hands and gripped the saddlehorn, then he put his left foot in the stirrup. Lightning nickered, jerked his head and danced sideways to the left with his rear legs, knocking Dutch off balance and into the corral fence. Wili reached for the horse's bridle to try to control him, but Lightning swung his front end after his rear.

"Ahh," Dutch groaned, as the big horse pressed him against the fence rails. Wili pulled on the horse's head, and Lightning, excited now, jerked his head up and down and stamped his feet. He danced again to the left. Dutch groaned and shoved against the horse's side.

"Ho! Ho!" said Wili. "Come on! Settle down!"

Then the top rail of the corral fence snapped in two, and Dutch fell through it, back over the second rail, landing hard on his back on the frosty ground. Wili turned loose of the horse and jumped over the rail to his father's side.

"Are you hurt?" he asked.

Dutch started to sit up, and he groaned out loud and lay back down. "Oh," he said, "I'll be all right. Give me a hand up."

Even with Wili's assistance, it was more difficult for Dutch to get to his feet than he expected. He stood with an arm around his son's shoulder, and they walked slowly, painfully for Dutch, back to the house. As they stepped through the doorway, Susanna rushed over to them.

"What is it?" she said. "What's happened?"

"It's all right," said Dutch. "I took a fall. Let me rest a bit, and then I'll go."

They helped him to the bed, and then they had to help him to lie down and stretch out his legs. He started to suck in a deep breath, but the breathing hurt his chest. Maybe a broken rib or two, he thought.

"What can I do?" Susanna asked. She looked terribly worried, and Dutch didn't want her to worry.

"Nothing," he said. "I'm all right. Just let me rest awhile." He smiled, trying his best to cover up the pain in his chest and back and sides. She still looked worried, but she turned and walked away.

"Shall I take the saddle off of Lightning?" Wili asked her in a low voice, but Dutch did not hear Susanna's answer. He groaned low, and he thought of the irony of his situation. He thought of all the horses he had ridden, all the horses he had stolen from the Osages and from other Indians on the plains. He thought of the fights he had been in, and the one single wound he had ever received, and he touched his fingers to the scar along his cheek.

He wondered who that Osage woman had been whose rifle ball had cut his cheek, and he thought about another Osage woman long ago. And then he slept.

Susanna had sent Wili out for help, so when the time came, she was in the house alone. She draped a blanket around her shoulders and walked to the home of her nearest neighbor, just over the hill. It was cold out, and the wind was blowing. She held the blanket close around her as she walked.

She wasn't crying. She was determined. She knew that they would be wondering when it was time for the meeting to get started in Tahlequah. He was never late. He took his responsibilities as a councilman very seriously, and he would not want them sitting there, ready to start the meeting and wondering where he was, why he was late. He would want them to know.

She saw the smoke rising out of the chimney of the log house just ahead, and she saw the horses in the small corral nearby. She knew that everyone was still at home. She walked on, pulling the blanket tight against the cold. When she reached the house she pushed on the door, and it opened just a little. She called a name. A man came to the door and pulled it open. He looked surprised to see her.

"Susanna," he said. "Come in. Come over by the fire."

"Are you going to Tahlequah for the council meeting?" she asked.

Many people did attend the meetings, even though they were not members of the council, just to observe and find out what was going on, or to visit, for council meetings almost always drew large crowds from all over the Cherokee Nation. It was a social event as well as a political event, a time for people to visit with friends they rarely saw.

"I'm going to leave here in a little while," he said. "I thought I'd go over there and look around."

"When you get there," said Susanna, "go to the council for me. They'll want to know. Tell them for me that Captain Dutch won't be there. Tell them that Captain Dutch is dead."

Afterword

Because this novel is peopled with so many minor characters who are, in fact, significant, if not major, historical figures, it seems somehow appropriate to offer the reader a little follow-up information on some of the people, places, and things that help to make up the story of Captain Dutch. Also included in the following list are explanations of some of the Cherokee and Osage words and phrases that appear in the book.

Ani-Wasasi. This is a combination of the Cherokee pronunciation of the Osage word *Washashe* and the Cherokee plural prefix *Ani*. The translation is therefore simply *Osages*.

Beatte, Pierre. This scout first gained national attention when Washington Irving's *A Tour of the Prairies* was published in 1835. Irving describes him more or less as he appears here, a French-Osage half-breed. However, Foreman quotes Catlin and another source who, taken together, maintain that Beatte

431

was a Frenchman with no Osage blood, who had an Osage wife and half-breed children. Furthermore, according to these sources, his given name was Alexo, not Pierre.

Boudinot, Elias. Born Buck Oowatie in 1802 in the old Cherokee country in Georgia, he attended school in Cornwall, Connecticut, where he met his wife, Harriet Gold and took the name of his benefactor, Elias Boudinot. He had a classical education, was bilingual, and became the first editor of the official Cherokee Nation newspaper, *The Cherokee Phoenix*. In 1835, with his uncle, Major Ridge, and others, he signed the Treaty of New Echota, for which he was assassinated following the Trail of Tears. He was also the brother of Stand Watie, Cherokee general in the army of the Confederate States of America and the last Confederate general to surrender.

Catlin, George. Catlin did indeed survive both his illness and his trip back to St. Louis, to complete many more paintings as well as his two-volume study of American Indians. He went to Europe in 1840 to lecture and exhibit for eight years, wrote several more books, and made a trip to South America. He remains to this day one of the best known early painters of the American West and of American Indians. Catlin died in New Jersey in 1872 at the age of seventy-six. Reproductions of many of his paintings, including those he did while on the Dodge expedition, of the Comanche village, the Wichita village, and Dutch can be easily found in numerous picture books on American Indians. (Dutch was also painted, while on one of his trips to Washington, by artist Charles Bird King for the famous McKenney-Hall portrait gallery.)

Chisholm, Jesse. Chisholm did go on to become a trader in the West. It has been said that he eventually became fluent in fourteen languages, most of them languages of Plains Indian tribes. He served both the Republic of Texas, under the presidency of Sam Houston, and the United States on numerous occasions as scout and interpreter on expeditions to the Plains Indian tribes and at various treaty conferences. He is best remembered, of course, as the man who blazed the Chisholm Trail. He died in 1868. John Chisholm, who appears in some of the earlier years in the course of this tale, was Jesse's grandfather. John was a white man who married a Cherokee woman. Their son Ignatius was Jesse's father.

Chouteau. Brothers Auguste and Pierre Chouteau wrote to the Spanish governor in New Orleans in 1794 offering to establish a fort for the control of the Osage Indians in exchange for a monopoly on Osage trade until the year 1800. The governor agreed. When the monopoly expired, and following the Louisiana Purchase, the Chouteaus moved from what is now Arkansas to the Three Forks area in what is now Oklahoma, convincing the Osages to move with them. Chouteau's Trading Post had several different sites, but eventually was located near the present town of Chouteau, Oklahoma, which has retained the name. Several tales of massacres of Osages by the Western Cherokees were first told to one of the Chouteaus or to Pryor (see below), who then relayed the stories to the army. The details as given originally by Osages then went into the records of the war department. Historians have repeated them, usually without question.

Clermont. John Joseph Mathews, himself an Osage, said that Clermont's name was Gra-Mo'n, Gle-Mo'n, or Gleh-Mo'n, meaning Arrow Going Home. The Clermont prominent in this story was Clermont II. The present town of Claremore, Oklahoma, bears an anglicized version of his name.

Davis, Jefferson. Davis did resign his commission and return to Kentucky, where he married the daughter of General Zachary Taylor. He went on to become secretary of war, and later, of course, president of the Confederate States of America.

Degadoga. As with many Cherokee names, this one has been spelled variously in historical records and by historians. Washburn spelled it Ta-kah-to-kuh, Foreman used Takatoka, and most have followed his example. One historian came up with Tick-e-toke. The name is fairly common and still in use. It was also carried by General Stand Watie and, much more recently, by Cherokee artist Cecil Dick. I have chosen to use the common current spelling of the name, which more closely reflects Cherokee pronunciation. The name has been translated as *they* (meaning two men) *are standing together so close in sympathy as to form but one body.*

Diwali. The Cherokee name of the man known in history as the Bowl, Bowles, Chief Bowles, Colonel Bowles, or John Bowles. Names often present a problem for the scholar. Handed down from generation to generation, meanings sometimes get lost as the language changes. In contemporary

Cherokee usage bowl is *atlisdodi* or *ganuhwedadeligo*. *Dawoli* (close) is a mushroom.

Dodge, Henry. Colonel Dodge was not unaffected by the general disgust with the army and with life in the West that plagued the surviving members of the Dodge expedition. He too resigned his commission, and he went on to become governor of Wisconsin Territory.

Dutch, Dutch's Settlement, Dutch's Creek. (Dutch is also referred to by historians as Tahchee, Tuch-ee, Datsi, Tatsi and William Dutch.) The original Cherokee (*Tahchee* by whatever spelling) is an old name, and as far as I know can no longer be translated. Not much more remains to be said about Captain Dutch, except that he would probably have been totally forgotten had it not been for George Catlin. Even so, he has become obscure. Dutch's Settlement became the small town of Texanna, Oklahoma, and even there Dutch has been so much forgotten that local residents eventually could no longer recall why the creek that ran beside his house was called what it was called and began pronouncing and spelling it Duchess Creek.

Ehiyu ha. Come in. (Cherokee)

Hlesdi. Sometimes *hesdi*. Stop it. (Cherokee)

Houston, Sam. Not many know about the years Sam Houston spent with the Cherokees, but they have been admirably dealt with by Gregory and Strickland. (See Author's Note at the beginning of this novel.) Best known as the Father of Texas, Houston probably held more high offices than any other man in the history of the United States. He was adjutant general of the state of Tennessee, U.S. Congressman from Tennessee, governor of the state of Tennessee, general of the Texas army, president of the Republic of Texas, and governor of the state of Texas. He was also, at different times of his life, a citizen of three different sovereign nations: the United States, the Western Cherokee Nation, and the Republic of Texas. Houston, Texas, is, of course, named for him.

Irving, Washington. Born in 1783 in New York, Irving was admitted to the bar in New York at the age of twenty-three, but he proceeded to live the life of a literary vagabond. His first big success was *A History of New York by Diedrich Knickerbocker*, published in

1809. In 1819 and 1820 his *Sketch Book* appeared serially and shortly thereafter in book form and was an international success. Irving traveled widely in Europe. After having spent seventeen years abroad, he returned to the United States in 1831. His trip west, during which he stopped at Fort Gibson and became acquainted with Pierre (or Alexo) Beatte, Sam Houston, and others, resulted in the publication of *A Tour on the Prairies* in 1835. Best remembered for "Rip Van Winkle" and "The Legend of Sleepy Hollow," Irving died in 1859.

Kanohena. A traditional Cherokee dish made of hominy, the reason for its frequent appearance in this story is that it was once the dish customarily served to welcome a guest to one's home.

Mad Buffalo. According to Grant Foreman, Mad Buffalo, one of the sons of Clermont the second, "bore the Osage names of Cha-to-kah-wa-she-pe-she and Skitok." Mathews identifies him as Tse-To-Gah Wah-Shi'n-Pische, or Bad Tempered Buffalo.

Pryor, Nathaniel. Pryor was an early trader to and a friend of the Osages. For a time he was acting sub-agent to the Osages. Like the

Chouteaus, Pryor sometimes brought the tales of Cherokee atrocities against the Osages to the attention of the army. Pryor, Oklahoma, has his name today.

Ridge, Major. A full-blood Cherokee, Ridge, along with eight hundred other Cherokees, served with Andrew Jackson during the 1814 Creek War. Known as progressives, he and his brother Oowatie sent their sons north to school. Eventually, believing removal to be inevitable, Major Ridge became the leader of the political faction called the Treaty Party. He signed the Treaty of New Echota, and for that he was assassinated following the Trail of Tears. His Cherokee name was Ka-nunda-cla-ga or Ganun-da-le-gi, meaning something like *he walks along the mountaintop*. In English it became Ridge, and during the Creek War, Ridge received the title or rank of major, which he began using as a first name. Major Ridge's son John became a prominent Cherokee leader, but he, too, was assassinated for being a treaty signer. John's son, John Rollin Ridge, went to California and became a well known poet and journalist. He also wrote a novel, *The Life and Adventures of Joaquin Murieta*, which, though it was but suggested by actual events occurring in California, has been taken by many as genuine history or biography. It is still in print.

Ross, John. Born in 1790, Ross was the elected principal chief of the Cherokee Nation from 1828 until his death in 1866 in Washington, D.C. He staunchly resisted the removal of the Cherokees from their homelands until the last possible moment. During the removal, he lost his first wife, Quatie, on the Trail of Tears. Ross is a controversial figure in history, but he was unquestionably a powerful and influential politician, serving as principal chief for thirty-eight years during some very trying times.

Sequoyah, also known as George Guess or Gist. Famous as the inventor of the Cherokee syllabary, Sequoyah remains shrouded in controversy and obscurity. He has generally been thought to be the son of trader Nathaniel Gist and a Cherokee woman by the name of Wurteh. He walked with a limp, it is said, possibly because of a wound received during the Creek War of 1814. He went west with John Jolly in 1818. Various stories have been told about the pains he went through to develop a writing system for the Cherokees. His invention, if such it was, was extremely successful, making the Cherokee Nation into a literate nation in a matter of months. However there are those who believe that the writing system was an ancient one and had simply fallen into disuse and been largely forgotten. Sequoyah, according to these, knew the old system and made it public once more. According to Jack Kilpatrick ("Sequoyah of Earth and Intellect"), Sequoyah and Dutch were half brothers. Leon Gilmore of Tahlequah claims to have seen an old family bible that lists the two men as brothers. These claims are difficult to reconcile with other sources, but, who knows? Sequoyah is one of only two American Indians represented in the National Statuary Hall of Fame in Washington, D.C. (the other is Will Rogers, also Cherokee), and his name has been attached to parks and businesses all over the country. Even a tree has been given his name. (So far, as far as I know, no one has yet called a car a Sequoyah.) The meaning of the name is controversial. It has been translated Pig in a Pen, from the Cherokee *sikwa* (pig) and the locative suffix *yi*. However, *sikwa* originally meant opossum and *ya* is a suffix meaning real or original. The name could mean the real or original opossum. Some scholars have suggested that *sequoyah* is not even a Cherokee word and probably came into usage from some other language.

'Siyo. A common Cherokee greeting, this is a contraction of the word *osiyo.*

Starr, Tom. Tom Starr has been held responsible by many historians for most of the violence in the Cherokee Nation between the years of 1842 and 1846. His bold and daring deeds became legendary, even in his own lifetime, and he was said to have killed one hundred men. He would probably have been better remembered had not one of his sons, Sam, married a white woman named Myra Belle Shirley, who went on to become notoriously famous as Belle Starr, her legend far overshadowing that of the rest of the family.

Tsiyu-utana. (Cherokee) *Tsiyu* is a boat or canoe. *Utana* means big.

Wasasi. Cherokee for Osage. See *Ani-Wasasi* above.

Washashe. Osage. According to Mathews, *Washashe* or *Wah-Sha-She,* means The Water People and was originally a designation of one branch of the Osage People. The

Osages' own name for themselves is *Ni-U-Ko'n-Ska*, Children of the Middle Waters. A French missionary, upon meeting the Washashe, assumed their name to indicate the entire nation. He called them in his notes *Ouazhaghi*. From that original error, English speakers came up with Osage, and the designation stuck.

ABOUT THE AUTHOR

ROBERT J. CONLEY was born in Cushing, Oklahoma, in 1940. He received a bachelor's degree in drama and art and a master's in English from Midwestern University. He has taught English at Northern Illinois University, Southwest Missouri State University, and Morningside College. He has also served as director of Indian Studies at Eastern Montana College and as assistant programs manager for the Cherokee Nation of Oklahoma.

Since the publication of his first novel in 1986, Mr. Conley has written sixteen novels and a collection of short stories. He received a Spur Award for Best Short Story from the Western Writers of America for "Yellow Bird: An Imaginary Autobiography," and another for his novel *Nickajack*. Among his other works acclaimed for their unique voice and Cherokee perspective are Spur Award finalist *Ned Christie's War*, *The Way of Priests*, and *Mountain Windsong*, which Tony Hillerman said "is beautiful and heartwarming as well as tragic. . . . Deserves to become an American classic."

Robert J. Conley lives in Tahlequah, Oklahoma, with his wife Evelyn, also Cherokee. He has been named the Official Historian of the Cherokee Nation.

The employees of Thorndike Press hope you have enjoyed this Large Print book. All our Thorndike and Wheeler Large Print titles are designed for easy reading, and all our books are made to last. Other Thorndike Press Large Print books are available at your library, through selected bookstores, or directly from us.

For information about titles, please call:

(800) 223-1244

or visit our Web site at:

www.gale.com/thorndike
www.gale.com/wheeler

To share your comments, please write:

Publisher
Thorndike Press
295 Kennedy Memorial Drive
Waterville, ME   04901